SOLD TO THE SILVERFOX DADDY

A DARK VIRGIN AUCTION SECRET BABY AGE GAP DARK ROMANCE

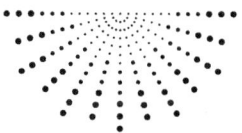

A.J. BLACK

UNTITLED

Copyright © 2025 by A.J. Black

All rights reserved.

No portion of this book may be reproduced in any form without written permission from the publisher or author, except as permitted by U.S. copyright law.

CHAPTER ONE

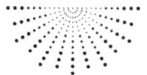

Celia

G<small>LOVED FINGERS PROBED</small> my most intimate places. My legs forced apart, humiliation rising in my throat like bile, burning me from within.

"Relax, sweetheart. The more you tense up, the harder this becomes." The long-haired woman patted my inner thigh.

I didn't respond. I forced myself to stare at a spot on the ceiling—I had to focus on that, on anything that would pull my mind away from this room, this cold examination table, these two women inspecting me like livestock.

"Nice and tight. She's still a virgin." The short-haired woman spoke to her colleague.

The long-haired woman made a sound—approval mixed with envy. I didn't know which. Didn't care. My jaw clenched so tight I thought my teeth might shatter.

When they finished, they hauled me up and shoved me into the bathroom. Water blasted at full force, scalding drops pounding my skin. I stood there numb while they scrubbed me raw with exfoliating cream. Coarse grains scraped from neck to ankles, searing every inch of flesh.

When the torture finally ended, my skin was red and raw. Then they slathered me with lotions and essential oils before producing something I couldn't even call clothing.

A few black strings. Scraps of lace that barely covered anything. They forced me into it. I felt more exposed than naked.

The door opened. A man in a suit with slicked-back hair walked in. Sal—the manager of this damned underground auction.

His beady eyes crawled over me, that revolting smile spreading across his face.

"Maria, checked her out?" He glanced at the short-haired woman.

"Yes, boss. Perfectly intact." Maria's voice was deferential.

"Excellent." Sal's gaze slithered back to me. He licked his lips. "Look at you, Celia. Your body is a work of art. You're our grand finale tonight!"

I remained silent, staring at him coldly.

"Don't look at me like that, sweetheart." He stepped closer, rough fingers seizing my chin.

He forced my head up.

"If it weren't for some bigshot coming tonight—someone we can't afford to piss off—I swear I'd be first in line to taste you. You're the best stock I've seen here."

His thumb dragged across my lips. Nausea slammed into me. I jerked away from his touch.

"Don't touch me." My voice seethed with suppressed rage.

Sal chuckled. "Got some fire. I like that. But tonight, you'd better keep those claws sheathed."

He leaned closer, voice dropping to a whisper. "Listen carefully. Rick should be proud to have such a dutiful daughter. Fifty thousand —that's serious money. Without you, he'd be a cold corpse at the bottom of the river by now."

"You think I wanted this?" I couldn't stop myself from screaming. "It was you! Your thugs burst into our home, held guns to our heads, forced us into submission!"

My mind flashed back to two days ago—our decrepit apartment, guns pressed to our temples.

Terror consumed me, blood turning to ice. I was twenty years old. My life hadn't even begun. I'd never left Chicago, never seen other cities, never fallen in love... I wasn't ready to die.

"Fifty grand. Sal's rules. Debts must be paid—natural law." The lead enforcer tapped my father's cheek with his gun barrel.

My father knelt there, trembling.

"Or," the leader went on, "we could make things more entertaining—send you off with a bullet. As for your pretty daughter... me and my boys will show her what it's like to live worse than death."

In that moment, my father didn't even look at me. He mumbled through chattering teeth, "Don't kill me, please. I'll give her to you. She's a virgin—worth good money..."

My eyes widened in disbelief. I stared at my father, unable to comprehend.

The lead enforcer slowly lowered his weapon from my father's face. His eyes appraised me while he stroked his chin. He was actually considering it. He was genuinely fucking considering it.

I looked down, tears welling. That was my moment of complete devastation.

"Is she really a virgin?" the enforcer finally asked.

"Yes!" My father answered eagerly. "She's never had a boyfriend."

"No, you can't do this." Desperate pleas tore from my throat.

"We can. Sal has a taste for this kind of merchandise. Take her." He nodded to the enforcer covering me.

That was it. I had been sold by my own father—the same man who'd tossed me into the air laughing when I was a child—hollowed out by gambling and drugs, bargaining away his daughter to stay alive. They grabbed my arm and dragged me to the door.

I struggled desperately, screaming, "Let me go!"

The lead enforcer cocked his weapon at me. "Die, or obey."

The pressure crushed the air from my lungs. I stopped fighting.

"Sweetheart, those are just minor things you can brush off." Sal's voice pulled me from the memory back into the same dark present.

He looked me up and down with a greasy grin. "The point is, after tonight, your father's debt's wiped clean. He's safe. And you..." His eyes lingered on me, slimy. "You might have a very bright future—depends on how well you perform."

"I don't want your so-called future," I said through gritted teeth. "I just want your word. After tonight, you'll release us."

Fine. Pay Rick off for twenty years of a fucked-up 'fatherhood.'

"Of course." Sal turned to leave, pausing at the doorway.

He pointed at me in warning, "Behave, Celia. Don't screw this up. That guest—he's not someone we can mess with."

The door slammed shut behind him.

Maria positioned me before the mirror, working through my tangled hair. "Listen to me, Celia. Just one night. Think of it as a dream. When you wake up, you can return to your life."

I said nothing. I had no better alternatives anyway. The flames of anger had died, leaving only the ashes of despair. My tears had run dry when I was forced into this place. All I could do was stare at my pale face in the mirror.

"Easy for you to say," the long-haired woman scoffed. "If she's lucky enough to catch that New York big shot's attention, think she'll want to leave?"

Her eyes gleamed with gossip as she lowered her voice, "I heard that big shot has connections to the Bratva."

Bratva. Russian mafia. The word hit my stomach like a block of ice. Christ, this was even worse than I'd imagined. I knew of them—they were true darkness, the kind that made street-level predators like Sal grovel.

"Keep your mouth shut, Lina!" Maria shot the long-haired woman a sharp look.

"I'm not making it up," Lina retorted. "I saw the boss meet him at the door—practically bowed. Bartender said his name was—what was it—Kirill Zaitsev. The name alone makes your knees go weak. Handsome as a movie star, but with killer's eyes."

"So what?" Maria worked hair oil through my strands efficiently.

"Mob boss or president, tonight they're all just clients. Our job is providing premium service."

She paused, meeting my eyes in the mirror with something approaching sympathy. "You're beautiful, Celia. Use that. Make this Zaitsev obsessed with you. Let him claim you. Being his mistress beats being sold to some old pervert."

Lina added bitterly, "Exactly. Guys like Zaitsev give their women everything—money, jewels, mansions... Just be compliant, keep him satisfied, and you're set for life."

The sharp jasmine scent of the essential oil hit my stomach, churning my insides.

Seeing my continued silence, Lina rolled her eyes. "Ungrateful bitch. When you're living that life, you'll realize we were right."

"I don't want to be anyone's mistress. I just want this nightmare over so I can escape this hellhole." My voice was emotionless.

Leaping from one hell into another wasn't an improvement.

"Time's up," Maria announced.

They flanked me, escorting me through a narrow, dimly lit corridor. Their grip on my arms was uncompromising—resistance was futile.

The corridor terminated at a circular lift platform. Chaos echoed from above—nothing like the refined atmosphere of legitimate auction houses.

Dread knotted my stomach.

"Gentlemen, prepare to witness tonight's crowning treasure!" The auctioneer's voice assaulted my nerves. "She's merely twenty—fresh, pristine, ready to be claimed by tonight's most distinguished victor!"

My stomach cramped violently. My legs felt leaden. I froze at the platform's edge, unable to advance.

"Up you go!" Lina shoved me from behind.

I stumbled forward onto the metal disc.

Blazing white spotlights crashed down, engulfing me completely. I raised my hand to shield my eyes. When they finally adjusted, I saw the scene below.

A black sea of faces. Countless eyes—greedy, leering, curious, contemptuous—all fixated on me. Nauseating.

"Look at those legs! God, I can imagine them wrapped around my waist!"

"Start the bidding! I need her tonight!"

"I bet she's good in bed. I love hearing virgins weep and beg on their first time."

The filthy words crashed over me, stripping away what remained of my dignity. I stood rigid, fingers clenched into fists, tasting copper in my mouth.

The auctioneer's voice sliced through again like a cleaver.

"As you can observe, absolute perfection. Opening bid—ten thousand dollars. Let the bidding commence!"

CHAPTER TWO

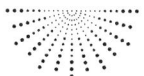

Kirill

I HELD A GLASS OF AMBER—MACALLAN 25—the only thing in this shithole that could be called classy.

"Kirill, my friend." The man beside me spoke with eagerness. Theodore Moretti. Chicago's underground kingpin, head of the Moretti Family.

"Not bad, huh?" Theodore kept babbling. "Sal did a hell of a job—always manages to dig up the right...amusement."

I didn't look at him. My eyes remained fixed on the auctioneer onstage, presenting some antique vase—a clumsy fake. The original sat in my estate.

I sipped my whiskey. I hadn't come to Chicago for this third-rate spectacle. The Zaitsev Group was launching a new shipping route through the Great Lakes, a golden waterway that would channel our cargo straight into America's heartland. The only problem? That route ran directly through Moretti territory.

I could have started a war. My Bratva could wipe the Moretti Family off Chicago's map in two weeks. But war is costly, chaotic, and draws too much attention. A business alliance—a clean, signed contract—beats piles of corpses every time.

So here I sat, enduring Theodore's flattery and this mind-numbing auction. Business foreplay. A tedious but necessary social ritual.

"How about that vase?" Theodore persisted. "Might make a nice centerpiece."

"Fake." My voice carried no emotion.

Theodore's smile froze. He cleared his throat awkwardly, signaling a waiter for more champagne. "Ha! Thought so! Your eye is razor-sharp as always."

I ignored his ass-kissing. My patience was wearing dangerously thin. Finally, some pretentious fool bought the counterfeit vase for forty grand. Next came firearms, jewelry. All unremarkable.

"Don't worry, Kirill. The real piece is coming up," Theodore said, sensing my impatience. He leaned in, smeared with a greasy grin. "Sal swore this one's prime. Never been touched."

I didn't bother to raise an eyebrow. Women. To me, they were no different from the items we'd been watching. I enjoyed their bodies, admired their beauty, but never invested emotionally.

The stage lights suddenly dimmed, leaving only a spotlight on the slowly ascending circular platform center stage. The auctioneer's voice grew even more theatrical.

"She's merely twenty—fresh, pristine, ready to be claimed by tonight's most distinguished victor!"

I settled back in my chair, prepared to endure this final act before leaving this cesspit.

The platform stopped. In the harsh spotlight, a silhouette appeared. Very young.

She wore practically nothing—scraps of black lace that traced her flawless curves. Her raven hair cascaded like dark silk, slightly wavy, spilling over bare shoulders. Her body possessed that raw, untainted beauty unique to youth.

I found myself straightening unconsciously, my throat tightening.

Stunning. Especially her face. Exquisitely sculpted features, full lips, a perfect nose, and emerald eyes.

I could see her terror—her complexion was ghostly pale, yet those eyes blazed with defiant light.

Heat spread through my lower body. I loosened my tie.

Around us, the room stirred. Lewd talk buzzed like flies. I frowned, a primitive disgust rising. These men were mangy dogs fighting over prime meat; their greed fouled whatever they craved.

Theodore whispered in my ear, voice dripping with perverted glee, "What do you think, Kirill? Told you—prime. A virgin. You know how it is, first time's always the tightest, and they make the most delicious sounds..."

I ignored Theodore completely, my gaze locked on the girl as she bit her lip in anguish.

The auctioneer announced the opening bid—ten thousand dollars.

"Twenty!"

"Twenty-one! Back off!"

"Twenty-five!"

The price spiraled upward. When it reached sixty grand, a man stood with triumphant laughter. I tracked the sound to a scarred brute with a sickly flush staining his face.

"Ah, Maloni. That guy's a sick bastard in bed—likes things way past the line. A month ago a girl died in his sheets." Theodore's tone carried malicious satisfaction.

My lip curled in disgust. I despised these crude beasts.

The auctioneer raised his gavel, calling the price. He surveyed the room, but no new bids emerged. Sixty grand for a girl's first time—not exactly pocket change for most here.

Maloni clearly couldn't contain his anticipation. He preened smugly, basking in the attention.

Then he wheeled toward his companions, bellowing, "Hear that, you bastards? This little beauty belongs to me tonight!"

His table erupted in obscene laughter and catcalls.

"Don't be so fucking stingy, Maloni!" someone shouted. "Quality goods like that—think you can handle her alone?"

"Relax, guys! I'll take the first bite—there'll be extras for you. We'll all have our fun—turn this little virgin into our bitch!" Maloni's laugh was guttural and savage.

Something vicious clawed through my chest. Hearing his fantasies about that girl made me want to crush his windpipe.

The girl began trembling at those words. Despair and horror consumed her features, those brilliant eyes threatening to dim forever.

Possessiveness surged within me. I refused to let her show that expression because of another man. More than that, I wouldn't allow it.

I wouldn't allow those luminous eyes to be extinguished.

If they were destined to go dark, it would be by my hand alone.

"Sixty thousand, going twice!" The auctioneer's gavel hovered menacingly.

Maloni raised his glass in premature celebration.

"Sixty thousand, going three times—"

I lifted my chin fractionally. My assistant immediately raised paddle number one.

"One hundred thousand."

My voice cut through the noise like a blade.

Maloni's face turned purple with rage. His mouth worked soundlessly.

After three calls, the gavel crashed down. Transaction complete.

The girl onstage appeared shell-shocked. When she realized she'd escaped Maloni's clutches, I watched her rigid shoulders crumble with relief—relief so absolute it looked like survival.

Then she saw me. Our eyes met. For a heartbeat she brightened, like I'd been a savior. Pleasure sparked down my spine. But when she read my face, her relief froze; it shifted into a new, wary anxiety.

Smart girl. She recognized I was hardly a savior.

A smile ghosted across my lips. I arched an eyebrow at her.

"Congratulations, Kirill! You bagged a beauty tonight." Theodore offered his felicitations.

I nodded curtly, acknowledging his sentiment.

"I've reserved the finest booth at Bull's Horn Club," Theodore shifted to business. "Tomorrow evening, seven sharp. We'll have ample time to discuss the new shipping route properly."

I rose, adjusting my cufflinks with deliberate precision.

"I'll be there." Leaving him with those words, I cast one final glance at the girl still watching me from the stage and silently mouthed my message.

"I'll wait."

She understood perfectly, her lips parting in shock. She looked like a startled doe. I smirked and turned away, my assistant falling into step behind me.

I knew the staff would deliver her to my suite, where I could savor her at my complete leisure.

CHAPTER THREE

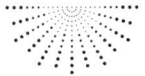

Celia

T̲h̲e̲ ̲m̲o̲m̲e̲n̲t̲ ̲t̲h̲e̲ ̲g̲a̲v̲e̲l̲ ̲f̲e̲l̲l̲, I knew I was saved.

The thought pierced through the terror in my mind like dawn breaking. I wouldn't be dragged away by that disgusting man. I wouldn't have to imagine what kind of hell it would be to be used by a crowd of men.

My nerves, stretched to their breaking point, finally relaxed. I took a deep breath, as if trying to reclaim all the oxygen I'd lost.

Then I lifted my head, instinctively searching for the man who'd pulled me back from the edge of hell.

My eyes locked onto the front row center, on the man who seemed so out of place in this world.

It was him.

The man who'd paid a hundred thousand dollars to buy me.

The moment our eyes met, my heart—which had just settled back into my chest—was seized again by an invisible fist.

He was nothing like any buyer I'd ever imagined. He just sat there quietly, as if he owned the entire world.

He was handsome, though not young. He wore a perfectly tailored dark suit that outlined broad shoulders and a lean, powerful frame. His hair was dark brown, cut with military precision. His facial features were as hard and cold as marble sculpture.

He had gray-blue eyes, deep and sharp. A scar cut through his left eyebrow, creating a distinctive break. Rather than marring his handsome face, it added something dangerous and untamed.

A wave of unease hit me. My mind went blank.

I'd escaped one hell, but I felt like I'd crashed into another, more unpredictable abyss.

The corner of his mouth curved into an amused smile. Then he raised that scarred eyebrow at me.

My scalp tingled. Heat pooled between my legs.

I read his lips—"I'll wait."

My eyes widened in surprise. He didn't seem as terrifying as I'd imagined.

I don't remember walking off that stage. Sal came up to collect me, his face stretched into a smile that made me sick.

"Nice work, Celia! You hooked tonight's most distinguished guest." His words stung.

He handed me a coat and escorted me out of the club, into a car.

I stared numbly at the passing scenery, my mind replaying that man over and over. Even now, my heart was beating at an irregular rhythm.

The car soon stopped in front of an impressive hotel.

I kept my head down as I followed the driver into an elevator, watching the floors climb. Finally, the numbers stopped at thirty-three—the top floor. The driver led me into a presidential suite so spacious it was almost absurd, then closed the door and left.

This suite was twice the size of my house, decorated with a brightness and luxury I'd never seen. Thick wool carpets covered the floor, massive floor-to-ceiling windows revealed Chicago's glittering night skyline. The room was quiet—so quiet I could hear my own heartbeat and the sound of rushing water from the bathroom.

I knew the man who'd bought me was in there.

I stood frozen in place, clutching my coat, swallowing hard.

What should I do? Stand by the door and wait, or take off my coat and lie on the bed...

No time to think.

The water stopped abruptly. The bathroom door swung open.

He walked out.

My breath was stolen instantly.

The man wore only a white towel loosely wrapped around his waist. Water droplets traced the defined muscles of his chest, sliding down toward the towel's edge, leaving everything to imagination.

His body was like a masterpiece crafted by ancient Greek sculptors. Broad shoulders, thick chest, eight-pack abs carved in sharp relief, powerful thighs... His skin was perfectly tanned, covered in intricate black tattoos that screamed mystery and danger.

He dried his wet brown hair with a towel as he approached me. Each step carried crushing presence.

My palms sweated with nerves. I instinctively stepped back.

He stopped a few feet away, those gray-blue eyes raking me from head to toe.

"Name?" His voice was deep and rough, carrying the lazy aftermath of a shower.

"...Anna." I lied. I couldn't let him know my real name. Too dangerous.

His brow furrowed. "Doesn't suit you."

My breath caught. I stayed silent. Thankfully, he didn't press.

"Kirill Zaitsev." He gave his name, then moved closer.

My pupils dilated wildly. Kirill Zaitsev? I realized with shock—he was the important guest Lina had mentioned, the one connected to the Bratva!

We were barely a foot apart now. I could smell his body wash and that unique masculine scent. The smell wrapped around me like a net.

"Say my name." His command was absolute.

"Ki-Kirill." My voice came out dry and raspy, barely squeezed from my throat.

He was a big shot. The kind of man who made Sal grovel. Maybe...

maybe if I pleased him, I could get something out of this. At least make tonight bearable.

The thought gave me courage. I stood on my tiptoes and clumsily pressed a kiss to his hard cheek. I'd never been intimate with any man. I didn't know what to do. I could only copy what I'd seen in movies.

I heard him chuckle low in his throat, clearly amused.

"That's it?"

Before I could react, one large hand cupped the back of my head while the other wrapped around my waist, pulling me against him. I gasped, crashing into his hard chest.

The next second, his lips came down on mine.

His kiss was like him—completely aggressive. His tongue easily pried open my teeth, driving deep, claiming every inch of my mouth with ruthless dominance. He kissed me until I was dizzy and breathless, could only whimper helplessly.

He pulled back slightly, lips still touching mine, hot breath washing over me.

"Breathe, good girl." When he spoke, the vibration of his lips against mine made them tingle.

"So inexperienced. Never been kissed?" His words carried teasing mockery, stroking my sensitive nerves like feathers. My face burned instantly, heat crawling down from the back of my neck.

I lowered my head in embarrassment. "I've never... this was my first kiss."

I watched Kirill's smile widen. Brief, but enough to outshine the entire room.

Clearly, my answer pleased him.

"Good." He smiled.

He grabbed the remote and dimmed the main lights, bathing the room in warm, golden tones. Then he stripped off my coat, swept me up in his arms, and carried me toward that impossibly large bed.

I instinctively wrapped my arms around his neck.

He laid me gently on the soft mattress, then leaned over me, caging me in.

"So, Anna." He twirled a strand of my hair around his finger. "Let me see how many more firsts you have to give me tonight."

Kirill's lips crashed against mine, hungry and demanding, his tongue sweeping into my mouth with a fervor that made my head spin. I kissed him back, my hands clutching at his broad shoulders, trying to match his intensity despite my inexperience. His kisses were relentless, each one deeper than the last, pulling soft whimpers from my throat. My body felt like it was on fire, every nerve alight as his hands roamed my sides, grazing the curve of my waist.

He pulled back just enough to look at me, his dark eyes glinting with a mix of mischief and desire. "You're so sweet, Anna," he murmured, his voice low and rough. "I'm gonna ruin you tonight." His words sent a shiver down my spine, and I felt my cheeks flush even hotter, but I didn't look away. I wanted this—wanted him.

His hands moved to his waist, and with a swift tug, he yanked off the bath towel wrapped around him. It fell to the floor, revealing his erection, hard and straining. My breath caught in my throat. His cock was thick, veins prominent along its length, the head flushed a deep pink. It was bigger than I'd imagined—intimidatingly so, easily eight inches, maybe more. My eyes widened, and I swallowed hard, my heart pounding. How was that supposed to... fit?

Kirill noticed my reaction, a smirk curling his lips. "Scared, baby?" he teased, his voice dripping with confidence. "Don't worry, you'll take it just fine."

I bit my lip, torn between nervousness and a strange, burning need to please him. I wanted to make him feel good, to see that smile of his widen again. Tentatively, I reached out, my fingers brushing against his shaft. It was hot to the touch, pulsing under my fingertips. Kirill let out a low groan, encouraging me. Emboldened, I leaned forward, my lips hovering just above him. I'd never done this before, but I'd seen enough to have a vague idea. I pressed a soft kiss to the tip, tasting the faint saltiness of his skin.

"Fuck, Anna," he growled, his hand tangling in my hair. "Go on, take me in your mouth."

I parted my lips, sliding him in slowly, my tongue brushing against the underside. He was so thick, my jaw stretched to accommodate him. My movements were clumsy, uncertain, as I tried to find a rhythm. I bobbed my head, taking him deeper each time, but my inexperience showed. My teeth grazed him accidentally, and he hissed, his hand tightening in my hair.

"Easy, sweetheart," he said, his voice strained but gentle. He tapped my cheek lightly. "Keep those teeth tucked away, yeah?"

I nodded as best I could, my lips still wrapped around him, and focused on keeping my teeth out of the way. I glanced up at him, desperate to see if I was doing it right. His head was tilted back, eyes half-closed, a look of pure bliss on his face. "Goddamn, Anna," he muttered. "No one's ever made me feel like this. You're so fucking perfect."

His words lit something inside me, urging me to try harder. I moved faster, my tongue swirling around him, my hands gripping his thighs for balance. I could feel him throbbing in my mouth, his breathing growing ragged. I kept stealing glances at his face, watching the way his jaw clenched, the way his eyes darkened with need. The more he groaned, the more I wanted to please him.

"Fuck, baby, you're gonna make me come," he growled, his hand tightening in my hair. He guided my head, moving me faster, his hips rocking slightly. "You ready for me, Anna? Gonna take it all?"

I hummed around him, the vibration making him curse under his breath. His grip tightened, and suddenly he was thrusting into my mouth, shallow but firm. I tried to keep up, my eyes watering as he hit the back of my throat. With a low, guttural moan, he came, hot and thick, spilling into my mouth. I swallowed instinctively, the taste bitter and unfamiliar, making me grimace slightly.

Kirill chuckled, his thumb brushing my cheek as he pulled out. "Look at you, so eager but so damn innocent," he said, his voice dripping with heat. "That little frown is gonna be the death of me."

Before I could respond, he was on me, his hands ripping apart the skimpy black fabric on my body until I was bare beneath him. My heart raced, my body exposed to his hungry gaze. He didn't give me time to feel shy. His mouth was on my chest, kissing and sucking at my breasts, his teeth grazing my nipples until I gasped. The sensation was overwhelming, pleasure mixed with a sharp edge that made me arch into him.

"Kirill," I whimpered, my hands clutching at the sheets.

He didn't stop, his tongue swirling around one nipple while his hand pinched the other, just hard enough to make me cry out. Then he moved lower, his lips trailing down my stomach, leaving a path of fire in their wake. When his mouth reached the apex of my thighs, I tensed, my breath hitching.

"Relax, baby," he murmured against my skin. "I'm gonna make you feel so good."

His tongue flicked against me, and I nearly came off the bed. He licked slowly at first, teasing, then with more purpose, his lips closing around my clit. I moaned, my hips bucking involuntarily. His fingers joined in, one sliding inside me, then two, stretching me gently. It felt strange but incredible, the pressure building as he worked me with his mouth and hands.

"You're so fucking wet," he growled, his voice muffled against me. "Can't wait to be inside you, Anna. Gonna fuck you so good you'll never forget it."

His words were filthy, but they only made me want him more. My body was trembling, every touch pushing me closer to the edge. I was so wet I could hear it, the slick sounds of his fingers moving inside me. My hands fisted in his hair, pulling him closer as I chased the release building inside me.

"Kirill, please," I gasped, my voice barely recognizable.

He chuckled, the vibration sending another jolt through me. "That's it, baby. Beg for me."

I was too far gone to care about pride. "Please, Kirill, I need you."

He didn't make me wait. His fingers curled inside me, hitting a spot that made stars burst behind my eyes. His tongue flicked faster, and I shattered, my orgasm crashing over me like a wave. I cried out, my body shaking as he kept going, drawing out every last bit of pleasure.

When I finally caught my breath, he was above me again, his cock hard and ready once more. He positioned himself between my legs, the tip brushing against my entrance. "You ready for me, Anna?" he asked, his voice thick with lust. "Gonna fill you up, make you mine."

I nodded, my body still buzzing from my climax. He leaned down, kissing me deeply, and I could taste myself on his lips. Then he pushed forward, just the tip at first, and I tensed, the stretch unfamiliar and intense.

CHAPTER FOUR

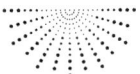

Kirill

FUCK, she was tight. So tight I could barely think straight as I eased into her, inch by agonizing inch. Anna's breath hitched, her nails digging into my shoulders, and I had to grit my teeth to keep from thrusting too fast. Her pussy gripped me like a vice, hot and wet and perfect. This gorgeous, fiery woman, who could've had any man she wanted, was giving me her first everything.

"Jesus, Anna," I rasped, pausing to look at her. Her eyes were wide, a mix of nervousness and desire, her lips parted as she panted. "I need you to relax a bit for me."

She blushed, her cheeks a deep pink. "Okay, just..." she whispered, her voice trembling but bold. "Just tell me what to do."

Her words did something to me, twisted something deep in my chest. I leaned down, kissing her softly, trying to ease her nerves. "I've got you, baby," I murmured against her lips. "Gonna make this so good for you."

She nodded, her hands sliding down my back, urging me closer. I could see the tension in her face, the slight wince as I pushed a little deeper. It was killing me to go slow, my cock throbbing with the need to bury myself in her, but I didn't want to hurt her. I kissed her again, deeper this time, my tongue tangling with hers as I waited for her to relax.

When her brows smoothed out, her body softening beneath me, I took it as my cue. I pushed in further, slow and steady, until I broke through. She gasped, her nails biting into my skin, and I froze, giving her time to adjust. "You okay, sweetheart?" I asked, my voice rough.

"It hurts," she admitted, her voice small but not panicked. "But… keep going."

I kissed her forehead, her cheeks, her lips, whispering filthy promises to distract her. "You're so fucking tight, Anna. Gonna feel so good when I'm all the way in. You're gonna love it, I promise."

She nodded, her legs wrapping around my waist, pulling me closer. I thrust slowly, deeper each time, until I was fully seated inside her. The sound she made—half moan, half whimper—nearly undid me. I groaned, the pleasure of her tight heat overwhelming. "Fuck, you feel incredible," I said, my voice strained. "So perfect, so mine."

I started moving, slow at first, watching her face for any sign of discomfort. But her expression shifted, the pain giving way to pleasure. Her hips rocked against mine, tentative but eager, and I couldn't hold back anymore. I picked up the pace, thrusting harder, deeper, each movement pulling a moan from her lips.

"Look at you, taking my cock like you were made for it," I growled, my hands gripping her hips. "You love this, don't you? Tell me how much you love it."

Her cheeks flushed, but she didn't shy away. "I love it," she gasped, her voice shaky but bold. "It feels so good, Kirill."

Her words were like gasoline on a fire. I fucked her harder, the bed creaking beneath us, her legs tightening around me. "That's it, baby," I said, my voice low and dirty. "Squeeze me tight. Let me feel how much you want it."

She moaned louder, her hands clawing at my back as she met my thrusts. I could feel her getting close, her pussy fluttering around me.

"Come for me, Anna," I urged, my thumb finding her clit, rubbing in tight circles. "Come all over my cock."

She cried out, her body arching as her orgasm hit, her walls clenching around me so tight I nearly lost it. I slowed my thrusts, letting her ride it out, her moans filling the room. But I wasn't done with her yet.

I pulled out, ignoring her whimper of protest, and flipped her over. "On your knees, baby," I said, my voice rough with need. She obeyed, her movements a little shaky but eager, presenting herself to me. Her ass was perfect, round and soft, and I couldn't resist giving it a sharp smack. She gasped, her body jerking, but she pushed back against me, silently begging for more.

"Fuck, you're so hot like this," I said, lining myself up and thrusting into her from behind. The new angle was even tighter, and I groaned, my hands gripping her hips. I spanked her again, harder this time, loving the way her skin pinked up under my hand. "You like that, don't you? My dirty little virgin."

"Yes," she moaned, her voice muffled against the sheets. "Please, Kirill, more."

I gave it to her, fucking her hard and fast, each thrust punctuated by another smack to her ass. Her moans grew louder, more desperate, and I could feel her building toward another climax. I leaned forward, my teeth grazing her neck, biting down just enough to make her gasp. "Come again for me, Anna," I growled. "Let me feel you."

She did, her body shaking as her second orgasm hit, her pussy pulsing around me. The sensation was too much, pushing me over the edge. I bit down harder on her neck, marking her as mine, and came with a groan, spilling deep inside her. We collapsed together, panting, our bodies slick with sweat.

I LEANED back against the headboard, my gaze settling on the girl sleeping beside me. Her face still held traces of a blush, innocent in slumber.

She was so damn young, wasn't she? Twenty years old—barely half my age. College age. Fresh and untouched.

She had no business being here. No business in a stranger's bed.

It was surreal. Two hours ago, this same inexperienced body had unraveled beneath me with wild abandon.

I'd been with more women than I could count. Blonde models, A-list actresses—they performed in bed as professionally as the checks I wrote them.

But she was different. Every response was clumsy, untrained. Yet she learned fast. Or maybe her body was simply honest.

I'd never experienced anything like it with any woman—that perfect fit. She was like a lock crafted specifically for me, and I was the only key that could open her.

She'd driven me to the brink. Once, twice... until she finally shattered in my arms and collapsed into sleep.

But my bed had always belonged to me alone. After passion faded, my usual partners would dress themselves and leave before I had to ask. No one ever stayed until dawn.

So should I wake Anna now? Have Volkov send someone to escort her away? The thought lasted maybe a second before I dismissed it. Too much trouble to wake her.

I convinced myself with that simple excuse, pulled her against me, and drifted into sleep.

* * *

MORNING LIGHT SLICED a narrow band across the room.

I woke first. She was still naked in my arms, marks on her skin testimony to how wild we'd been.

I slipped my arm free and rose silently, stepping on the torn black lace from last night. I kicked it aside and headed for the shower.

When I emerged, she was awake. She blinked sleepily, confusion clouding her features as she tried to place where she was. Then her eyes focused on me.

She bolted upright, wrapping the sheet around her naked form.

"No need for that. You were laid bare long before now. We did worse, Miss Anna." My voice carried lazy amusement.

Her face flushed crimson.

I texted my assistant to collect twenty grand from the bank and bring Anna decent clothing.

Everything arrived before Anna finished getting ready.

I handed her the new clothes. After she dressed, I placed the envelope containing twenty thousand dollars on the table before her.

She stared at it, bewildered. "What's this?"

"Twenty thousand. Payment for last night." My tone remained casual.

I watched her face drain of color. She bit her lip hard. When I expected her to refuse, she accepted after a prolonged silence.

"Thank you... but this is too much."

"You earned every penny."

"Thank you, Mr. Zaitsev." This time she accepted quickly.

"Why were you at the underground auction?" I asked.

"My father owed fifty grand in gambling debts. He put me up as collateral. If I didn't comply, he said we'd both be killed." Her expression was downcast, her voice hollow and fragile.

Something uncomfortable stirred in my chest, but I pushed it aside.

"What's your plan now? I can handle your father's situation."

I never meddled in others' affairs. I had no idea why I was offering.

"Handle?" Confusion flickered in her eyes.

"Yes, you know who I am, don't you? I could have his hands and legs broken. If you'd like."

I flashed a roguish smile.

"I know you're connected to the Bratva. But no, thank you. He's still my father." Her lips pressed into a tight line.

"Unfortunate." I drew out the word.

After a moment, I asked directly, "What do you want? A house, car, money?"

"What do you mean?"

"I mean I'm satisfied with your body," I stated it bluntly. "Stay with me as my woman. I'll give you whatever you desire. All you need to do is service me like last night whenever I require it."

Disbelief flashed across her features. She refused immediately, "No, thank you. I don't want anything. I'm leaving."

She started toward the door.

"Wait." I stopped her. "Are you certain? I'm never stingy with women."

She whirled around, her voice suddenly sharp, "Yes! I'm sure. Your tip was enough. And I'm not—God, I'm not some damn whore!"

Frustration descended like a dark cloud. I always get what I want. No woman had ever refused me so decisively. Twice.

Anger coiled in my chest, but I didn't let it show. I desired her body, yes. But I wasn't desperate. My world was full of women. If I wished, I could have a dozen more beautiful women lined up naked on this bed within the hour.

I never favored force. Too undignified.

"Very well," I said coolly. "If you have that much backbone, take your pay and go."

Only then did she remember to grab the twenty thousand and rush out without a backward glance.

I released a deep, frustrated breath.

* * *

In the private booth at Bull's Horn Club, Theodore and I sat across from each other, our subordinates positioned behind us.

"Seventy-thirty?" Theodore barked. "Kirill, that's not fair. That Shipping Route runs through my turf. My men will do the work and shoulder the risk. Fifty-fifty at least."

I drained my whiskey glass. Since that girl departed this morning, rage had been smoldering in my chest, making me increasingly irritable.

"Fair?" I scoffed. "Theodore, my people will handle whatever risk you're whining about. Your job is to keep your boys at the docks. Zaitsev Group is paying for every bit of the shipping route buildout—

the costs, the logistics, the push to get it moving. You'd be handed thirty percent pure profit for doing almost nothing. You're complaining to me?"

"No, of course not, I just—"

"You think my money's easy? Thirty percent is my bottom line. Take it or I'll start a war you don't want. I doubt either of us wants that." I interrupted him, my voice laden with menace. My men behind me straightened, fixing him with intimidating stares.

Theodore's face went ashen. War meant blood flooding the streets, and Moretti Family's influence paled compared to Bratva.

"Agreed. Seventy-thirty. We'll do it your way." Theodore gave in.

"A wise decision." I reclined back into the sofa, resuming my languid posture.

My phone vibrated. Volkov, my right hand, calling.

"Speak."

"Boss, trouble. A bunch of Irish at Brighton Beach stepped on our people. It's getting out of hand. You need to come back." Volkov's voice carried urgency.

I frowned. Damn pests.

"I'm on my way." I terminated the call and stood.

"Leaving already?" Theodore rose as well.

"I must return to New York to squash some flies. My guy will coordinate contract details with you." I retrieved my coat and strode toward the exit without looking back.

Back in New York, it was simpler than I expected.

One night was enough. I made those arrogant Irish understand who ran Brooklyn. When I put the boss's broken hand under my boot and told him to leave New York or die, he chose to leave.

Problem resolved. Yet the irritation burning in my chest remained undiminished.

My usual girl visited my office. I used her body to vent my frustration. But even as I moved within her, my mind conjured that girl's face—how she'd clung to me with desperate intensity, gazing at me with those watery, bright, green eyes as though I were the sole anchor she could grasp in that ocean of desire. That sensation had completely satisfied me.

Perhaps I just like her type? Inexperienced, green-eyed, dark-haired. Yes, that must be it.

Over the following days, I had Volkov locate several girls resembling her. I brought them to my bed. I could perform, my body still derived pleasure. But something felt fundamentally wrong. Like wine with the alcohol burned away—the flavor remained, but the essence had vanished. That perfect, wild synchronization with that girl never materialized again.

A month later, I was compelled to send Volkov to Chicago to locate her using only her name. But she had vanished like smoke, leaving no trace.

BANG!

The heavy bag swung violently from my savage right hook, the impact reverberating through the space.

Sweat streamed down my forehead into my eyes, stinging sharply, but I remained indifferent. I regulated my breathing, preparing for the next assault.

"Whoa there, easy, man." An amused voice drifted from nearby. "You got a vendetta against that bag or you picturing someone's face?"

I didn't turn around, delivering another devastating punch to the bag. "Shut up, Viktor."

Viktor Petrov. One of my few genuine friends. Former Russian special forces elite sniper, currently leading a semi-retired existence. The sole individual I knew who dared jest when I was in a foul mood.

He approached, wrapping his hands. "What's troubling you? Those Irish vermin in New York still causing problems?"

"A bunch of bugs. Handled long ago." I took off my gloves and wiped my face.

"It's strange seeing you like this," Viktor said as he warmed up. His movements were clean, efficient.

I remained silent. I walked to the octagon's edge and took a long sip of water.

Viktor followed, leaning against the cage, studying me with perceptive eyes. "Let me guess. Not business. Woman trouble?"

I slammed the water bottle down forcefully. "Care for a round?"

"I was hoping you'd ask." Viktor grinned broadly, showing teeth.

We entered the octagon and secured the door.

After touching gloves respectfully, combat commenced.

Viktor's assault was rapid and relentless, each punch and kick carrying that special forces lethality—designed for elimination.

The percussion of fist meeting flesh, labored breathing, echoed throughout Novak Club's combat arena.

Sweat soaked our clothes, muscles burned, but we kept going.

Throughout our exchange of blows, I finally let it out.

"Then she refused me," I said—the sentence that'd been gnawing at me for a week—and I drove a straight right that pushed him back.

We opened space.

Viktor hung there for a beat, then burst into a laugh that filled the room.

"She turned you down?" He laughed until he doubled over. "She turned down Kirill Zaitsev? Jesus. What planet did she fall from? Doesn't she know what you are?"

"She kind of did." My face darkened.

"And still turned you down? Fuck, now I'm curious. What's her name? What does she look like?"

"Anna."

"Anna? That's a boring name."

"After that I had people look for her. Couldn't find her."

"For a one-night thing you went to war over? Kirill, that's not you." Viktor ribbed.

We clashed again. He caught my punch and threw a perfect shoulder toss, slamming me to the mat. I spun and locked my legs around his neck, trying to flip the script.

"You hooked?" Viktor asked, muffled by my legs, teasing despite the choke.

"Fuck no," I snapped. "I was into her body."

"Just the body?" He raised an eyebrow.

I shut up.

"I wasn't satisfied," I said finally.

Not just because she'd rejected me. I couldn't accept that, after what we'd shared, she'd say no and vanish. That wasn't how things went with me.

"Fine. So what now? Dig up every hole until you find her? Tie her to your bed until you get bored?" Viktor asked.

I didn't have an answer. All I knew was I had to find her.

I had to make her understand who it was she'd refused.

I had to taste her again.

CHAPTER FIVE

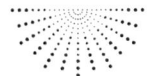

Celia

I STARED at the heavy twenty thousand dollars lying on the bed. Generous payment for a whore.

His words still echoed in my ears.

"Be my woman." Be my on-call prostitute.

Humiliation washed over me.

For a moment, I even wanted to be like some proud heroine—refuse his tip, hold my head high, and walk away. But I couldn't. I needed the money. I needed it to start over.

I was grateful he'd outbid everyone at the auction, that he'd saved me from that scarred brute and spared me from something truly horrific.

Sleeping with him had felt incredible. I'd experienced pleasure I never knew existed. But I also hated myself for losing control beneath him, for getting lost in a one-night stand. That wasn't what an "auction item" was supposed to do.

I took a deep breath, pushed down these feelings, and got to work before my father came home.

I pulled out a hundred-dollar bill and slipped it into the locked drawer of my nightstand. Bait.

The rest went into the metal box under my bed—my escape money.

The moment I finished, I heard the front door.

He was back.

My father appeared in my doorway soon enough. When he saw me, calculation flickered in his bloodshot eyes.

"You're back? How'd it go? You service him good last night?"

My lungs swelled with rage. I stared at him with ice-cold eyes.

He didn't seem to mind my silence, just kept talking. "Having a daughter really pays off. Look at that—one night with some rich old bastard and daddy's debt is gone."

His words cut like a dull knife, slicing open the rawest parts of my heart over and over.

"Shut up!" My voice shook with fury. "You shouldn't talk about your daughter like that!"

"I shouldn't?" His laugh was grating and ugly. "I gave you life, gave you a safe warm home. What shouldn't I do? If it wasn't for me, you think you'd still be standing here? You'd probably be raped by those loan shark bastards in some back alley—"

"Enough!" I screamed, cutting him off. "Why did you become like this? Why!"

I stared at his twisted face, searching for any trace of the father I remembered.

When did he change?

Was it after Mom died of cancer and he started drinking all day? Or was he always this selfish piece of shit deep down?

I didn't know. And I didn't need to know anymore.

"What the fuck did I become?" He swayed toward me. "I'm still me. You're the one who changed, Celia. You used to be a good girl. You never used to fucking scream at your old man like this."

Then he showed his real purpose. "Where's the money? Those guys pay big. You were a virgin—they must've tipped you good. Hand it over."

"There isn't any." My answer was cold.

"No money?" His eyes narrowed. "You think I'm fucking stupid? Come on, fork it over! I'm on a hot streak lately—perfect time to double down!"

"I told you, there isn't any!"

He stopped talking and started tearing through my room like a madman. Everything he touched looked ransacked. Finally, his eyes landed on the locked drawer.

"What's in here?" He pointed at the drawer.

"Nothing. Just old stuff." I blocked his way.

"Open it!"

"No."

"I said fucking open it!"

"No!"

SMACK!

A sharp slap cracked across my face. My head snapped to the side, ears ringing, cheek burning. I stared at him in disbelief. First time he'd ever hit me.

Looking into his impatient eyes, I knew I couldn't fight anymore. I pulled out the key and opened the drawer.

He shoved me aside and grabbed the hundred dollars. When he saw that's all there was, his face twisted with disappointment and disgust.

"That's fucking it?" He spat. "You locked this shit up like it was treasure. This wouldn't even last me a few hands at the table."

He pocketed the money and stormed out without looking back.

The door slammed shut. The world went quiet.

I slowly sank to the floor, the pain in my face nothing compared to what was tearing through my heart.

I curled up, hugging my knees, and sobbed. For my dead mother. For my rotten father. For my damned life that couldn't see a single ray of light.

I don't know how long I cried. Until the tears ran dry and my throat was raw.

I got up and went to my bedroom, pulling out an old picture frame from the nightstand.

It was a photo of our family. Mom smiling warm and bright, holding little me, while Dad looked at us with pure adoration.

It used to be such a warm, happy home.

Now it was all destroyed.

I took scissors and cut Dad out of the photo, keeping just me and Mom.

Then I bought a one-way ticket to New York and started packing. I didn't have much. A few changes of clothes, some things Mom left me, and the metal box under my bed with all my hope inside—that man's tip, nineteen thousand nine hundred dollars.

Before leaving the apartment, I snapped my phone card in half and flushed it down the toilet.

I didn't know what I could do in New York. But I remembered Mom always talking about that place. She said it was where she and Dad first met, a city full of opportunities and miracles.

* * *

IN NEW YORK, I rented a shabby apartment with cheap rent. Then I got two jobs—serving coffee during the day, washing dishes at a restaurant at night. Life was hard and exhausting, but I felt safer than I ever had.

Here, no one knew me. No one knew my past. I was so tired every day I collapsed into bed, no time to think about painful memories.

That's where I met Mia Carter.

She was a regular at the coffee shop, a sweet girl as warm as sunshine. She was a social media blogger, always holding up her phone, capturing moments. She seemed interested in this quiet waitress, always finding ways to chat with me.

We became friends. She'd drag me out for cheap pizza, buy me lattes when I was broke before payday, pretending it was no big deal.

She never asked about my past. I was grateful for her thoughtfulness.

Days passed in this quiet rhythm.

"When was your last period?" the doctor asked.

I stared at the uterus anatomy chart on the wall, trying to remember exactly.

"About... a month ago?" I said uncertainly. "My periods have never been regular, so..."

"Besides missing your period, any other symptoms? Nausea, fatigue, increased appetite?"

"No," I answered immediately. "I feel pretty normal."

I was telling the truth. My body felt fine, which was why I'd waited so long to come to the hospital.

The doctor nodded, expression unchanged. "Let's draw some blood for an HCG test, see if you're pregnant. Results come back quickly."

"Pregnant?" I frowned. No, impossible. Just that one time.

The twenty-minute wait felt endless. I sat on the hallway bench staring at my phone screen but couldn't read a word. My brain started spinning out of control. I thought about that man I'd slept with, Kirill Zaitsev. I thought about that wild night.

We hadn't used protection. My palms started sweating.

"Celia Cole?"

The nurse's voice cut through my thoughts. I jumped up, heart hammering against my ribs.

When I sat across from the doctor again, anxiety crystallized under my skin. She pushed a lab report toward me. I couldn't even look at it.

"Celia, the results are clear. You're pregnant." The doctor looked into my eyes.

"What?" Two dry syllables squeezed from my throat. My brain shut down. The doctor's words sounded muffled, like through frosted glass.

Pregnant.

"Based on your last period, about eight weeks along." The doctor's voice pulled me back from the chaos.

Eight weeks. Without me knowing, this little thing had been quietly growing inside me for two months.

"What... what should I do?" My voice shook. The second the question left my mouth, I wanted to bite my tongue off. What should I do? What could I do? I didn't have enough money to raise a child. The words "single mother" flashed through my mind—that kind of struggle wasn't something a twenty-year-old could handle.

"An abortion... how much would that cost?" I heard myself ask in a stranger's voice.

The doctor looked at me without judgment, just calm understanding. "Before making any decision, I recommend an ultrasound first. We need to confirm it's an intrauterine pregnancy and rule out ectopic pregnancy. That's important for your safety."

Her words were professional and reasonable. I nodded like a puppet, letting the nurse lead me to the ultrasound room again.

Cold gel on my stomach made me shiver. The doctor moved the probe and black and white images appeared on the screen.

"Look, that's your baby." The doctor pointed to a shadow on the screen. "About eight weeks, developing well."

I stared at that blurry image, mouth hanging open. Only now did I truly feel there was a little life inside me.

"Listen, this is the fetal heartbeat." The doctor adjusted the equipment.

Thump-thump, thump-thump...

That rapid, rhythmic sound like a little train racing by made my eyes well up instantly. This was part of me, connected to me in the most intimate way possible. Even though I wasn't ready to be a mother, I couldn't bring myself to get rid of this beautiful little one in my belly.

"Very strong fetal heartbeat, 158 beats per minute. Very healthy." The doctor recorded while describing. "You'll need regular checkups, proper nutrition..."

The doctor's words quickly faded. My eyes stayed locked on the little one on the screen.

I had no family left. He would be my only family from now on. I would love him, protect him.

My life might get harder because of this, but I didn't care. I only knew that from now on, I wouldn't be alone anymore.

CHAPTER SIX

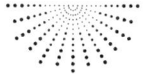

Celia

FIVE YEARS LATER.

"Mommy, is dinosaur poop round or square?"

I nearly launched that overcooked egg straight onto the floor. I turned to look at Lucas, who was sitting in his chair with his little legs swinging in the air. Those gray-blue eyes... God, he had inherited that man's eyes completely.

"I'm guessing round, sweetheart. Like big rocks." I slid the egg onto his plate with the T-rex print.

"Whoa," he marveled, "that must be huge."

"Very huge." I poured the last of the coffee into my mug—the one that said "World's Best Mom," a gift from Mia last Christmas. The thing was already chipping.

After Lucas was born, that money was long gone—diapers, formula, and everything else a kid needs. I swore I'd give Lucas the best, even if it meant splitting myself into three pieces.

"Hurry up and eat, little dinosaur. We're going to Mia's." I ruffled his soft hair.

I had a ten o'clock interview, and I needed Mia to watch Lucas.

Five years ago, when Mia found out I was pregnant, she didn't pry. She knew I'd talk when I was ready, and honestly, I wasn't prepared to spill everything about that auction and one-night stand.

When I first got pregnant, I was completely clueless. Mia was there the whole time, helping and supporting me. She went to doctor's appointments with me, stayed by my side when I gave birth, made me nutritious meals after delivery, and took care of me. She treated Lucas like her own child. For five years, whenever I was working and couldn't watch Lucas, Mia would edit her videos while carefully looking after him. In my heart, she was Lucas's second mother.

I drove my beat-up secondhand Toyota through the streets, feeling like I was piloting a moving tin can. I always worried it would break down on me someday.

I parked my faithful old buddy downstairs from Mia's building, then took Lucas's hand and walked up the stairs, knocking on Mia's door. Mia had become a minor YouTube celebrity now, doing way better financially than me, living in a decent apartment.

"Hey, super mom!" Mia opened the door and gave me a big hug.

"Hey!" I hugged her back.

"Little guy, come let Mia hug you!" Mia crouched down and gave Lucas a big squeeze, even lifting him up and bouncing him a couple times.

"How do you feel heavier? What good stuff have you been eating in that round little belly?" Mia said as she started tickling Lucas's stomach.

Lucas burst into giggles, his body writhing as he tried to escape those mischievous fingers.

I smiled and pulled out my phone to capture the moment.

"No... stop tickling... Mia... help me, Mommy!"

"Okay, okay, let's go inside." I tried to rescue Lucas.

Finally, after my son was laughing himself to tears, Mia mercifully stopped.

Lucas rushed into the living room and pulled out the toy box Mia always kept there for him.

"All set? Your Fortune 500 company interview?" Mia handed me a steaming cup of coffee.

I took the coffee and answered, "Please, it's just a simple typing clerk job. And I'm so nervous I might throw up."

"Zaitsev Group is a major company with global operations. Even if you're interviewing for a clerk position, you'd be a high-end company clerk." She patted my shoulder. "This is a real start—steady salary, and you won't have to work three jobs anymore. You'll actually have time to spend with Lucas after work."

Zaitsev Group. My heart still skipped when I heard that name. I'd wondered if this company might be connected to that man. But he lived in Chicago and was connected to the Bratva. Why would the Bratva come to New York to run a legitimate company? In my mind, those dangerous people dealt in gray areas—drugs, casinos, loan sharking.

"I know, Mia. I'll work super hard to nail this interview."

"Go get 'em, honey! For Lucas, you can do this!" She gave me her most sincere encouragement as I prepared to leave.

I nodded. Mia's blessing temporarily settled the nerves in my stomach.

But when my car stopped in front of Zaitsev Group's skyscraper that pierced the clouds, my pathetic courage evaporated instantly.

The company lobby was blindingly luxurious—marble floors you could see your reflection in, even the wall reliefs looked like they'd been polished with money. The men and women coming and going wore sharp suits and moved briskly, carrying briefcases, looking thoroughly professional. Honestly, everything here excluded someone like me standing at the entrance, completely lost.

The interview outfit I'd gritted my teeth to buy had looked decent enough in the department store's fitting room mirror, but now, compared to the receptionist's uniform, it looked like something from a street vendor.

"Hello, I'm Celia Cole. I have a ten o'clock interview appointment." I fought to keep my voice steady.

The receptionist directed me to follow the instructions to the interview location.

Thank God, the interview went smoother than I'd expected. The HR manager was a sharp middle-aged woman who asked questions all within my preparation range.

"Very well, Ms. Cole. You're hired. Please report next Monday morning at nine sharp." She finally closed the interview folder and gave me a professional smile.

I practically floated out of that building on clouds. The moment I stepped past the entrance, sunlight enveloped me. I'd always thought sunlight was ordinary, but now I felt its brilliance.

I'd done it! I'd landed a real job! Stable, respectable, with good pay. More importantly, I'd have more time to spend with Lucas.

That night, we cooked a big meal at Mia's to celebrate—the main course was steak, something we rarely ate because of our tight budget.

Watching Lucas eat with his eyes squinted in pleasure, I felt happy and fulfilled, but also guilty.

Monday morning after reporting in, HR led me to my workstation. My marketing department was on the seventeenth floor—an open office area with dozens of cubicles arranged neatly.

I turned on my brand-new computer and logged into my company email. Everything was full of hope. Colleagues trickled in and greeted me warmly. The atmosphere was relaxed. I quickly dove into the tedious work of organizing files, but even repetitive work excited me.

Around ten o'clock, the office chatter suddenly cut off like someone had hit mute, leaving only the mechanical sound of keyboard clicks. An invisible pressure descended. I felt strange and looked up from my cubicle.

Then my world stopped spinning—I crashed into a pair of gray-blue eyes.

The instant our eyes met, it felt like tiny electric currents raced through my limbs. My eyes were wide open. I didn't dare move.

I was so shocked I forgot to breathe!

It was him. Kirill Zaitsev! The man who'd bought my virginity five years ago! What were the odds? How could he be here?

Was he looking at me? How long had he been watching? Did he recognize me? How could he?

I quickly ducked my head, burying it below the cubicle wall. Why was that man standing by the elevator? Zaitsev Group... could he really be someone from this company? Wasn't he in Chicago?

After a few seconds, afraid I'd mistaken him for someone else, I carefully lifted my head to look at that spot again.

The man stood at the front of the group, wearing a charcoal gray suit with fabric pressed to perfection, making his already powerful frame even more imposing, his broad shoulders radiating authority.

Compared to five years ago, his hair was cut shorter, neatly combed back to reveal a smooth, full forehead and that scar through his eyebrow I'd remembered too long.

Time had barely touched his face, just adding fine lines at the corners of his eyes and a few silver threads in his dark brown hair. This only made his presence shift from the fierce intensity of five years ago to current composure, making him look more experienced and charismatic.

But what made me feel suffocated was that he was still looking at me, his eyes holding depths I couldn't read.

Finally, his gaze shifted, his body turning toward the suited man beside him.

"This floor houses our company's marketing department." His voice was low and steady as he addressed his companion. "Last quarter, this department successfully partnered with three Boston enterprises and secured long-term contracts."

As soon as he finished speaking, the entourage behind him immediately started recording something on their tablets.

After what felt like a damn eternity, the whole group left. The moment they were gone, the office's oppressive atmosphere instantly lifted, and whispered conversations spread.

"My God, that was terrifying." Emily, who sat in the cubicle next to mine, dramatically patted her chest. "The boss's presence is really intimidating. I didn't even dare breathe loudly."

"Boss?" My tongue felt thick.

"Yeah! You didn't know?" Emily looked at me like I was an alien. "Mr. Kirill Zaitsev, our group's CEO. He's a total workaholic, and... very intimidating."

Kirill Zaitsev.

The man who bought my virginity, my one-night stand, Lucas's father... he was actually my new company's boss!

This was insane!

"He's really handsome, though! Did you see him in that suit? He's like a walking clothes hanger." Another female colleague joined our chat.

"His physique is incredible, so much masculinity. Even though his presence is intimidating, if I could get with him..." Emily said, her face flushing.

"Dream on, ladies." Our marketing supervisor, O'Neil, walked over and leaned his arm on the cubicle wall, bursting their bubble. "A man like that has more women around him than you've had cups of coffee. You better just focus on your work."

After O'Neil spoke, everyone quickly shut up and returned to work.

I stared blankly at my computer, my stomach churning uneasily.

I was terrified he'd recognize me. What if he discovered Lucas's existence? Would he try to take Lucas away from me? He was connected to gangs—if he really wanted to do that, calling the police wouldn't help.

But seeing this man again, some part of my body became a traitor. It welcomed this reunion, it led me back to that night five years ago, it made me think about new possibilities with him.

Just when fear and anxiety were about to drive me insane, the supervisor came back and knocked on my desk.

"Celia." His expression was odd. "The big boss wants to see you upstairs. Top floor office."

My breath caught in my throat.

Colleagues immediately turned to look, murmuring among themselves.

"What's going on? Getting summoned by the CEO on her first day?"

"She is really pretty... the boss was looking in her direction earlier."

I ignored the chatter. I mechanically stood up and followed the supervisor to the private elevator that led to the top floor.

The supervisor brought me to the top-floor office door and left.

I took a deep breath and knocked.

"Come in."

The steady voice penetrated the door and crawled up my spine, sending shivers through me.

I pushed open the door.

This office was bigger than my entire apartment. One whole wall was floor-to-ceiling glass with a panoramic view of the city skyline.

He sat behind his desk reading some documents.

He'd removed his suit jacket, leaving only a white shirt that draped smoothly over his strong torso. His sleeves were casually rolled up to his elbows, revealing solid forearms. The authority he radiated was almost tangible, even more commanding than five years ago.

I stood there like an idiot, not knowing what to do with my hands and feet.

He finally finished reading and looked up, those gray-blue eyes fixing me with their intensity.

"Celia Cole?" He spoke my name like he was tasting an unfamiliar word.

"Yes, sir." It took me forever to find my voice.

"Not Anna?" He leaned back in his chair, hands crossed in front of him.

Pressure pushed against my eardrums, an invisible force dragging me into a spiral of unease.

"I'm-I'm sorry, sir. I was—" I tried to explain as quickly as possible.

"You don't need to explain," he cut me off. "HR made a mistake."

"...What?" The topic shifted too fast for me to follow.

"They hired you. But you're not qualified." His tone was as flat as if he were stating the weather.

Hot blood rushed to my head, overriding my fear. "I don't understand. I already passed the interview. The HR manager said—"

"I said," he cut me off again, "you're not qualified. Don't come in tomorrow."

Tears almost spilled over. I bit my tongue hard. Anger, confusion, and despair crashed over me like mixed paint. I'd finally gotten this job—it was hope for me and Lucas! How could he... how could he so casually take it away? Was this his punishment for me using a fake name to deceive him?

"Why?" My voice shook. "You haven't even looked at my résumé! What gives you the right to say I'm not qualified? Just because... just because you don't like the sight of me?"

He looked at me, the corner of his mouth curving into a mocking smile. "I don't need a reason, Ms. Cole. In this building, my will is reason enough."

He was right. What was I? An ant he could crush with his bare hand. My dignity, my efforts—worthless in front of him. Overwhelming sadness and helplessness crushed me. My job, my hope—all shattered.

Just as I was about to turn and leave, he suddenly stood up and pulled me into his arms.

Kirill was tall, his imposing presence making me forget to resist.

He raised his hand, and I fearfully closed my eyes. But he didn't strike me. His hand touched my lips.

My whole body stiffened, blood roaring in my ears.

His thumb rubbed against my trembling lips, making them red and swollen. His eyes locked onto mine, churning with dark currents. I even had the absurd illusion that he was going to kiss me.

"Perhaps." His voice was like a devil's whisper. "There's one way you could stay."

I stared wide-eyed, only able to look at him mutely.

"Be my mistress, Celia. If you agree, I'll let you stay at Zaitsev Group." His voice carried husky magnetism, his blatant gaze seeming to strip away my clothes.

The humiliation of being priced like an object five years ago, the humiliation of being treated like a whore—it all came flooding back.

I understood now. He was getting revenge on me, revenge for refusing to be his mistress five years ago!

Anger erupted inside me like a volcano, giving me the strength to break free. I shoved him away, my chest heaving violently.

"In your dreams! I'm not your whore!" I practically screamed the words.

He staggered back a step, surprise flashing across his face.

Tears filled my eyes, but I forced myself not to let them fall. "You bastard!"

After cursing him, I refused to look at him anymore. I bolted out of there.

CHAPTER SEVEN

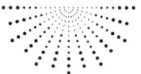

Kirill

I STOOD FROZEN IN PLACE. I should have had that woman in my arms to toy with, but now my embrace held nothing but empty air.

My fingertips still carried the warm, soft memory of her lips. Her scent still lingered in my nostrils—that fresh, distinctive citrus fragrance. I exhaled in frustration, this feeling of wanting what I couldn't have driving me to crave destruction.

She called me a bastard. Yeah, I was. I'd searched for her for so damn long, yet she acted like she'd never existed in my world.

She gave me a fake name—Anna. Fuck Anna.

I recognized her instantly in the marketing department. In five years, her appearance hadn't changed much—still beautiful. Her black hair was pulled back, revealing that delicate face, those green eyes like emerald lakes. She appeared often in my wet dreams, where I found her. I'd fuck her hard, punish her until she rolled her eyes back and begged me to stop.

In my dreams, she looked like she did five years ago—innocent and sweet. Today, reuniting with her, I saw a mature, gentle version of her.

I couldn't bear to think about who had transformed her into this more alluring woman. Was it time? Or some other damn man? If it was the latter, I'd make those bastards disappear.

Celia Cole. Her real name suited her perfectly.

But why had she deceived me? Five years of suppressed resentment desperately searched for an outlet. And earlier, that opportunity came.

When I said "you're not qualified," she looked both panicked and helpless. All her emotions were because of me, and I savored everything I made her feel. When she was about to cry from anger, I seized the moment and proposed making her my mistress. And again, she refused me. I didn't know whether to feel vindicated or surprised.

I told myself that after her repeated rejections, my latest invitation had nothing to do with interest anymore. This was purely about conquest.

My phone's vibration interrupted my turbulent thoughts. I walked back to my desk and picked it up. The screen showed a call from the Novak Club manager.

"Mr. Zaitsev, sorry to disturb you. Our racing facility just finished renovations on a new track with some really challenging features. If you're interested, we'd be honored to have you come experience it," the club manager said.

Racing. I hadn't done that in ages.

When I was young, I was obsessed with the sport. I loved that adrenaline rush at extreme speeds. That ultimate sense of control, holding life and death in my hands—more addictive than any drug.

But as I aged, I hadn't touched a steering wheel in years. Even after ascending to the Bratva boss position, I rarely drove myself.

Now, suddenly, my hands were itching. I needed speed. I needed sensory stimulation intense enough to make me forget how to breathe, to suppress this damn restlessness Celia had stirred up in me.

"Get things ready. I'm coming today." I hung up.

The black stretch Lincoln moved through traffic, reaching Novak Club in about thirty minutes. The driver immediately stepped out and respectfully opened my rear door.

The manager was already waiting outside the ornate iron gates. Seeing me, his face immediately lit up with a perfectly calibrated smile as he hurried over, bowing slightly.

"Mr. Zaitsev, what an honor to have you here!"

I acknowledged him with a grunt, adjusted my cufflinks, and walked inside.

"Seriously, how many years has it been since we've seen you on the track?" he said, following at my side while carefully maintaining half a step's distance. "I remember when you were in your twenties—God, the way you drove was simply... forgive me for saying this, sir, but it was like you were chasing death itself. Every turn was like gambling with your life."

Chasing death? He wasn't wrong. Back then I raced like I had a death wish. Racing was the only way to escape my mother's suffocating funeral and my father's guilt-free apologies.

"Then... you never came back to our club's track," he said with a sigh.

Images from the past flashed through my mind.

Back then, my old boss father's liver finally gave out completely, and he died in some mistress's bed. One day I was just Kirill, a fucked-up son who could escape reality through racing. The next day, I became the new boss. Hundreds of men and their families' lives suddenly weighed on my shoulders overnight.

A boss's life was no longer his own. My life belonged to Bratva, and the steering wheel was permanently taken from my hands.

The boss couldn't put himself in danger, especially during Bratva's most precarious times. When my father moved Bratva from Russia to New York, our power base wasn't stable. After his death, the situation became extremely volatile. Old enemies pursued us relentlessly, while New York's new laws cracked down harder on organized crime. Our people kept dying. Without change, without growing stronger, we were waiting to die.

So I led the brothers in brutally uprooting our enemies' power, then cloaked the entire Zaitsev family in legitimate business—developing real estate, defense contracts, and massive logistics operations.

I succeeded. Maybe because my father's blood ran through my veins, I accomplished it all naturally, without any damn training period or adjustment phase.

"The new track absolutely won't disappoint you," the manager's voice pulled me back to reality.

I nodded.

The manager had already led me to my private changing room where I put on a black racing suit. Then he guided me toward the racing facility while introducing the new track.

"The renovated track is shaped like a horse ready to charge. The number and types of turns vary dramatically, with some sections having elevation changes up to 32 feet."

"Definitely quite a challenge," I said.

The track might look dangerous, but I only felt excitement.

We reached the expansive racing area. The air seemed thick with restless energy that pumped me up. The starting line was packed with various race cars, the stands filled with spectators ready to go wild for this upcoming display of speed and passion.

The manager continued, "Exactly! It's attracted quite a few challengers and spectators, plus reporters. The track is about four kilometers per lap. Since we're not professional racing, our club races are just twenty laps!"

After learning the rules, the manager led me to the Lamborghini waiting at the starting line. I opened the gull-wing door and slid in, gripping the steering wheel and feeling the engine's roar as it started. A long-lost feeling surged back into my bloodstream.

Besides me, several other supercars of different colors lined the track—rich kids with money to burn, seeking thrills.

I put on my helmet and snapped down the visor, taking one last look at the red numbers dancing on the dashboard.

The signal lights came on. Red. Yellow. Green!

Before my brain could react, my body moved first. I slammed the gas pedal, and the car shot forward like an arrow released from a bow, leaving the other vehicles far behind.

Wind howled in my ears, the massive G-force pressing me deep into my seat. My world narrowed to nothing but that endless gray track stretching ahead.

First turn. I downshifted precisely, cranked the wheel, and slid through in a near-perfect drift, hugging the apex. The massive centrifugal force sent my adrenaline skyrocketing.

I could feel the cars behind desperately trying to catch up. I accelerated harder, tires screaming against asphalt with violent friction. Every drift pushed my limits. I loved this feeling—dancing on the edge of life and death, all senses amplified to their peak, my brain forcibly cleared. Nothing but the instinct to win could exist in this space.

Through a series of sharp consecutive turns, I felt my body almost thrown from the seat. The tires groaned in agony, as if they might lift off the ground any second.

But I felt no fear. I would conquer it, just like I conquered everything in my life that tried to obstruct me.

Finally, the car burst through the sharp turns onto the straightaway. I shifted to top gear—one lap completed.

The intense rush of achievement and pure pleasure made me smile. After adapting to the track conditions, I drove even faster. Lap after lap, my brain finally shed that woman's shadow. All the irritation, all the loss of control—everything was pulverized before this ultimate speed.

I finished first.

I drove into the pit area and stopped, killing the engine.

I pulled off my helmet and stepped out. Sweat had soaked through my hair, trickling down my cheeks. I felt completely exhilarated.

Those scantily clad, statuesque models immediately swarmed around me.

"Mr. Zaitsev, you were incredible!"

"God, I was terrified watching, but you never slowed down!"

"Your driving skills are the best I've ever seen!"

They chattered away, wrapping me in various flattering words. I frowned in annoyance.

My gaze swept across their nearly identical faces. Then my eyes stopped on one particular girl.

She bore some resemblance to today's Celia—hair pulled back, green eyes.

I nodded at that girl. She froze momentarily, then her face lit up with ecstatic joy as she quickly walked over to me.

"Mr. Zaitsev." Her voice was sickeningly sweet.

Still in my racing suit, I put my arm around her and walked into the club's exclusive lounge reserved for me.

The door had barely closed when a body reeking of heavy rose perfume wrapped around me like a vine.

"Now, let's enjoy this moment." The woman's voice was sticky, her fingers deliberately provocative as they roamed restlessly over my body.

Her perfume was amplified countless times in the enclosed space, like spilled cheap fragrance. My nasal passages flooded with the scent, making my temples pound violently.

In that suffocating sweetness, another scent crashed into my mind without warning—sunshine-warmed citrus mixed with a hint of soap. Clean, crisp, just like Celia herself.

"Get off." The icy words erupted from my throat before I realized I'd frowned deeply and shoved her away with considerable force.

The woman staggered back two steps, her deliberately seductive smile instantly freezing, confusion flooding her eyes. "Sir?"

I ignored her and strode to the table where a checkbook and pen lay. I quickly tore off a check, scrawled a thousand-dollar amount, and threw it at her.

"Take the money and get out. Now."

Resentment flashed across the woman's face. She wanted to approach me again, but seeing the cold menace in my eyes, she only dared to bend down, snatch up the check, and flee the room in panic.

The door slammed shut, leaving me finally alone. But that nauseating rose scent stubbornly lingered in the air, as if mocking my foolishness.

I roughly tore off my racing suit and strode to the bar, twisting open a bottle of premium vodka and putting it directly to my lips for a savage gulp.

The burning liquid blazed a trail from my throat straight to my stomach. That searing sensation actually sharpened my thoughts.

I was wrong. Completely wrong.

When that woman approached me, I was physically revolted. The perfumes and deliberate pandering I once found meaningless now disgusted me utterly.

I could no longer settle for other women's bodies. I couldn't accept any substitutes.

I only wanted to sleep with one woman I'd once possessed—her, Celia.

I was rock hard and aching now. My erection strained painfully against my pants.

The racing suit pants were skin-tight, and I struggled to get them off, especially in my current state of peak arousal. When I finally sat naked on the soft couch, I exhaled in relief.

My hand gripped my already erect cock, fingers working with brutal force. When was the last time I'd masturbated? I couldn't remember—I had plenty of women to handle this for me. Now no one could help me unless she was Celia.

Thinking of Celia made my muscles tense even more. I was acting like some desperate teenager, all because of that goddamn Celia! My grip intensified, bringing exquisite pain and pleasure.

My mind was consumed with her. Her pink lips, her crisp citrus scent.

I still remembered vividly how it felt to fuck her five years ago. I remembered how her pussy wrapped around me, tight enough to nearly snap my dick off. I remembered how she rocked and writhed, moaning and screaming in rhythm with my thrusts.

My movements became more violent. I stroked fast and brutally like I couldn't feel pain, until I finally roared and released.

CHAPTER EIGHT

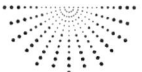

Celia

I LAY on my side next to Lucas's little bed, the room lit only by a tiny dinosaur nightlight. The warm yellow glow enveloped us like a gentle embrace.

"...and then T-Rex Dino used his long, long tail and SWOOSH! He swept all those naughty little raptors right into that sticky mud pit!" I told the bedtime story with exaggerated flair.

Lucas, clutching his well-worn dinosaur plushie, giggled at this part.

"Mommy, what happened to the little raptors after that?" he asked curiously, those gray-blue eyes sparkling.

"They all turned into little mud babies, crying and calling for their mommies to give them baths!"

"They're so silly!" Lucas laughed even harder. "Dino is so cool! I want a tail that awesome too!"

"You already have one," I smiled, tapping his little head. "Your tail is this smart little brain of yours. It can help you defeat all the little monsters in life."

He nodded vigorously, then yawned like a satisfied kitten. "Mommy, I want to hear more Dino stories tomorrow."

"Okay," I whispered, planting a gentle kiss on his forehead. Soon after, I heard his steady breathing.

I quietly closed Lucas's door and returned to my own room—a cramped space cluttered with belongings—then collapsed onto the bed, exhausted.

In my life, I was split in two. When I was with Lucas, I was the perfect mom—positive, energetic, full of life. The rest of the time, I was just another loser who'd barely found decent work only to get fired by my one-night-stand boss.

My brain became a broken projector, replaying that office scene over and over.

His voice echoed like a curse in my ears. The rough texture of his thumb brushing my lips felt like it was still there. His familiar masculine scent seemed to still envelop me.

My body reacted against my will. A shameful heat rose from deep in my belly.

I shot upright, yanking at my hair in frustration. Damn it! Celia, what the hell are you thinking?

He humiliated you. He treated you like some whore who could be bought with money and a job. How could you... how could you feel anything for him?

I rushed into the tiny bathroom with its peeling wallpaper and cranked the faucet wide open. Water gushed out as I cupped my hands and splashed it hard against my face. The cool shock helped clear my head somewhat.

But it was useless. I remembered that incredible night five years ago. His kisses all over my body, the dirty things he whispered in my ear, that feeling of being completely filled when he entered me.

I'd refused him. Yes, I'd used every ounce of strength to push him away and fled that office.

But only I knew that when I turned to leave, my legs were weak.

Just like now, I truly wanted him.

I bit my lip hard. Somehow my hand had already slipped into my pajama pants. I pushed my panties aside, fingers sliding over my folds —I was already wet and hot between my legs. I closed my eyes, placing my fingers on my clit. I found a comfortable rhythm, fingertips circling slowly around my clit, imagining it was Kirill's fingers touching me. Just thinking about Kirill sent shivers down my spine.

I fantasized about his gray-blue eyes watching me, telling me, "You're already so wet, Celia." I let out a satisfied sigh.

I imagined him pressing harder, so my fingers moved more intensely, and then I arched like a fish. Pleasure crashed over me. I couldn't help clamping my legs together, and in my body's violent spasms, I cried out as I reached my peak.

I melted into the bed. I hadn't released like this in so long. These past five years, caring for Lucas and working day and night, I'd had no time for boyfriends. I'd occasionally remember that night five years ago, but desire had never hit this hard.

I exhaled and resignedly grabbed some tissues to clean up the mess between my legs.

It was definitely because the "living" Kirill was too damn sexy. Absolutely! I pounded the bed in frustration.

The next morning, a brutal phone ring jolted me from shallow sleep.

I groggily answered. It was my landlady's voice, sharp enough to puncture eardrums.

"Celia Cole! Do you still want to live here or not?" She was practically roaring. "Rent's three months overdue. I'm telling you, this is your final notice! If you don't have that eighteen hundred dollars by Friday, you and your kid better pack up and get the hell out of my house!"

"Ma'am, please just give me a few more days!"

"I don't care! Friday! You hear me!"

"Beep—beep—beep—"

The phone slammed down. I held it, ice cold all over.

Another crushing reality pressed down on me. Lucas was almost five—way past kindergarten age. I'd been putting it off because I couldn't afford the steep tuition. But I couldn't wait anymore. This month was the final deadline to register for that decent public kindergarten nearby. Miss it, and we'd have to wait another year.

I couldn't let my failures rob Lucas of his right to education and friendship.

Money. Money, money, money!

It loomed like an insurmountable mountain, blocking the path to happiness for me and Lucas.

I tried calling the employment agency that had placed me in my last three jobs—all low-barrier, daily-pay gigs. But they said there were no openings.

My heart sank like an anchor into my chest.

Desperate, I took Lucas to Mia's place, hoping to find some breathing room with my friend.

Lucas charged straight for the bathroom the moment we walked in.

My shoulders collapsed instantly, all my energy draining away. Mia and I sank into her soft couch together, lavender scent filling the air.

"Hey, are you okay? You're whiter than the milk I just drank. What happened?" Mia frowned with worry, seeing my apocalyptic expression.

My emotions crumbled completely. I couldn't help spilling everything I'd bottled up for five years. From my father selling me to that underground auction five years ago, to Kirill buying me and sleeping with me, to struggling alone in New York, yesterday's reunion at the company, the landlady's ultimatum, kindergarten registration deadlines, and my job hunt failures.

"...so I got fired," I concluded miserably. "The job I finally found—gone on day one."

Mia listened quietly throughout.

When I finished, she wrapped me in a huge hug.

"Listen, honey." She rubbed my back. "The sky isn't falling. Don't worry about money—I've got savings to help you out. And housing? Easy. You and Lucas just move in with me! I've been saying this place is too big anyway. Two more people would liven things up."

"No, Mia, I can't..." I shook my head immediately. "I've already caused you too much trouble. I can't—"

"Shut up," she cut me off firmly. "We're friends. We're family. Family doesn't say that bullshit."

My eyes welled up, deeply moved. But I wouldn't accept it. Lucas and I couldn't keep imposing on her.

"But..." Mia's tone shifted, a mischievous, gossipy smile spreading across her face. "Dear Celia Cole, look at you go. Sleeping with the Zaitsev Group CEO? Come on, tell me—how was it? Is he really as gifted as the rumors say, able to make every woman—"

"Mia!" I interrupted, mortified. "This isn't the time for jokes!"

"I'm not joking." She looked at me seriously. "Really, Celia, why don't you tell him about Lucas? He's a Forbes-listed billionaire. Even just out of humanitarian duty, he wouldn't hesitate to pay child support. That's serious money! Enough for you and Lucas to live comfortably forever!"

"No." I rejected the idea instantly.

"Why not?" Mia looked confused.

"Because..." I hesitated. "Because his background isn't simple. He's not just any businessman."

"What do you mean?"

"He's connected to the Bratva. I'm afraid he'd take Lucas away." I voiced my deepest fear. "Lucas is everything to me. I can't risk it. I looked him up online last night—all his public records show he's unmarried with no children. A man like that, if he suddenly found out he had a son, God knows what he'd do."

Seeing the weight on my face, Mia finally grasped the seriousness. Her playful expression faded.

"Okay." She sighed. "But don't panic. Like I said, you and Lucas move in here first. I'll cover Lucas's tuition."

She started getting up, heading toward her bedroom. My heart tightened—knowing her, she was definitely going to get money right now.

"Really, no." My voice was pleading. "You've already helped us so much. And even if you have savings, they won't last forever with us draining them. What I need most is steady work. That would solve everything from the root."

Mia paused, understanding my stubbornness, and sat back down.

"So what now? I don't have the connections to help with job hunting either."

I couldn't answer. We both fell silent.

My life felt like it had hit a dead end.

No. There was one option. One I least wanted but had to face.

Kirill. Yesterday he'd said if I became his mistress, he'd let me stay at Zaitsev Group.

The thought took root and grew wildly in my mind.

Humiliating. But reality's weight could crush that completely.

I could see the landlady throwing Lucas and me out. I could see Lucas's longing eyes when we passed that kindergarten.

I'd promised Lucas the best, but I couldn't even give him stable housing or kindergarten at the right age.

I had to accept Kirill's offer. It was a dangerous and desperate decision, but maybe from the moment this thought occurred to me, my future was already out of my control.

"Mia," I finally spoke. "I think... I might know what to do."

The Zaitsev Group skyscraper appeared in my sight again. Sunlight reflecting off the glass facade nearly blinded me.

My stomach churned uneasily. Mostly from selling my dignity, but partly from undeniable excitement.

I knew it was crazy—two completely different emotions coexisting irrationally.

Facing Kirill, this handsome, commanding man with incredible appeal to women, my body seemed to rebel with a mind of its own.

I pushed down the chaotic thoughts and entered the opulent, heavily air-conditioned lobby again, walking straight to reception.

"Hello, how may I help you?" the receptionist smiled.

She wasn't yesterday's receptionist, but that wasn't unusual for a big company.

"I... I'd like to see Mr. Zaitsev." My heart pounded, saying his name.

"Do you have an appointment?"

"No." I clenched my fists. "But I have something very important to discuss with him. Could you please—"

"I'm sorry, ma'am." She politely interrupted. "Without an appointment, I can't let you up. Company policy."

"Could you call his office? Tell him Celia Cole is here to see him." I begged, placing my last hope in her.

"Ma'am, I really can't do that. If you truly have important business, please make an appointment through proper channels." Her smile had grown stiff.

My heart sank bit by bit. I stood there like a fool, blocked by this invisible wall, not even qualified for an announcement. Just as I was about to leave in despair, a familiar voice called from behind.

"Celia? What are you doing here?"

I spun around to see supervisor O'Neil carrying breakfast, looking surprised.

I rushed to him like he was a lifeline. "O'Neil!"

O'Neil frowned, confused. "What happened yesterday? After you were called to the CEO's office, you never came back. HR didn't send any notices either."

I opened my mouth but didn't know how to explain. I couldn't exactly say I'd refused the president's advances yesterday and was now back to accept them.

I took a deep breath. "O'Neil, please help me. I need to see Mr. Zaitsev. It's very important."

His expression grew hesitant. "What's so important that has you this desperate?"

"It's about my job. Please, just this once." I clasped my hands together.

He adjusted his glasses, then sighed. "Fine, but don't say I helped."

"I promise I won't!" I thanked him sincerely.

He turned to the receptionist. "Connect me to the president's office."

The receptionist looked surprised but complied. The call connected quickly. She gave my name, then handed me the phone.

"Speak." The magnetic voice on the other end sent tiny tremors through my body with just one word.

"It's me." My voice shook slightly. "Celia Cole."

"I know." He indicated for me to continue.

"I..." I struggled to speak. "I've thought it over. I accept."

"I'll have my secretary come down for you."

The line went dead. I could finally breathe.

"Alright, thanks." I returned the phone. The receptionist's expression had completely changed—from professional courtesy to subtle scrutiny.

O'Neil also studied me with curious eyes, but I didn't care anymore.

Within two minutes, an impeccably dressed woman approached from the elevators. She came straight to me and nodded slightly. "Ms. Cole, please follow me."

I followed her to the president's private elevator. With a soft "ding," the mirror-like doors closed smoothly.

The elevator reached the top floor. The secretary smiled and nodded before leaving. I stood alone outside the president's office, knocking as I had yesterday, entering after receiving permission.

Kirill still sat behind that desk, but surprisingly, he wasn't reading documents.

He leaned back in his chair, studying me with those deep eyes at his leisure.

My mouth went dry. I could only force myself forward under his gaze.

I reached his desk and stood there. After a moment of continued silence from him, I bit my lip and broke the silence first.

"Mr. Zaitsev, I accept your proposal from yesterday."

"My proposal yesterday? What was that?" He feigned confusion.

He clearly wanted me to say outright that I wanted to be his mistress. My cheeks burned.

"I agree to be your mistress." I nearly bit my tongue off.

He finally deigned to speak. "You're sure you want to accept?"

"Absolutely sure."

I actually felt relieved afterward. No turning back now. I didn't have to pay for those complicated emotions anymore. This was reality—my conflicted feelings couldn't change anything, right?

"Completely voluntary?" He raised an eyebrow, the gesture striking my heart.

"Of course," I answered quickly.

He seemed to be pondering something, stroking his chin thoughtfully.

"But—" he drawled, "Ms. Cole, you seem to have misunderstood something."

"What?" I was confused.

"Now, you're the one asking me for favors, delivering yourself to my door. I hold all the cards." He spoke ruthlessly, flashing a dangerous smile.

My stomach plummeted. He didn't seem to want me as his mistress anymore. I couldn't even sell myself?

"What... what do you mean?" I asked in disbelief.

"I mean, if you can service me well, I'll consider it." His voice carried sexy temptation, pulling me from despair even though this demand was equally humiliating.

One choice was to leave and continue living in embarrassing poverty, unable to give Lucas a decent future.

The other was to please him in exchange for respectable work and a truly bright future for Lucas.

My mental scales tipped toward the latter. I made my decision.

I walked around the desk to his side. His legs were long, so there was enough space between his chair and desk for me to squeeze in. I knelt between his legs.

I looked up at him from this angle, backlit. His features looked even sharper, his nose perfectly defined in the shadows, eyes buried in darkness revealing danger and depth. I clearly saw his Adam's apple move, and heat surged in my lower belly.

I swallowed and unzipped his incredibly smooth suit pants, pulling out his cock.

His penis was very energetic—I couldn't grip it with one hand. Slap! It bounced squarely against my cheek.

I stared at it in bewilderment.

Light laughter came from above. "Looks like my cock really likes you."

Getting such an up-close look at his cock hit me with the most intense visual shock. It was massive, veins bulging, pulsing with his every breath. My pussy was soaked in no time.

I could feel Kirill's gaze on me, heavy, almost tangible. But he didn't rush me—he was like a patient hunter, waiting for his prey to make the first move.

I licked and sucked the tip of his dick, teasing it with my tongue. Above me, Kirill's breathing got rougher, and that sexy sound pulled me in deeper. I opened my mouth wide, trying to take his cock in, but it was so thick and long that I had to relax my throat just to manage part of it.

I started moving, mimicking what I remembered. I kept my teeth out of the way, bobbing up and down. Kirill's low, husky moans drove me wild.

I worked harder, sucking with more focus.

Knock, knock, knock.

The sudden sound of knocking made my body freeze.

"Come in," Kirill's raspy voice called out.

Panic shot through me, and I instinctively started to pull away. But a strong hand landed on my shoulder—not hard, but firm enough to keep me in place.

Kirill slid his chair forward, forcing me to shuffle back on my knees, still with his cock in my mouth, until I was completely hidden under the desk.

I heard the door open, followed by the sharp click of high heels on the floor. They stopped somewhere behind me.

A shiver crawled up my spine. I wanted to pull his dick out of my mouth, but Kirill tapped my cheek lightly.

I figured he was telling me to keep going. I hesitated, but I'd come this far—there was no stopping now. I started moving again, slower this time, careful not to make any lewd sounds that might give me away.

"Boss, here's the latest report on the NTIA project..."

It was Kirill's secretary, the same woman who'd brought me up earlier. Did she think I'd left? Or did she know I was still here?

"And about next week's dinner with the congressman..."

This was insane, but fuck, it was thrilling. The secretary was standing there, giving her boss a serious work update, while I was under the desk, sucking him off?

I felt Kirill's cock swell even more in my throat. My God, he was getting harder, thicker, almost choking me. My head spun from the wild mix of nerves and adrenaline.

CHAPTER NINE

Kirill

What was my secretary saying? Something about the latest NTIA report? Dinner with some damn congressman next week?

I couldn't hear where the hell the venue was anymore. Every auditory nerve in my brain had been hijacked by the wet heat below, all my attention concentrated on my cock. I could feel exactly how that slick mouth under the desk was pleasing me.

Celia had to be at her limit. After all this time and I still hadn't come, her mouth must be aching. The moment I sensed her about to pull off, I placed my hand on her head, pressed her deeper, and controlled the rhythm of her movements.

The vein at my temple throbbed uncontrollably.

Damn it. This woman—she was nothing but a slut. A slut in innocent clothing, born to torment me.

"...the project is progressing steadily." My secretary's report came to a stop.

I heard myself respond in a deliberately measured tone, "I know. You may go."

My secretary bowed slightly and exited, closing the door behind her.

Almost instantly, I thrust upward and released into Celia's mouth.

Celia coughed violently.

I pulled her out from under the desk and lifted her onto it.

She'd stopped coughing now. Her lips were flushed red, looking thoroughly used. For once, I felt a rare pang of guilt.

"Are you alright?" My voice came out husky.

She nodded. So I pressed my lips gently against hers.

My lips lingered on Celia's, soft and deliberate, the kiss a slow burn that sent heat curling through my veins. Her mouth was warm, pliant, yielding to the gentle pressure of mine. I tilted my head, deepening the kiss, my tongue slipping past her lips to taste her. She sighed into me, a quiet sound that vibrated against my mouth, and our tongues met, sliding against each other in a lazy, sensual dance. Saliva mingled, slick and intimate, as I explored her mouth, savoring the way she responded, her tongue chasing mine with a hesitant hunger that made my pulse spike. Each brush of our lips, each wet glide of our tongues, felt like a conversation—raw, unspoken, and electric.

My hands, resting on her hips, began to wander. I slid them up her sides, feeling the worn fabric of her faded T-shirt under my palms. My fingers found the swell of her breasts, and I cupped them, squeezing gently at first, then with more intent. The fabric stretched taut as I kneaded her, my thumbs brushing over the hard peaks of her nipples. Celia moaned into my mouth, the sound muffled but desperate, her body arching into my touch. The kiss grew messier, our breaths mingling as I pressed harder, rolling her nipples between my fingers through the thin cotton. Her moans grew louder, vibrating against my lips, and I drank them in, my cock stirring at the way she melted under me.

I pulled back, breaking the kiss with a wet sound, my lips hovering just above hers. Her eyes were half-lidded, glassy with want, her lips swollen and glistening. I smirked, my voice low and rough. "Look at you, Celia. So fucking needy already. You love this, don't you? My hands on your tits, making you squirm on my desk like a good little slut."

Her cheeks flushed a deeper red, but she didn't look away. "Kirill..." she whispered, her voice shaky but thick with desire. "You're... you're terrible."

"Terrible?" I chuckled, my hands sliding down her body, fingers hooking under the waistband of her skirt. "You're gonna love how terrible I can be." I pushed the fabric up, exposing her thighs, and my hand dipped between her legs. My fingers brushed against the damp fabric of her panties, and I groaned at the heat radiating from her. "Fuck, you're soaked," I said, my voice dripping with smug satisfaction. "This wet just from a kiss? You're practically begging for me, aren't you?"

She bit her lip, her thighs trembling as she tried to close them, but I held them apart with a firm grip. "Kirill, please..." Her voice was small, embarrassed, but her hips shifted toward my hand, betraying her. "Not here. What if someone walks in? Can we... can we go to the break room?"

I shook my head, my fingers tracing the edge of her panties, teasing the sensitive skin where thigh met core. "No, baby. Right here. Right on this desk." I leaned in, my lips brushing her ear as I whispered, "Don't worry. No one's gonna barge in. They'll knock first. And if they don't..." I nipped her earlobe, making her gasp. "Let them see how fucking gorgeous you look when you're falling apart for me."

She whimpered, her protests fading as my fingers slipped beneath the fabric of her panties. Her slick heat coated my fingertips, and I groaned, circling her clit with slow, deliberate strokes. Her head fell back, a soft moan escaping her lips as I worked her, my touch precise, knowing exactly how to build her up. Her hips bucked, chasing my fingers, and I watched her face—eyes squeezed shut, lips parted, completely lost in the pleasure I was giving her.

"God, you're so sensitive," I murmured, my free hand gripping her thigh to keep her spread open. "I could make you come just like this, couldn't I? My fingers playing with your pretty little clit until you're screaming my name."

Her moans grew louder, her body trembling as I increased the pressure, rubbing tight circles that had her gasping. Her hands gripped the edge of the desk, knuckles white, and I could feel her getting close, her pussy clenching around nothing as her thighs shook. Just as her breaths turned ragged, I stopped, pulling my hand away.

Her eyes snapped open, wide and desperate. "Kirill, no—please, don't stop!" Her voice was raw, pleading, and the sound went straight to my cock.

I grinned, leaning back to watch her squirm. "What's that, Celia? You want more? Gotta beg a little louder than that."

Her face flushed, but her need overpowered her shyness. She grabbed my wrist, pulling my hand back to her. "Please, Kirill. I need it. I need you to... to make me come. Please."

The desperation in her voice was fucking intoxicating. I laughed softly, my fingers returning to her clit, rubbing faster now, harder. "That's my girl," I said, my voice thick with lust. "Look at you, so greedy for it. Come for me, Celia. Let me feel that tight little pussy fall apart."

Her moans turned into cries, her body shuddering as I pushed her over the edge. Her orgasm hit hard, her thighs clamping around my hand as she arched off the desk, her nails digging into my arm. I kept rubbing, drawing out every wave of pleasure until she was panting, boneless, her head resting against my shoulder.

I didn't give her time to recover. Hooking my fingers into her panties, I tugged them down her legs, letting them pool on the floor. "Up," I said, patting her thigh. She obeyed, still dazed, and I lifted her legs, draping them over my shoulders as I sank to my knees. Her pussy was glistening, pink and swollen, and I groaned at the sight. "Fuck, you're perfect," I said, before leaning in and dragging my tongue along her slit.

Celia gasped, her hands flying to my hair as I licked her, slow and deep, savoring her taste. My tongue circled her clit, then dipped lower, fucking into her as she squirmed. Her moans were louder now, unrestrained, and I loved every second of it. I sucked her clit into my mouth, flicking it with my tongue, and her hips bucked against my face. "Kirill, oh God," she whimpered, her fingers tightening in my hair. I didn't let up, eating her out with a hunger that had her trembling, her second orgasm building fast. When she came again, her thighs clamped around my head, her cries echoing in the quiet office.

I stood, wiping my mouth with the back of my hand, my cock straining against my pants. I pulled her legs down, wrapping them around my waist as I positioned myself between her thighs. "You taste so fucking good," I said, unbuckling my belt and freeing myself. My cock sprang free, hard and aching, and I rubbed the tip against her slick entrance. "You ready for me, baby? Ready to take every inch?"

She nodded, her eyes wide, her voice breathy. "Yes, Kirill. Please. I want you inside me."

I didn't need more encouragement. I pushed into her, slow at first, letting her feel every inch as I stretched her. She was tight, hot, and so fucking wet, and I groaned as I bottomed out, my hips flush against hers. "Fuck, Celia," I said, my voice rough. "You feel like heaven. You know, I've been thinking about this for years. That night five years ago... I fucked you so good, didn't I? And I've been dreaming about this pussy ever since. Jerking off to the memory of you, imagining bending you over and fucking you just like this."

Her eyes fluttered shut, her lips parting as she moaned. "God, Kirill, yes. I remember that night too. I've... I've thought about you too. About how you made me feel. Do it again. Fuck me like you did then."

Her words set me off. I thrust into her, hard and deep, setting a rhythm that had her gasping. My hands gripped her hips, pulling her into me with every stroke, my cock hitting that spot inside her that made her cry out. "That's it, baby," I growled. "Take it. Take my cock like the good girl you are. You love this, don't you? Love me fucking you on my desk where anyone could walk in."

"Yes," she gasped, her legs tightening around my waist. "I love it. I love you inside me."

Her words pushed me over the edge. I fucked her harder, my thrusts relentless, and when I felt her clench around me, her third orgasm ripping through her, I couldn't hold back. I came hard, spilling inside her, my groans mixing with her cries as we rode out the pleasure together.

But I wasn't done. I pulled out, my cum dripping down her thighs, and sat back in my chair, pulling her with me. "Ride me," I said, my voice low and commanding. I guided her onto my lap, her knees straddling me as she sank down onto my still-hard cock. The angle was deeper, tighter, and she gasped, her hands gripping my shoulders as she adjusted.

"Fuck, Kirill," she whimpered, her hips rocking as she started to move. "It's so deep."

"Yeah?" I grinned, my hands on her ass, guiding her movements. "You like that? Like feeling me so deep you can't think straight? Ride me, Celia. Show me how much you want this cock."

She moaned, her movements growing faster, more desperate. Her breasts bounced under her T-shirt, and I yanked the fabric up, exposing them. I sucked a nipple into my mouth, biting gently as she rode me, her cries growing louder. "Kirill, I'm... I'm gonna come again," she gasped, her nails digging into my shoulders.

"Do it," I growled against her skin. "Come all over my cock. Let me feel you."

She shattered, her body shaking as she came, her pussy clenching around me so tight it pulled my own release from me. I groaned, thrusting up into her one last time as I spilled inside her again, our bodies locked together in the aftermath.

We stayed like that for a moment, panting, her forehead resting against mine. "Fuck, Celia," I murmured, my hands still on her hips. "You're gonna be the death of me."

She laughed softly, breathless. "Worth it."

Afterward, only our intertwined breathing filled the office. I withdrew from Celia's body and placed her on the desk, where she immediately went limp.

She didn't even have the strength to lift her legs. I gripped her ankles, helped her into her panties, then smoothed out her rumpled skirt. I straightened my own pants, resuming my CEO appearance as if the man who'd just been completely unhinged wasn't me.

"Tomorrow morning at nine, come straight to work." I looked at Celia lying on the desk.

She bolted upright, asking cautiously, "Do I... do I still need to complete the hiring paperwork, Mr. Zaitsev?"

Mr. Zaitsev?

When we were making love, she was fine calling me Kirill, but now that we're done, she just suddenly acts so distant? Like she's the one calling the shots in this relationship.

"No need. I haven't notified HR," I replied. "And call me Kirill from now on."

One moment she was still basking in the afterglow, tired and drowsy. The next, she'd instantly perked up. Was getting this job really that thrilling?

"Thank you, Kirill." She looked at me with sparkling eyes, her voice sincere, then broke into a heartfelt smile.

That smile was radiant and brilliant, so pure it was blinding, catching me completely off guard and piercing straight into the most vulnerable part of my heart.

A strange, tender ache spread through me, making my breath catch. Fuck. What the hell had I just done?

Celia was still wearing that cheap T-shirt, washed until it was wrinkled and faded. The neckline sagged, edges frayed—completely out of place in this office.

Why was I treating her this way? She was so pitiful, driven by her worthless gambling father to sell her own body. Yet I was using employment to coerce her, making her my mistress. I'd manipulated her into pleasing me, into having sex with me in my office. And I was actually savoring her confusion and helplessness, secretly congratulating myself.

What was I doing? Being cruel to her, threatening her, toying with her—all just to sleep with her?

I raked my fingers through my hair in frustration. No. I'd never treated my lovers this way. My behavior toward her these past two days baffled even me.

My gaze returned to her face, to that smile so content from

receiving a job opportunity, as if she'd been given the entire world. A thought suddenly struck me, perhaps she was different to me.

The realization made me freeze, then grow even more agitated. Different how? Because the innocence in her eyes pierced through me? Because her submissiveness stirred some misguided compassion?

I didn't know. All I knew was that something was now blocking my chest, making me feel stifled and restless.

CHAPTER TEN

Kirill

IT WAS three in the afternoon. I was due to meet a Qatari buyer about a large shipment of AK-47s—he'd picked a bar across town—so I figured I'd grab lunch nearby first. My driver of ten years had called in sick. I didn't trust the replacements, so I drove myself.

The Mercedes wasn't nearly as thrilling as a race car, but there was something satisfying about having the wheel in my own hands.

"Boss, something's off with the Chicago route." Volkov's voice came through the phone, heavy with concern.

I pulled into the emergency lane of the congested street, fingers unconsciously drumming the steering wheel. "Spell it out."

"During the dock inventory, we're missing an entire container from the Eastern European shipment of fancy liquor." Volkov's breathing hitched. "The boys estimate we're looking at over two million in losses."

I stepped out of the car. Gray-white pigeons were pecking at breadcrumbs on the plaza, fluttering up when they saw me approaching, settling on top of the monument nearby.

The noon sun was harsh. I squinted against the glare.

"What's Theodore saying?" I asked coldly, walking briskly across the plaza.

"Claims it was some small-time thieves at the dock. Says he's got people looking into it." Volkov's voice dripped with skepticism. "But I don't think it's that simple."

"Of course not." I let out a bitter laugh. "Thieves who can make an entire container vanish from Theodore's turf without a trace? They'd have to be fucking Superman."

"Send more of our own people to investigate."

"Yes, boss. I'm on it now."

I'd just hung up when something slammed into my leg. Looking down, I saw a small figure stumbling backward before landing on his ass.

He looked about four or five, with soft black curls framing his forehead and pale gray-blue eyes. He wore a blue T-shirt with a cartoon T-Rex and denim overalls.

He looked up at me, somewhat dazed.

I'd never liked kids. They were loud, troublesome, and fragile as hell—exactly the kind of creatures I preferred to avoid. But this little guy didn't even cry after falling, and strangely, I felt no irritation. Instead, there was something inexplicably familiar and comforting about him.

Weird. I was certain I'd never seen him before.

"Lucas!"

A panicked, urgent female voice called from nearby. I looked up, following the sound. Celia.

She was running toward us, worry written all over her face. Her hair was pulled back in a simple ponytail, revealing her smooth forehead and that face that was stunning even without makeup.

After what happened in the office a few days ago, the suffocating feeling in my chest made me want to run. She'd been coming to work normally since then, and despite being in the same building, I hadn't sought her out.

"Mommy!" The little guy had already gotten to his feet, calling out in that sweet, childish voice when he saw her.

Mommy? The word hit me like a sledgehammer. Celia... had a child?

A surge of inexplicable displeasure spread through me.

She had a kid? A family? Then why the hell had she accepted my proposition to be my mistress? Why did she come back to my office, kneel before me?

Wait. HR said Celia was unmarried, so this child was... her bastard?

My throat felt constricted. Celia, the poor single mother. No wonder she'd requested a three-month salary advance just two days ago. Raising a kid alone must cost a fortune.

Celia reached us but didn't even glance at me. She crouched down, anxiously checking over the little boy named Lucas.

"Baby, are you okay? Did you hurt yourself anywhere? Let Mommy see."

"I'm fine, Mommy." Lucas shook his head, pointing at me with his small finger. "I bumped into this uncle."

Only then did Celia slowly stand and look up. The moment our eyes met, she tensed like a startled hedgehog. She immediately pulled Lucas protectively into her arms, her wariness practically radiating from her.

Her reaction puzzled me. I was just standing here, hadn't done anything. Why was she looking at me like that?

"Hi, Kirill." Her voice was tight, unnaturally stiff.

"Celia. What a coincidence." My gaze fell on Lucas, who was curiously studying me from her arms. "This is your son?"

"Yes." Her eyes darted away, avoiding my gaze.

The tightness in my chest pressed against me. I didn't want to see her look at me like that, like I was some kind of monster.

"Don't worry, this won't affect our cooperation." I emphasized the word cooperation, making sure she understood. "If you still want to work with me after thinking it through, then whatever you have going on doesn't get in the way. Right?"

With the kid here, some things could only be implied. If she'd ultimately chosen to be my lover, she should have considered all the consequences. I didn't need to worry about her past or her son.

"Ah? Y-yes." Celia clearly understood. "It won't affect anything."

For some reason, I felt relieved.

"Mommy, what's your cooperation about?" Lucas asked, looking up with bright eyes.

I saw Celia's smile freeze, like she'd been caught off guard.

"Our cooperation is that your mommy works for me, and I pay her." I crouched down to Lucas's eye level, trying to make my voice sound gentle.

I was surprised by how naturally I made that gesture. Was I usually this patient with children?

Lucas tilted his head thoughtfully, then nodded vigorously. "Then I like cooperation!"

"I like cooperation too." After saying that, we bumped fists lightly.

As I stood up, I remembered to ask, "Where are you two headed?"

"Just finished his enrollment paperwork, planning to grab something to eat." Celia's voice relaxed slightly, though her hand still gripped Lucas's tightly.

"Perfect, I haven't eaten either. Let's go together. My treat."

"Don't bother!" She refused almost instantly, reacting like a cat whose tail had been stepped on. "We'll just find somewhere casual. Don't want to trouble you."

"It's no trouble. Just a meal. As your boss, since we happened to meet, I should buy this little guy lunch." I looked at her face. "Besides, Lucas is starting kindergarten. That's worth celebrating."

She pressed her lips together but didn't argue further.

"Thank you, Kirill." Her voice dropped. "And... thank you for approving my three-month advance. Otherwise, I couldn't make rent, and Lucas couldn't start kindergarten."

Something stabbed at my chest. She was struggling more than I'd imagined. An emotion I barely recognized—something close to tenderness—churned in my heart.

"Mommy, I'm hungry." Lucas tugged at Celia's hand, whispering.

The kid was well-behaved. While the adults talked, he'd stood quietly without making a fuss, unlike most children his age. That surprised me.

"I will take you for something delicious." I looked at Lucas, my gaze unconsciously studying his features. The straight little nose, the pressed thin lips, those gray-blue eyes... too familiar.

A vague image suddenly flashed through my mind. A childhood photo of mine—a little boy with pursed lips, staring seriously at the camera, eyes holding a gravity beyond his years.

Lucas, aside from his black curls and innocent demeanor, looked almost identical to that photo of me.

A thought struck me, making my breath catch.

Could he... be my child?

I drove them to an upscale Italian restaurant nearby.

The décor was understated luxury, the air fragrant with truffle and premium olive oil. Gentle violin music floated through the space.

The moment Celia walked in, she looked uncomfortable, gripping Lucas's hand tightly.

When the waiter handed over the leather-bound menus, I saw her flip through a few pages quickly, then bite her lip hard, like she'd seen something distressing.

"Um... Kirill." She set down the menu, her voice barely audible. "Isn't this place too expensive? Maybe we should find somewhere else?"

"No need." I calmly took the menu that was making her squirm, my finger tracing the gold-embossed dish names. "Black truffle risotto, seared foie gras with fig compote, Sicilian prawn linguine..." I rattled off several signature dishes, then looked up at them. "Any dislikes?"

Mother and son shook their heads almost simultaneously, like they'd rehearsed it.

Before the food arrived, I watched the little guy craning his neck to study the crystal chandelier, my heart skipping unexpectedly. I had to know for sure.

"Lucas," I called his name.

He immediately looked at me. "Uh-huh?"

"How old are you?"

"He just turned four." Celia jumped in, her voice a bit rushed. "Had his birthday last month."

Just turned four? My heart sank. That night in Chicago was five years and two months ago. If Lucas were my child, he'd be almost five now, not barely four. Maybe I really was overthinking this.

"Is that so?" I looked at Celia, trying to find some crack in her story. But I came up empty.

"Yeah, I had my birthday last month!" Lucas's little face beamed with pride. "I can go to kindergarten now! The teacher says I'm a big boy!"

The kid's words were like cold water, dousing my unrealistic speculation. Maybe it really was just coincidence. The world was full of people who looked alike.

The food arrived quickly.

When the waiter placed the aromatic black truffle risotto in front of him, I saw Lucas swallow hard. He carefully scooped a small spoonful, put it in his mouth, and his eyes went wide as saucers.

"Wow... so good!" he whispered in amazement.

But he didn't continue eating. Instead, he pushed his small bowl toward Celia. "Mommy, try it. This is really good."

I saw Celia's eyes well up in that instant.

"I'm fine, Lucas. You eat. Eat more so you can grow tall." She smiled, pushing the bowl back to him, but that smile held an unmistakable sadness.

My heart felt like it had been run over by a truck.

"Another black truffle risotto," I told the waiter.

"Right away, sir."

"Don't!" Celia's voice overlapped with the waiter's.

"Really, we have enough. We can't finish all this." Celia frowned at me.

"It's fine. One more."

"Yes, sir."

I caught the waiter's puzzled expression as he left—he'd already served all three of us risotto, just at different times, with Lucas first and Celia last. Mother and son didn't need to share at all.

And I had no fucking clue what I was doing! That huge plate of risotto was more than enough, not to mention all the other dishes on the table. So why did I feel compelled to order another? What the hell was I trying to prove?

Still, the meal was surprisingly pleasant. Lucas wasn't shy at all. He'd gesture excitedly while telling me about his T-Rex Dino, "Dino swishes his tail, but he doesn't bite people. He's a good dinosaur."

I listened intently, occasionally asking, "So what does Dino like to eat?"

"He likes eating leaves!" Lucas said seriously. "Just like giraffes!"

He made me laugh, and I reached out to ruffle his hair. Celia smiled warmly too.

After dinner, I drove them back to Celia's apartment building. The place looked old, with peeling paint on the walls, dark and damp.

I frowned. This wasn't a suitable environment for a young woman with a child.

Before getting out, Lucas suddenly tugged at my sleeve, looking at me expectantly. "Kirill, can you play with us again next time?"

"Yes." I heard myself say. "Two weeks from now, this weekend. I'll take you both to an amusement park."

"Amusement park!" Lucas's eyes lit up like stars. "I've never been to an amusement park!"

I smiled and pulled a personal business card from my suit pocket, handing it to Celia. I rarely gave these out—it only had my private number.

"Add my number when you get home."

Celia hesitated before taking it. Her fingertip brushed mine and quickly pulled away.

"I have another client waiting. Got to go." I started the car, glancing in the rearview mirror—Celia was walking into the building with Lucas, the little guy still waving at me.

My fingers drummed the steering wheel. That inexplicable sense of connection crept up again.

CHAPTER ELEVEN

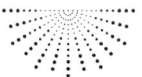

Celia

"...Mommy, when we go to the amusement park with Kirill, can we bring my dinosaur? Kirill will definitely love it!"

Lucas's voice danced through the dim, humid hallway like bouncing sunlight. He was already so pumped to see Kirill again before I even realized it.

Was this what blood meant? This damned invisible, untouchable, yet unbreakable bond?

Just two hours ago, my son—my well-behaved little boy who never ran wild in public—had bolted from kindergarten like an untamed colt when we passed the square. He'd charged straight for the pigeons, then somehow, out of hundreds of strange faces, crashed right into his biological father's arms with pinpoint accuracy.

What twisted my stomach even more was how Lucas had never been this affectionate with someone he'd just met. And Kirill? He was probably already suspecting Lucas was his child. He'd been probing about Lucas's age. Thank God Lucas's birthday was just last month—

when he heard me mention birthday, he jumped on my half-truth and accidentally threw Kirill off the scent.

"Of course, sweetheart. But you have to take good care of it—don't lose it." I finally found my voice, fishing out my keys to unlock the apartment door. "Now, we need to change into pajamas. It's nap time."

"I'll take care of Dino!" Lucas patted his chest, said good afternoon, then bounced off to his room.

Lucas was an angel baby who never gave me trouble. I didn't need to worry about his nap, but I did need to figure out how to handle the relationship between Lucas and Kirill.

I sank onto the faded little couch with a heavy sigh, clutching Kirill's business card—his private number.

Add him or not? If I added his contact, Lucas and Kirill would connect more, increasing the chances of Lucas's identity being exposed. If I didn't add him, their magnetic pull toward each other was already there. I'd bet money this wouldn't be their only meeting after the amusement park.

Either way, the outcome would be similar. The important thing was to keep Kirill stable for now. He'd dropped his suspicions—suddenly changing course might draw more attention.

I bit the soft flesh inside my mouth. Besides, I couldn't disappoint the little guy, could I?

My fingers flew across the phone screen, saving Kirill's number.

Me: Lucas will bring his dinosaur to the amusement park next time. He thinks you'll like it.

No reply. Probably still with clients. I set the phone down, curled up on the couch, and dozed off without realizing it.

When I woke from my nap, I saw Kirill's response.

Kirill: He really knows me well. I'll treat his dinosaur friend like my own good buddy.

I couldn't help laughing out loud. God, I must have woken up confused. Did Kirill sound like someone who'd say that? Had someone stolen his phone? Could he actually be some kind of kid whisperer?

Imagining Kirill with his silver-streaked hair surrounded by a bunch of knee-high kids made my stomach hurt from laughing.

I was certain Kirill and Lucas would get along perfectly.

Me: Thanks for treating us to lunch. Lucas loved that restaurant—the food was amazing.

Kirill: Just Lucas?

Heat rushed to my cheeks.

Me: Lucas and I both loved it. Best lunch we've ever had. Thank you!

Kirill: There'll be more. Maybe we can try a different cuisine next time.

Bubbles rose in my chest. I was supposed to be afraid of him and Lucas getting too close! So why did the thought of a next time make me happy?

WE STARTED CHATTING LIKE THAT. I'd share Lucas's drawings, and he'd seriously reply, "He'll definitely be a great artist someday."

I'd send pictures of Lucas's goofy crafts, and he'd comment, "Very much Lucas's style. Such a little cutie."

It felt like... like a real family, parents sharing their child's daily life. The panic about my child's parentage got pushed down by this strange warmth.

When he asked about other things involving Lucas, I tried to keep my replies formulaic, like two adults forced to communicate for a child's sake. But my heart betrayed me—before sending each message, I'd read those few lines over and over.

The turning point came when Kirill shared a photo from some banquet—well-dressed elites clinking glasses.

Kirill: Boring celebration dinner. Nothing but people making pointless small talk. Really want to flip the table.

My fingers froze over the keyboard. What was this? This crossed our unspoken boundary of kid-related topics only.

I hesitated for ages before replying.

Me: Maybe you could pretend they're NPCs you have to deal with for a mission.

The screen went quiet for so long I started regretting my stupid joke. Just as I was about to turn off my phone, it buzzed.

Kirill: That actually works. This idea makes me feel much better.

A strange tingle spread through my stomach.

After that, our conversations weren't limited to Lucas. We started sharing daily life. I'd share my cooking; he'd share his weekend overtime coffee. I began anticipating every phone buzz.

In just a day and a half, we'd exchanged dozens of mundane messages.

Sunday night, lying in bed scrolling through our texts, thinking about facing Kirill tomorrow, emotions surged through me that nearly drove me crazy. Even though we were just in the same office building—he rarely came down to the employee floors.

What was this? What were we to each other?

Did lovers share non-sexual daily life like this? Chat like friends, even make harmless jokes?

This blurred boundary terrified me. I'd rather our relationship be pure transaction—at least then I could guard my heart. But now Kirill was using this slow-pacing strategy, infiltrating my life bit by bit, breaking down my defenses.

And I didn't know his real intentions. Did he find this amusing? Did he become friends with all his lovers?

A man like Kirill never lacked women. To them, women were like clothes—get bored, toss them out. I didn't think I'd be any exception to becoming one of the many women who got replaced. This relationship was like walking a tightrope. One wrong step and I'd plummet into the abyss. I had to be ready to pull back anytime.

My phone buzzed like a curse. I buried my head in the pillow, trying to ignore the message. I was certain it was from Kirill.

Can't look. Can't reply. Can't continue. I need to go back to being just a bed partner.

But my willpower betrayed me. Just one peek? I bit my lip and opened the message.

Kirill: Work finished on time. Good night.

The text included a photo of the night view from his office floor-to-ceiling windows.

The familiar office made me instantly think of our intense encounter—Kirill putting me on his desk, thrusting hard.

My lower belly ignited.

Damn it! Sleep. Now.

Monday was always like warfare. After processing mountains of emails and reports, my head was spinning. I grabbed my mug and headed to the break room, hoping strong coffee could resurrect my dying brain cells.

"Hey Celia, you okay? You look like you just got run over by a truck."

Josh—our department's star salesman, a golden-haired, blue-eyed guy as sunny as a golden retriever. He leaned against the counter, offering me a cookie.

"Thanks," I took the cookie, biting it weakly. "Trust me, I feel worse than that. I think my soul ran away around email number 100."

Josh laughed, showing perfect white teeth. "Sounds like you need a vacation. Or at least some tequila. How about Friday night? There's this new bar downtown—supposedly the bartender's ridiculously good-looking."

"Oh yeah?" I raised an eyebrow, making coffee while playing along with his joke. This was just harmless office flirtation, seasoning to combat boring work. We both knew it wouldn't go anywhere.

"Put it this way," Josh lowered his voice mysteriously, "if good looks generated electricity, he could light up all of Times Square by himself."

He made me laugh, and I relaxed against the wall. I sipped my coffee, giving him a thumb-up. "You really are an excellent salesman, Josh."

"Always have been. It's my job." He winked at me.

Just then, the break room temperature seemed to drop ten degrees. That familiar, spine-tingling pressure emanated from the doorway.

Shit! I didn't need to turn around to know who it was. I'd only felt this aura from one person.

"B-boss." Josh's voice stuttered as he straightened up after seeing Kirill.

I turned around. Kirill stood a few steps behind us.

He wore a sharp black suit with no tie, the top two shirt buttons casually undone, revealing his dark, muscular chest and a hint of tattoo. His face was stormy, making his scar more prominent and dangerous. I suddenly realized his scar wasn't some sexy decoration—it was a real wound.

But why was he here? This was the seventeenth floor, the marketing department's employee break room, not his penthouse.

"The marketing department seems to have it easy, chatting during work hours." His oppressive gaze swept over Josh.

Josh's face instantly froze as he fumbled to explain. "Boss, I... we were just—"

"Get back to work." His interruption cut like ice through our eardrums.

"Sure!" Josh fled like he'd been granted amnesty.

Kirill didn't spare Josh another second. He turned those stormy gray-blue eyes directly on me.

Only the two of us remained in the break room. Deathly silence.

I could hear my heart pounding so loud I wondered if Kirill heard it too.

He still didn't speak. The suffocating silence made me grip my mug handle tight.

"I..." I started awkwardly, trying to explain. "We were just talking about work matters."

"Were you?" He stepped closer, his powerful aura enveloping me. "What I heard was you flirting with that golden boy."

I bristled. What right did he have to interrogate me like this?

"So what?" I lifted my head, meeting his gaze. "It doesn't affect my work."

"No, it doesn't affect work." His low voice was dangerously husky. "But it affects my mood. You ignored my message to flirt with some insignificant little clerk. You'll learn your place, Celia."

He grabbed my wrist with crushing force.

"What are you doing? Let go!" I hissed under my breath, and the ceramic mug slipped from my grip, shattering on the floor as coffee splashed everywhere.

High heels clicked on the floor—someone was coming! I struggled to break free, not wanting coworkers to see me tangled up with the boss, but Kirill's grip was iron.

Emily! She hummed a tune, carrying an empty cup. When she saw the scene—the company's big boss roughly gripping her little clerk colleague's wrist—her mouth formed a perfect O, frozen in the doorway.

Kirill didn't even glance at her, dragging me toward the exit without a care. He hauled me through the marketing department's open office area.

This was definitely public humiliation. Dozens of eyes shot toward us like lasers. I felt shock, curiosity, gossip, and disbelief in those stares. Josh's complex gaze pierced through me too. My cheeks burned like fire—I wanted to crawl into a hole and disappear.

I saw O'Neil, who'd been instructing a new intern, look our way when he sensed something amiss. When he saw Kirill dragging my stumbling form, his expression froze. He quickly removed his glasses, breathed on the lenses, carefully wiped them with his shirt, then put them back on—like he was confirming he wasn't seeing things.

But this wasn't a hallucination. This humiliating parade starring me was absolutely real.

We finally left the marketing department and entered Kirill's private elevator.

"Kirill! Are you insane? Everyone was watching!" My anger gave me strength—I actually broke free from his grip.

I rubbed my reddened wrist, years of shame and fury exploding. "What the hell was that supposed to mean? What did you want to prove? How am I supposed to face my coworkers now?"

"Face them?" He sneered, advancing to trap me between him and the elevator wall. "You should worry about how to be my woman."

"I'm not your woman!" I practically screamed. "What's our relationship? You helped me get this job smoothly, I provide sexual services.

That's it! What right do you have to control who I talk to, who I flirt with? What right do you have to demand I answer your messages?"

When those words left my mouth, I saw something dark explode in his eyes.

"What right?" He growled, gripping my chin and forcing me to look up. "This gives me the right!"

The next moment, his scorching lips crashed down on mine.

The kiss was punishing, rough, and wild. His tongue forced its way past my teeth, claiming every bit of my mouth, stealing my breath. My brain short-circuited, and all I could do was whimper in protest, my hands uselessly pushing against his rock-hard chest.

My resistance only seemed to piss him off more. One hand gripped the back of my head, deepening the kiss, while the other slid under my skirt, his hot palm grazing the sensitive skin of my inner thigh, making my whole body shudder.

"No, not here…" I gasped, barely finding a moment to breathe and beg as the kiss broke.

The elevator had reached the top floor. The doors opened, then closed again.

"Right here," Kirill growled, his voice low and menacing, his hot breath hitting my face. "I'm gonna make sure you remember who you belong to."

Kirill's body pressed closer, caging me in his shadow. He grabbed my wrists with one hand, pinning them above my head. His other hand yanked my panties aside, his fingers pressing hard against my clit.

"Ah, no!" I yelped. It was insane—no warning, just him attacking my most sensitive spot, pain and pleasure hitting me so hard I nearly convulsed.

I was just getting used to his rhythm, my pussy getting wetter by the second, when he pulled his fingers back and, without hesitation, plunged his index and middle fingers deep inside me.

"This is too much, Kirill, please stop," I begged, my legs trembling, trying to close, but his knee between them kept me spread open.

"Stop?" Kirill smirked coldly. "Your pussy's saying something else. Listen to how fucking wet you are."

His fingers moved relentlessly inside me, the slick, obscene sounds filling my ears, making me shut my eyes in embarrassment.

Even though his touch was rough, waves of mind-numbing pleasure radiated from my core.

"Open your eyes, Celia," Kirill ordered.

Then he yanked his fingers out, and before I could process it, the world spun. I gasped, my eyes flying open as he lifted me, my legs instinctively wrapping around his waist. Afraid I'd fall, I clung to his shoulders, completely at his mercy.

He tugged my panties off, letting them dangle around my ankle, then unzipped his pants, pulling out his cock. He rubbed it against my entrance, teasing, not entering.

"Kirill…" My voice broke, half a plea for him to fuck me, half a desperate wish for him to stop torturing me.

"I'm right here," he said. "Feel me take you."

With one thrust, he buried himself inside me, and we both let out a groan of satisfaction.

"Tell me, Celia," he growled, his cock slamming into me. "That little punk from earlier—could he do this to you? Could he make you this fucking wet? Make you want it this bad?"

"No…" I bit my lip, trying to hold back the shameful moans.

The elevator stayed stuck on the top floor, but I was terrified someone could walk in and see us fucking like this.

This would be all over the tabloids, right? Fear and thrill twisted together, messing with my head.

"Say it!" he demanded, pounding into that sensitive spot deep inside me.

"He can't," I admitted, the pleasure overwhelming me.

"Then you better fucking remember who your man is!"

He grabbed my hips, lifting me higher so he could drive even deeper. Each brutal thrust felt like it was tearing through my soul.

"You love this, don't you?" His voice was low, dripping with sex.

"You love me fucking you like this, right here in this elevator where anyone could catch us."

The mix of shame and forbidden pleasure trapped me. My brain was crumbling, and I didn't care about getting caught anymore. All I could think about was wanting Kirill.

"Yeah, I love you fucking me like this," I moaned.

"Your pussy's gripping me so tight, like it was made for me."

"It is! Please, Kirill, give me more!"

Kirill didn't answer, but his thrusts turned frantic, the sound of skin slapping and wet noises echoing in the elevator.

I moaned, lost in a haze, every one of his thrusts pushing me closer to the edge.

I don't know how long it went on, but when the overwhelming wave of pleasure hit, it felt like my body and soul shattered together. He came right after, spilling deep inside me.

He held my weakening body tight, then completely removed my panties and put them in his suit pocket, smoothing down my skirt. I rolled my eyes, too tired to comment on his perverted behavior. Post-climax exhaustion made me too lazy to speak. Plus, the puzzle of our relationship occupied my mind again—I needed to think.

"Celia, you're mine. Have been since that night five years ago. Don't ever say we have no relationship again."

Kirill's words made me jerk up from his embrace, staring at him in disbelief. "What did you say?"

"I said you're mine. You belong only to me. I won't fucking let you think about other bastards!" Kirill practically roared.

Kirill's words cut through all the fog in my heart. He was jealous. This powerful man was jealous over me.

So he did care about me. We weren't just a transaction after all.

This both moved and delighted me. I leaned against his solid chest, feeling his heartbeat, my whole being like it was soaking in honey.

CHAPTER TWELVE

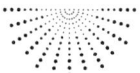

Kirill

CELIA WRAPPED her arms obediently around my neck, her head resting against my chest, clinging to me as if I were her entire world.

Damn, I loved seeing her like this.

When Celia had been laughing and chatting with that blonde kid, I felt a volcano erupting in my chest, something dark burning through my sanity. How could she? How dare she?

When I kissed her in the elevator, I knew this was what I'd been craving all along—Celia's lips, Celia's body, Celia's smile. Every piece of her belonged to me.

From that night in Chicago five years ago, the moment she cried and bloomed beneath me, her body and soul had been branded with my mark.

She was mine. Only mine.

Lost in thought, I carried Celia into my office's private lounge.

The space was equally expansive, centered around an absurdly large bed. Floor-to-ceiling windows were draped with silk curtains that blocked out the light completely, keeping the room dimly lit.

Perfect for rest, though rest wasn't what I had in mind.

I carried Celia to the bed and gently placed her on the soft mattress.

"This is where you usually rest?" She looked around curiously at the furnishings.

"Sometimes when work gets too exhausting, I come here to recharge." I leaned closer as I spoke, brushing the hair that had fallen across her cheek behind her ear.

Celia stared at me, seeming completely unaccustomed to this gentle version of me—after all, I'd been playing tyrant just moments before.

My lips traced the swollen outline of her mouth from my earlier kisses, then I captured her earlobe and murmured roughly, "How do you like me to treat you during sex? Rough, or gentle?"

I felt Celia shudder at my words.

"Or do you like both? As long as it's coming from me, you'll take it all, won't you? Tell me, Celia."

Celia's cheeks had turned crimson, but she answered anyway, "I like everything you give me, Kirill."

I chuckled low. "You just gave me the perfect answer, Celia."

I kissed her again.

Then I pulled back from the kiss, my lips tingling from the heat of Celia's mouth, her breath still mingling with mine. Her eyes, half-lidded and glassy with desire, locked onto me, and I could feel the pulse of her need radiating from her. The air between us was thick, charged with an electricity that made my skin hum. She was wearing that thin, flowing skirt that clung to her hips, and I already knew—God, I knew—she wasn't wearing anything underneath. The thought alone sent a jolt of heat straight to my cock, but I wanted to take my time with her. I wanted to worship her, to make her feel every ounce of devotion I had for her body, her soul, her everything.

"Celia," I murmured, my voice low and warm as I cupped her face, brushing my thumb along her cheekbone. "You're so fucking beautiful like this, you know that? All flushed and needy for me." Her cheeks darkened further, but she leaned into my touch, her lips parting on a soft gasp. I kissed her again, slow and deliberate, my tongue sliding against hers in a gentle dance that promised so much more. She responded eagerly, her hands fisting in my shirt, pulling me closer as if she couldn't get enough. Her enthusiasm lit a fire in me, but I kept my movements tender, savoring the way her body melted against mine.

I trailed my kisses down her jaw, her neck, lingering at the sensitive spot just below her ear. "You taste so sweet, baby," I whispered, my breath hot against her skin. "I could spend all day just kissing you, but I've got other plans for you." She let out a soft whimper, her hands sliding up to grip my shoulders, and I grinned against her skin. Slowly, I began to peel off her clothes, starting with her messed-up shirt. The fabric slipped down her shoulders, revealing the soft curve of her breasts, her nipples already hard and begging for attention. I didn't rush. I took my time, kissing every inch of exposed skin as I worked her top off completely, letting it pool at her feet.

Her skirt was next, and I knelt as I slid it down her hips, my lips brushing the smooth skin of her thighs. The absence of her panties made my breath catch, my cock throbbing painfully in my pants. "Fuck, Celia," I growled softly, looking up at her. "You're gonna kill me, walking around like this. So perfect, so ready for me." She bit her lip, her eyes shimmering with a mix of shyness and raw desire, and I couldn't resist pressing a kiss to the soft mound just above her core, teasing her with the promise of what was to come.

I stood, shedding my own clothes quickly until I was as bare as she was. Her gaze roamed over me, hungry and unashamed, and I felt a surge of pride at the way she looked at me, like I was everything she wanted. I pulled her close, her naked body pressing against mine, and kissed her again, deeper this time, letting her feel the heat of my arousal against her stomach. "You're mine tonight, sweetheart," I murmured against her lips. "And I'm gonna take such good care of you."

I I paused to admire her stunning body, her slightly flushed skin a silent invitation to me. Her legs parted instinctively as I knelt between them, and I couldn't help but admire the sight of her—glistening, open, and so damn inviting. I hooked her legs over my shoulders, my hands gripping her thighs gently as I lowered my mouth to her. The first touch of my tongue against her slick folds drew a sharp gasp from her, and I groaned at her taste, sweet and heady, like honey laced with something uniquely her. "God, you taste so good," I murmured, my voice muffled against her skin. "I could do this forever, baby."

I took my time, lapping at her slowly, circling her clit with the tip of my tongue before dipping lower to tease her entrance. Her hips bucked, and I tightened my grip on her thighs, holding her steady as I worked her with long, languid strokes. Her moans filled the room, soft and desperate, and I glanced up to see her head thrown back, her hands clutching the sheets. "That's it, Celia," I whispered, blowing a soft breath against her sensitive flesh. "Let me hear you. Let me know how good this feels."

"Kirill," she gasped, her voice trembling with need. "Please... don't stop."

"Never, baby," I promised, my lips brushing her clit as I spoke. "I'm gonna make you feel so good." I doubled my efforts, sucking gently on her clit while sliding one finger inside her, curling it just right to hit that spot that made her cry out. Her walls clenched around me, and I added a second finger, pumping slowly as my tongue worked her clit in tight, relentless circles. Her thighs trembled against my shoulders, her breath coming in short, ragged pants, and I knew she was close.

But I wasn't done with her yet. I wanted to push her higher, to make her lose herself completely. I pulled back just enough to shift positions, lying flat on the bed and guiding her to straddle my face. "Come here, sweetheart," I said, my voice thick with desire. "Sit on me. Let me taste you like this." Her eyes widened, a flush spreading across her chest, but she obeyed, positioning herself above me. The sight of her hovering over my face, her slick folds so close, was almost too much. I gripped her hips and pulled her down, my mouth finding her again as she gasped and braced herself against the headboard.

I devoured her, my tongue plunging deep inside her before flicking back to her clit, alternating between soft licks and firm sucks. Her moans grew louder, more desperate, and she started to rock against my mouth, chasing her pleasure. "That's it, baby," I murmured against her, the vibrations making her shudder. "Ride my face. Take what you need." Her movements became frantic, her hands gripping the headboard as she ground against me, and I could feel her getting wetter, her thighs quaking as she neared the edge.

"Kirill... oh God, I'm gonna—" Her words cut off in a cry as her orgasm hit, her body trembling above me as her release coated my tongue. I didn't stop, lapping at her gently through the aftershocks, drawing out every last shudder until she was panting, her body limp with pleasure. I eased her down onto the bed beside me, kissing her thighs, her stomach, her breasts, until I reached her lips. "You're so perfect when you come," I whispered, kissing her softly. "So fucking beautiful."

She smiled, her eyes hazy with satisfaction, but I wasn't done with her yet. I positioned myself between her legs, my cock aching as I rubbed the tip against her slick entrance. "You ready for me, sweetheart?" I asked, my voice gentle but laced with hunger. She nodded, her hands reaching for me, pulling me closer. "I want you, Kirill," she whispered. "Please."

I pushed into her slowly, savoring the way her tight heat enveloped me, inch by inch. She gasped, her nails digging into my shoulders, and I groaned at the sensation, my control hanging by a thread. "Fuck, Celia, you feel so good," I murmured, my lips brushing her ear. "So tight, so perfect for me." I started to move, slow and deep, each thrust deliberate, letting her feel every inch of me. Her legs wrapped around my waist, pulling me closer, and I kissed her again, our tongues tangling as our bodies found a rhythm.

"You're everything to me," I whispered against her lips, my hands sliding up her sides to cup her breasts, my thumbs brushing her nipples. "I love how you take me, how you give yourself to me." She moaned, her hips meeting mine with every thrust, and I could feel her building again, her walls fluttering around me. I kept my pace steady, gentle but firm, wanting to draw out her pleasure as long as possible.

"Kirill," she gasped, her hands clutching at my back. "I'm so close… please, don't stop."

"I've got you, baby," I promised, kissing her deeply as I angled my hips to hit that perfect spot inside her. Her moans grew louder, her body arching beneath me, and I could feel my own release building, the heat coiling tight in my core. "Come for me, Celia," I whispered, my voice rough with need. "Let me feel you."

Her orgasm hit hard, her walls clenching around me as she cried out my name, her body shaking with the intensity of it. The sight of her, the feel of her, pushed me over the edge, and I followed her, my release spilling deep inside her as I groaned her name, my hips stuttering against hers. I held her close, kissing her softly as we both came down, our breaths mingling in the quiet aftermath.

Everything fell quiet.

Celia had fallen into an exhausted sleep. I tucked the covers around her, then grabbed my phone and walked to the floor-to-ceiling windows, dialing the HR director.

"Boss." The voice on the other end was respectful. "What can I do for you?"

"There's a blonde kid in marketing." I watched the tiny stream of traffic below, my tone flat. "I don't want to see him in headquarters anymore."

Silence for a few seconds—the director was obviously processing this information quickly. Smart man. He didn't ask any stupid questions about why.

"Understood, boss. Do you want me to fire him outright, or…"

"No need to fire him." I pulled at the corner of my mouth. "Don't we have that infrastructure project in Africa? They're short-staffed there. Have him pack his things and get over to the project site immediately. Tell him it's company training for junior staff."

Infrastructure projects were brutal, especially in Africa. Let's see if he still had the energy to flirt with female colleagues.

"Yes, boss. I'll handle it right away."

"Make it clean," I added, then hung up.

Only after handling that did the irritation in my chest finally settle.

Ever since that day, I'd found myself increasingly unable to stand not seeing Celia.

Whenever she wasn't within my sight, it felt like thousands of ants were crawling through my chest.

Would I feel this way about my bed partners? Impossible. Bed partners were just tools for release—use them and toss them aside.

But Celia? She was definitely more than just a booty call or lover.

Maybe I was falling for her? It would be perfectly normal for a woman like her to make me fall. Beautiful, stubborn, pitiful—everything about her felt unique.

I needed her constantly in my sight. So I did something even I found strange—I had the tech department route the surveillance feed from the marketing floor directly to a secondary screen in my office. Now I could see her just by looking up.

Celia in the video was just as captivating.

When she worked seriously, her brow would furrow slightly, her fingertips dancing across the keyboard like an elegant butterfly. When she hit a problem, she'd unconsciously bite her lower lip or tap her forehead with the end of her pen. That troubled expression was so damn cute I wanted to drag her over to me.

What the fuck was I doing? I was the company president, not some peeping pervert.

I didn't need some bullshit surveillance to see Celia. I just needed to use my authority to keep her close.

When I called her to my office and handed her a position transfer and salary adjustment agreement, her eyes went wide.

"This is..."

"Starting tomorrow, you're no longer a marketing clerk." I interlaced my fingers and leaned forward. "You'll be my personal assistant, handling all my daily affairs. Your office will be right here."

I pointed to the empty space beside my desk, where HR had already set up a brand new desk and chair.

Celia's lips moved as if she wanted to say something, but she stayed quiet. She read through the agreement carefully, and when she reached a certain page, her breathing stopped.

"$120,000 annual salary? That's four times what I make now!"

It was enough for her and Lucas to live much better. I knew she couldn't refuse.

Celia's desk was less than three meters from mine. The air around us was filled with her citrus scent, and it satisfied me completely.

The office had become our playground for flirtation.

When she brought me coffee, I'd take the cup and have a sip, then grab her wrist and pull her onto my lap for a sudden kiss.

"Too bitter," she'd protest with a frown.

That afternoon, she was organizing a report, her brow tight with concentration. I set down my work and silently walked up behind her.

"Running into trouble?"

Her body tensed instantly.

"No... no." She stubbornly denied it. "Just some numbers that don't add up."

I chuckled softly, wrapping my arms around her from behind and covering her hand that controlled the mouse. My chest pressed tight against her back, surrounding her completely with my presence.

"Here." I guided her hand to move the mouse, clicking on a cell in the spreadsheet. "This spot's wrong. You should..."

I deliberately spoke right against her ear, my lips barely brushing her sensitive earlobe. I could clearly see the tiny, fucking adorable goosebumps rising on her pale neck.

The office was quiet except for our increasingly heavy breathing.

"Kirill..." she finally couldn't hold back, her voice as weak as a kitten's mewl.

"Yeah?" I responded, taking her cute earlobe into my mouth to nibble and suck.

She trembled lightly, struggling. "...we're still at work."

"I know, but this is my office. I can have you whenever I want." My hand had already slipped under her skirt, kneading the soft flesh of her thigh. She instinctively pressed her legs together, trapping my hand between them. I wickedly used my fingers to probe through her panties.

"No, Kirill!" Her beautiful moan escaped.

"You need me." My fingers tried to push her panties aside—

Someone was knocking at the door. I had to give Celia's clit one hard press before pulling my hand away.

CHAPTER THIRTEEN

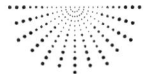

Celia

THE ATMOSPHERE in Kirill's office was the hardest thing to adjust to, aside from all the flirting during work hours.

In the marketing department, there was always this constant buzz in the air—keyboards clicking, coworkers whispering to each other.

Here, on the top floor of the Zaitsev Group, the only sounds came from Kirill himself. The rustle of papers as he flipped through documents, the scratch of his pen across paper when he signed contracts, and that low, sexy voice when he took calls in Russian.

I sat at the assistant desk just a few feet away from him, and every now and then I'd feel this burning gaze on my back. But at least when he was actually working, he didn't stare at me constantly. In fact, except for that first day when I moved up here, he spent most of his time focused on business.

My phone buzzed on the desk, pulling my attention. Emily.

She wasn't going to ask about me and Kirill again, was she? I could still picture the interrogation I faced when I went back after he dragged me away in front of everyone—

The second I walked back into the marketing department, the place exploded.

"Jesus, Celia, you better give us an explanation!" Emily was the first to rush over, eyes bright like she'd discovered buried treasure. "You and the boss... you two? I mean, the day he called you into his office, I knew something was off!"

"Is he promoting you? Or..." One of the male programmers couldn't help but lean in, his face screaming gossip.

A bunch of coworkers swarmed around me, waiting for answers.

I could only smile stiffly and deflect with bullshit like "I'm not really sure either." They didn't mean any harm—just pure curiosity—but I hated being the center of attention. I'd never been the focus of a crowd, and I never wanted to be. I just wanted to work quietly, make money, and raise Lucas.

But clearly, getting tangled up with Kirill Zaitsev meant "quiet" was permanently deleted from my vocabulary.

Thankfully, O'Neil showed up just in time, dispersing the crowd with a few dry coughs.

And when I moved upstairs later, I faced another round of "attacks." I practically fled with my cardboard box, leaving all the chatter behind.

I opened the message anyway.

Emily: Oh my God, Celia, did you hear? Josh got transferred to Africa! I heard the mosquito situation there is terrible!

I frowned.

Me: When did this happen? Why so sudden?

But I already had a sinking feeling.

Emily: Looks like he was transferred a few days ago, but we didn't think much of it then. Who knew it was Africa? I heard it's some infrastructure project... but his position is sales. So did he piss off some higher-up?

My stomach twisted. It had to be Kirill's doing. How could he just casually ship Josh off to Africa?

I felt guilty. An innocent man, because of me, because of Kirill's unreasonable possessiveness, got "exiled" to Africa.

I should be angry. I should be furious. But in that dark corner of myself I didn't want to acknowledge, a twisted pleasure bloomed.

It was sick satisfaction. Kirill had done something so domineering for me. He was declaring ownership over me. I wasn't his property—I screamed that in my head—but some beast inside me felt thrilled by the realization.

My hand gripped the phone tight. I couldn't bring myself to condemn what Kirill had done.

"If your phone is more interesting than my financial reports, Ms. Cole, maybe I should consider a position change. Social media director, perhaps?"

The teasing voice yanked me out of my thoughts so suddenly I nearly threw my phone. I looked up and crashed right into those bottomless gray-blue eyes. He'd somehow made it to my desk, arms crossed, watching me with amusement.

"No, I'm sorry." My cheeks flamed instantly. Getting caught like this was not an experience I wanted to repeat.

His mouth curved into a smirk.

"Oh? Then what had you so... absorbed?" He drew out the word.

"Just a message from a coworker."

"A coworker who could make you wear that expression?" He leaned forward slightly, and the pressure multiplied instantly. "Guilty, but also pleased with yourself. Interesting combination."

My breath hitched. How could he possibly... It was like he could see through my skin, straight into my soul.

"Pack up your things. We're traveling tomorrow afternoon for about two days." Thankfully, he didn't push, moving straight to the next topic. "As my personal assistant, your job includes going wherever I go."

Then he added, "Should I send someone to watch Lucas?"

"No need, it's fine. My friend will help me take care of him." I declined Kirill's offer, then asked, "So... where are we going?"

"Chicago. There's a real estate project to negotiate."

Chicago.

The word hit me like a bullet to the chest, making it hard to breathe.

That place I loved and hated. Where my most beautiful memories lived, where all my childhood happiness had been spent. Where I'd had parents who loved me most.

But it also held my worst nightmares. My father's face, twisted by alcohol and drugs. The humiliation I felt being forced onto that auction stage.

If I didn't bring it up, I'd almost managed to deliberately forget that city.

The private jet's luxury exceeded my imagination. Plush seats, spacious cabin, even a mini bar. I vaguely heard Kirill mention the plane carried a Bentley onboard. But I couldn't focus on any of it. From the moment we took off, my stomach had been tied in knots.

As we got closer to Chicago, the images I'd forcibly buried in my memory began surging up uncontrollably.

I felt like I was reliving being sold by my father, examined by those two women, auctioned off like merchandise.

I closed my eyes and breathed hard, trying to chase those images away.

"You're shaking."

Kirill's voice came from across the aisle. I opened my eyes to find him watching me, brow furrowed.

"I'm just... a little cold," I lied.

He didn't call me out. He grabbed a cashmere blanket from the seat beside him and draped it over me.

"Afraid to go back there?" His voice was soft.

I bit my lip and nodded. In front of him, any lie seemed pathetically transparent.

"I won't let him hurt you again," he said suddenly.

I froze, looking up. "Who?"

"Your father." Kirill's eyes darkened.

"It's not about him," I said quietly. "It's about me. There are too many bad memories there."

I wasn't afraid of my father. I just instinctively avoided memories that caused me pain.

"Then create new memories. Good ones. You can't stay trapped in the past forever, and you can't keep running." Kirill's tone was serious. "Like when my mother died from stress because of my father—I used racing to escape reality, but eventually I had to face her loss."

His face showed no expression as he spoke, but something stabbed at me, making my chest tighten sharply. So he'd had that kind of dark past too.

This was the first time he'd told me anything about himself. I'd always thought someone like him had lived a charmed life, born holding what others would fight their whole lives for, never understanding feelings like mine. But I was wrong. Beneath that polished exterior, he hid scars just as deep.

I opened my mouth, wanting to ask "what happened next," wanting to ask "did your father ever regret it," but the words stuck in my throat. I couldn't tear open his wounds again. I quietly pushed back the heat behind my eyes, drawing strength from his words.

He was right. I couldn't keep running. There were memories of me and my mother here too. I shouldn't abandon them. And I believed this trip with Kirill would become its own unique memory.

"Thank you, Kirill." I took a breath. "You're right. I can't keep hiding."

"This is the good place you wanted to bring me?" Kirill raised an eyebrow, clearly not expecting me to bring him to this unremarkable little restaurant.

It was tucked away on an old street, dim lighting with that vintage feel, red-and-white checkered tablecloths faded with age, black and white photos covering the walls, the air thick with the rich scent of baking bread. It looked exactly like I remembered. Nothing had changed.

When I was little, my mother brought me here once a month for our "secret dates." We'd order a huge plate of meat sauce pasta to share, then Mom would get us each a powdered tiramisu. Back then, Rick was still a gentle husband and father, watching us come home with full bellies, laughing about how we had snuck off to eat good food without him.

"Trust me, you'll love it!" I assured him.

Kirill sat down casually, no pretense at all. But his powerful presence still clashed with the humble surroundings.

The restaurant owner—a chubby, kindly-looking Italian man—clearly startled when he saw Kirill, but still warmly called for us to order.

"Robert, it's me, Celia. Do you remember me? My mother used to bring me here to eat when I was little." I hadn't been back to this restaurant since Mom was diagnosed with cancer, or after she died. I couldn't help asking Robert, though there was a good chance he'd forgotten me.

"Celia?" Robert frowned, leaning in to look at me. After a long moment, he clapped his hands in sudden recognition. "Oh, Celia! That chubby little girl Celia!"

I heard Kirill's unrestrained laughter and turned to glare at him, my whole body burning with embarrassment. God, his smile was the most beautiful thing I'd ever seen—those hard lines suddenly softening, the stern brow relaxing, like a melting iceberg. I'll admit I was dazzled.

"Kids that age tend to eat more," I explained, trying to salvage my image. Besides, I wasn't really fat then, just had round, chubby cheeks.

"How come you stopped coming here?" Robert asked.

My voice dropped. "The family went through some major changes, so I didn't come back."

Robert didn't pry, just said he was sorry to hear that.

I ordered normally, recommending the signature meat sauce pasta for Kirill and getting myself creamy mushroom pasta, then ordering tiramisu for both of us. While we waited, I couldn't help looking out the window at the familiar street.

"My mother loved the tiramisu here before she died." The words just came out. "She said it had more flavor than the cake shops."

Kirill didn't speak. He watched me intently with those gray-blue eyes, like he wanted to pull me in.

Under his gaze, I found I couldn't stop. Words I'd never told anyone, details I thought I'd forgotten, just flowed out naturally.

"She was such a gentle woman. She loved growing flowers—our tiny balcony was always full of colorful petunias. She'd tell me stories, hold me in her arms and sing. Back then, I thought life would always be that beautiful." My voice caught, my mother's gentle smile floating before my eyes.

A large hand covered mine—Kirill's. His palm was rough and warm, callused but with a comforting strength.

"My mother." He began, his voice lower and huskier than usual. "She was a traditional Russian woman. She gave me all her love, taught me to read, taught me to be strong, taught me how to be a better man. Even though she's gone, the qualities I learned from her will stay with me forever."

I looked up at him through tear-blurred eyes. Was he always so philosophical? No—I could feel his palm gripping mine tighter. He was suppressing his emotions. He hated his father, didn't he? He wasn't as at peace with his mother's death as he seemed.

"Your food is here!" Robert's appearance broke the heavy atmosphere.

We ate in silence. Neither of us spoke again. But something in the air had changed forever.

I felt like that invisible barrier between me and Kirill had shattered. The psychological distance between us had shrunk.

I also realized that everything Kirill had shown me was just the tip of the iceberg. He definitely had so much more for me to discover.

But I wasn't discouraged. We had time—I'd have plenty of opportunities to explore him in the future.

Just when I thought this meal would end quietly, everything went to hell.

The restaurant door got kicked open. Two men stumbled in, one clutching his abdomen with both hands, blood seeping through his fingers and staining his gray T-shirt. The other uninjured man carried a black briefcase, supporting his partner while frantically looking over his shoulder like someone was chasing them.

The restaurant erupted in screams, customers panicking.

"Nobody fucking move! Get down! Put your hands where I can see them!" The uninjured man pulled a black pistol from his waist, roaring.

The wounded one collapsed into an empty chair near us with a pained groan.

Were these gangsters? My body froze with fear. My first instinct was to look at Kirill.

He was the complete opposite of me.

He slowly set down his fork, then methodically wiped his mouth with his napkin. His face showed no expression, like these two armed thugs were no different from flies that had wandered into the restaurant.

Everyone else in the restaurant was on the ground as ordered, hands behind their heads. Only our table remained calmly seated.

Our composure clearly enraged the gunman.

"Hey! I'm talking to you! Are you deaf? Get the fuck down!" He pointed the gun at us, approaching step by step. His wounded partner struggled to lift his head, glaring at us with venom.

My stomach twisted, fear making my hands sweat as they gripped the tablecloth.

"Kirill..." I called his name shakily.

"Don't worry." His steady voice was reassuring, instinctively slowing my racing heart.

The moment the thug reached our table, Kirill moved.

That wasn't human speed. I watched him spring up and grab the gunman's wrist before the guy even realized what was happening.

Crack—the nauseating sound of breaking bone. The thug let out a piercing scream as his gun flew free, caught smoothly by Kirill's left hand. He even had the leisure to spin it once before pointing it at the thug, who was now pinned and didn't dare move.

"Frank!" The wounded thug saw what happened and struggled to pull another gun from his jacket, trembling as he aimed at Kirill.

"Bang!"

The gunshot exploded through the restaurant, making my ears

ring. I watched the wounded thug's wrist get blown apart by the bullet, his gun clattering to the floor. He stared at his bullet-torn hand in disbelief, and when he finally bent down to grab the fallen weapon, Kirill had already dragged the first thug over and kicked the gun to the corner of the restaurant.

It was over.

Start to finish, just a few minutes.

When the police burst in, they froze at the scene. Kirill explained briefly—these two were wanted for robbing a hardware store. The cops had been tracking them in the area before losing the trail, only following the gunshots here.

I couldn't take my eyes off Kirill. At the auction, I'd known he was connected to the Bratva. But that was all abstract concepts, distant legends. Tonight, I'd seen his world firsthand.

A world full of violence, danger, and death.

I should be terrified. Any normal woman seeing he—boss? lover?—so coldly and efficiently take down two armed thugs should be shaking with fear, wanting to run from him immediately.

But I wasn't. He'd been so incredible taking down those thugs! That calm control, that lethal grace... like the perfect action movie hero. He'd saved everyone in the restaurant, including me.

Bottom line—he was completely different from common gangsters. My heart pounded wildly.

CHAPTER FOURTEEN

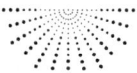

Celia

THE CHICAGO SKYLINE retreated behind us as we drove toward the hotel.

Kirill focused on driving, one hand casually resting on the steering wheel. That same hand had been gripping a gun just moments before.

"You were incredible back there taking down those guys," I said from the passenger seat. "Does this happen to you often?"

"How incredible?" he asked, not waiting for my answer. "If you mean getting held at gunpoint by two idiots, that's not exactly a regular occurrence in my life. If you mean gunfights, then too many to count."

My lungs felt compressed. Kirill's casual tone revealed a world where death could claim him at any moment.

"Scared?" Kirill broke the silence.

"I'm worried about your safety," I said, meaning every word. "I'm still scared, but not of you."

"Celia, you should worry about saying things like that." Something strained in Kirill's voice.

"What?" I didn't understand what was wrong with what I'd said. Was he annoyed that I was interfering? After all, he was the one dominating these fights, taking people out, even building his own business empire.

"You looking genuinely worried about me makes me want to fuck you in this car." Kirill's dangerous gaze swept over me.

The crude words swallowed my concern and sent heat coursing through my lower belly. I actually wanted him to pull over right now and do exactly what he said.

"So keep your heart where it belongs." His low voice cut through my fantasy. "If you're really that scared, I'll take you somewhere."

"We're not going back to the hotel? That's not according to plan." I looked at Kirill, confused. As his assistant, I'd made detailed plans, including booking the hotel to ensure we got enough sleep.

"Sometimes the best plan is no plan. This might be the start of a surprise." His voice was full of temptation.

The next moment, the car had already turned off our original route.

"So where are we going now?"

"Somewhere you won't find on any map."

The Bentley turned into what looked like a rundown alley. Red brick buildings lined both sides, walls covered in graffiti, dim streetlights making it feel like we'd driven into some abandoned district.

The car finally stopped in front of an unremarkable black iron door.

I don't know how Kirill did it, but a keypad emerged from the smooth iron surface. Kirill expertly entered the code, and the door slid inward with a soft chime.

I followed Kirill inside, through a long corridor, and a completely different world opened up before me.

The space was wider than I'd imagined. Two bars flanked either side—the left was a long marble bar with several bartenders expertly mixing drinks for customers. The right was a circular bar with no bartenders behind it, instead lined with rows of glassware and various fresh fruits, spices, and herbs.

Between the two bars was a stage where a band performed nineties jazz with complete absorption. Men and women swayed freely on the dance floor.

"Oh my God..." I couldn't help but whisper in amazement.

"Like it? This bar only opens to specific clients. No name, invitation only." Kirill's voice came near my ear.

I could only nod frantically. I'd never seen a bar like this. It perfectly matched Kirill's style—complex and mysterious.

A man with a carefully groomed silver beard, about fifty years old, walked over with a smile.

"Kirill, you bastard, I thought you'd died in New York." He opened his arms and gave Kirill a solid hug.

"Julian, hell isn't ready to take me in yet." Kirill's words couldn't hide their arrogant fire, but no one thought he was bluffing.

The man called Julian looked at me with benevolent scrutiny. "And this is?"

"Celia." Kirill introduced me, his hand naturally wrapping around my waist in a silent declaration.

"Pleasure to meet you, Celia." Julian winked at me. "Any lady Kirill brings here is something special."

I smiled and pressed my lips together, only I knew how fast my pulse was racing.

Kirill ignored Julian's teasing, but I felt the hand on my waist tighten.

"What'll you have?" Julian asked us.

"Tonight I want to do it myself." Kirill's voice came through.

Julian raised an eyebrow with a knowing expression, leading us to the circular bar while dramatically telling me, "Well, I should warn this beautiful lady—Kirill making drinks himself is rarer than spotting Halley's Comet. The last time I had one of his cocktails, I was probably still young. The taste of that drink, I still remember it—complex, potent, one sip could knock you on your ass."

My heart skipped a beat. I couldn't wait to taste a drink mixed by Kirill.

I watched Kirill remove his suit jacket, casually draping it over a bar stool, then start undoing his shirt cuffs, rolling his sleeves up to his elbows.

Julian tactfully left, giving Kirill and me the bar to ourselves.

"Sit." He pointed to a bar stool, then expertly walked behind the bar.

"Beautiful lady, all alone?" Kirill asked while taking several bottles from the liquor cabinet.

I froze. Was he pretending we were meeting for the first time?

"Maybe. I'm waiting for someone." I blinked at him, playing along with this charade.

"Who? He shouldn't leave you alone." Kirill used ice tongs to drop several ice cubes into a shaker. "Until he arrives, I hope I can have the honor of buying you one of my specials."

His words brushed across my skin, something hot coiling in my stomach.

I licked my suddenly dry lips, trying to make my voice sound lazy, "That depends on whether your work can impress me."

He chuckled low, the sound rumbling from his chest, sexy as hell.

He began his performance.

His fingers were long and powerful. He picked up a bottle of golden liquor, poured some in, then added a pale green liqueur with a berry fragrance. He cut open a citrus fruit, using skillful technique to slice it into nearly transparent pieces, the citrus scent filling the air.

He added more spirits and spices I couldn't name, the whole process flowing like water, full of rhythm. I watched mesmerized, completely forgetting to breathe.

He covered the shaker and began shaking. Not the flashy moves you'd see in regular bars, but something full of power and rhythm. His arms tensed with effort, strong muscles threatening to burst from his shirt.

This wasn't just mixing drinks—this was pure seduction. I felt fire burning deep in my belly.

Finally he stopped, straining the mixture through a fine mesh into a chilled glass. The liquid showed a mesmerizing jewel green.

Finally, he lightly rubbed the citrus peel around the rim, pushing the glass toward me. "Try it. I call it 'Chicago Dawn.'"

I brought the glass to my lips. The aroma immediately hit my nostrils—rich and fresh. I carefully took a small sip.

In that instant, my taste buds exploded.

The liquid went down smooth with a hint of sweetness. But then the burn bloomed across my tongue. Fortunately, the slightly tart citrus fragrance balanced the liquor's kick. When the drink slid down my throat, a subtle bitter aftertaste slowly emerged, long and complex, making me want to explore more.

"Complex, potent, one sip could knock you on your ass"—Julian's words echoed in my ears.

Exactly right! This drink was just like Kirill—complex, potent, and mysterious. One sip and I was completely hooked.

"How does it taste?" He'd somehow come around the bar and was sitting in the seat next to me, watching me with burning eyes.

"Absolutely delicious." I praised sincerely, taking another big sip. The alcohol flowed through my veins, making me feel light-headed.

"Well then," he turned my chair halfway so we faced each other, "beautiful lady, are you willing to tell me your name now?"

"Celia." This time I gave my real name. This felt like our true first meeting.

"Celia..." He savored my name in his mouth. "A name that suits you perfectly. I'm Kirill."

We looked into each other's eyes, lost in this game of role-playing.

"How much would it cost for you to stay the night with me?"

"I'm afraid I'll have to disappoint you, sir." I reached out one finger, lightly touching his chest. "I'm not for sale now. No amount of money could buy me."

He caught the hand I'd placed on his chest, bringing it to his lips for a kiss. Then he guided my hand to cover his left chest, right over his heart.

"If money won't work," he said word by word, his voice solemn and powerful, "what if I offer my heart instead?"

My breathing stopped completely. Through my palm I felt his

heart's vibration—rapid and strong, as if anxiously awaiting my response.

My heart was completely shattered in that moment. I stared into his deep gray-blue eyes, unable to say a word.

Before I realized it, I'd lifted my head and pressed my lips to his.

Kirill quickly bent down, gripping the back of my head as our lips met.

His tongue invaded my mouth, sweeping through my saliva. I closed my eyes, responding eagerly with my tongue.

We kissed deeper and deeper, our tongues intertwining like two vines.

"Whoo—!" Whistles and cheers came faintly from around us. Only then did I remember where we were.

Kirill didn't care at all, not stopping until he'd kissed me breathless.

"Let's go." He said huskily in my ear. "I'll take you to our room."

Kirill led me into an Italian-style room. I walked forward to explore—the arched windows, walnut tables and wardrobes, and perfectly placed oil paintings on the walls all felt fresh to me.

"This is where I stay sometimes." He wrapped his arms around me from behind, resting his chin on my shoulder and speaking in a low voice. "Before you, I never brought anyone here."

His rich voice seeped under my skin, spreading like wildfire through my body.

He turned me around to face him. Those gray-blue eyes were like passionate lakes where any woman who saw them would drown.

Kirill rubbed my lips with his rough fingertips. "We always seem to have unforgettable moments here in Chicago."

My body trembled from his low voice and intimate touch.

That night five years ago was so different from tonight.

That night, my body was falling but my soul was screaming to stop. Tonight, there was no fear in my body, only anticipation. Every cell in my body was crying out, craving more from Kirill.

"I never forgot that night five years ago." As if he could hear my thoughts, he whispered against my ear. "Almost every night I relive that evening, relive your body."

"Don't say that..." I moaned, the wetness between my legs impossible to ignore.

"Why?" His lips traced down from my ear, lightly kissing my sensitive neck. "Didn't you enjoy that night? I remember how wet and tight your pussy was, gripping me so hard it wouldn't let go."

"Kirill..." My legs started going weak.

CHAPTER FIFTEEN

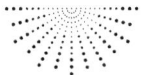

Kirill

HER MOAN, soft and desperate, vibrated through me, set my blood on fire. The way her body trembled under my lips, pressed against the delicate skin of her neck, told me everything I needed to know. She tried to fight it, but she was already mine—had been since that night five years ago. I could still feel the ghost of her tight, soaking heat wrapped around me, the way she had clung to me like she'd never let go. My cock twitched at the memory, strained against my slacks. I wasn't there to play gentle that night. I wanted her raw, honest, and unraveled beneath me.

"Do you like it when I talk about that night, sweetheart?" I murmured, my voice low and rough, lips brushing the curve of her jaw. "Tell me. Do you think about it? Do you touch yourself remembering how I fucked you?" My hand slid to her waist, gripped the fabric of her dress, bunched it slightly as I pressed myself closer, let her feel how hard I was already.

Her breath hitched, and her eyes fluttered shut, cheeks flushed a delicious shade of pink. She was trying to hold back, but her body betrayed her—those thighs pressed together, the way her lips parted like she was starving for air. "Kirill…" she whispered, her voice shaky, like she's pleading for me to stop and keep going all at once.

"No hiding from me," I growled, nipped at her earlobe, my teeth grazed just enough to make her gasp. "Answer me. Do you lie in bed at night, slipping your fingers between your legs, thinking about how I spread you open? How I made you scream my name?" I pulled back just enough to look into her eyes, dark and glassy with want. She was so fucking beautiful like this, caught between shame and desire.

"I…" She bit her lip, and I could see the war in her head—pride versus the truth I already knew. My hand slid lower, rested on her hip, thumb brushed the edge of her panties through the thin fabric of her dress. I didn't move further, not yet. I wanted her to say it.

"Tell me, baby," I coaxed, my voice a velvet threat. "Did you make yourself come thinking about my cock buried inside you? About how you begged me to fuck you harder?"

Her knees buckled slightly, and I caught her, pinned her against the wall with my body. Her scent—sweet, musky, and so fucking intoxicating—filled my lungs. "Yes," she finally admitted, her voice barely a whisper, her face burning with embarrassment. "I… I did. I thought about you. About that night."

A slow, wicked grin spread across my face. "Good girl," I purred, my cock throbbed at her confession. "Honesty deserves a reward." Before she could respond, I scooped her up in my arms, her legs dangled as I carried her to the bed. Her dress rode up slightly and revealed the smooth expanse of her thighs, and I had to fight the urge to rip it off her right then. Not yet. I wanted to savor this, make her beg like she did five years ago.

I laid her down on the bed, her dark hair fanned out against the sheets, her chest heaved as she looked up at me with those wide, needy eyes. I knelt between her legs, pushed her thighs apart, the fabric of her dress stretched tight across her hips. "You're still dressed," I said, my voice thick with lust. "Just like that night. You wore those skimpy scraps of fabric, teasing me with that pitiful look in your eyes until I couldn't take it anymore. Do you remember how I pushed it up and ate you out until you were shaking?"

She whimpered, her hands fisted the sheets. "Kirill... please..."

"Please what?" I leaned down, my lips hovered over the thin fabric covering her pussy, the heat radiated from her made my mouth water. "Tell me you want my mouth on you. Tell me you want me to make you come like I did before."

"I want it," she gasped, her voice breaking. "Please, Kirill, I need you."

That was all I needed to hear. I pushed her dress up just enough to expose her panties, soaked through and clung to her folds. Fuck, she was perfect. I pressed a slow, deliberate kiss to the wet fabric, tasted her through it, and her hips bucked against my mouth. "So fucking wet for me," I murmured, hooked my fingers under the lace and pulled it aside. Her pussy glistened, pink and swollen, begged for me. I didn't make her wait.

I dragged my tongue over her clit, slow and firm, and she cried out, her back arched off the bed. "Fuck, you taste even better than I remember," I growled, sucked her clit into my mouth, flicked my tongue against it until she was writhing. "You loved this, didn't you? Me licking this sweet little pussy until you couldn't think straight."

"Yes!" she moaned, her hands flew to my hair, tugged hard. "God, Kirill, yes!"

I chuckled against her, the vibration made her gasp. "You were so shy that night, trying to hide how much you wanted it. But your body didn't lie. Just like it's not lying now." I slid a finger inside her, curled it against her tight walls, and she clenched around me, so hot and slick I nearly lost it right there. I added another finger, pumped slowly, my tongue never stopped its assault on her clit. "You're still so fucking tight. Do you like this, baby? Like me eating you out while you're still in that pretty dress?"

She was incoherent now, just moans and gasps, her thighs trembled around my head. I could feel her getting close, her pussy fluttered around my fingers, her clit pulsed against my tongue. "Come for me," I demanded, my voice rough. "Come all over my face, just like you did five years ago."

She shattered with a scream, her body convulsed as her orgasm ripped through her. I kept licking, drew it out, until she was panting and limp beneath me. I pulled back, wiped my mouth with the back of my hand, my cock so hard it was painful. "Good girl," I said, my voice low and approving. "You're so fucking gorgeous when you come."

She was still catching her breath, her cheeks flushed, her eyes dazed. I stood, towered over her, my suit still pristine despite the heat coursed through me. "Your turn," I said, unbuckled my belt, the sound sharp in the quiet room. "Come here, sweetheart. Show me what you've learned since last time."

She scrambled to her knees, her dress still bunched around her hips, and reached for my zipper with trembling hands. I groaned as she freed my cock, hard and heavy in her grip. "Fuck, look at you," I murmured, brushed her hair back from her face. "So eager to please me."

She looked up at me, her lips parted, and I couldn't resist guiding my cock to her mouth. She took me in, her tongue swirled around the tip, and I hissed at the sensation. "Fuck, you're better at this than before," I said, my voice rough with pleasure. "You've been practicing, haven't you? Thinking about sucking my cock while you played with yourself?"

She moaned around me, the vibration sent a jolt through my body. She was so fucking good, her mouth hot and wet, took me deeper with every bob of her head. "That's it, baby," I groaned, my hand tightened in her hair. "Suck me like you've been dreaming about it for five years."

She did, her tongue worked me in ways that made my vision blur. I had to fight not to come right then, but I wasn't done with her yet. I pulled her off me, her lips swollen and glistened, and she lookedup at me with a mix of pride and desperation. "You're too fucking good at that," I said, my voice thick. "Now lie back. I'm going to fuck you just like I did that night."

She obeyed, lay back on the bed, her dress still on, her panties pushed to the side. I climbed over her, spread her thighs wide, my cock brushed against her slick entrance. "You were so tight that night," I murmured, teased her with the tip, not entered yet. "So wet, begging for me to fill you. Do you want that again? Want me to fuck you until you can't walk?"

"Yes," she gasped, her hands clutched my shoulders, her nails dug into my suit jacket. "Please, Kirill, fuck me."

I didn't make her wait. I thrust into her, hard and deep, and she cried out, her pussy clenched around me like a vice. "Fuck, you're still so tight," I groaned, pulled back and slammed into her again. "You feel so fucking good. Just like before. You love this, don't you? Love me fucking you hard?"

"Yes!" she moaned, her hips met mine, her body arched into me. "I love it, Kirill. I love how you fuck me."

Her words drove me wild, and I picked up the pace, pounded into her, the bed creaked under us. "You were made for my cock," I growled, my hands gripped her hips, pulled her into every thrust. "Five years ago, you took me so well, screaming my name. You're doing it again, aren't you? Screaming for me."

She was lost in it now, her moans loud and desperate, her pussy clenched tighter with every thrust. I pulled out suddenly, and she whimpered in protest. "Turn over," I commanded, my voice rough. "I want you on your hands and knees, just like that night."

She scrambled to obey, her dress rode up to her waist, her ass in the air. I groaned at the sight, my cock throbbed as I positioned myself behind her. "You looked so fucking good like this," I said, slid into her slowly, let her feel every inch. "Your pussy gripping me, your ass bouncing with every thrust. You loved it when I fucked you from behind, didn't you?"

"Yes," she moaned, pushed back against me, took me deeper. "I loved it. I love it now."

I gripped her hips, fucked her hard and fast, the sound of our bodies slapped together filled the room. "You're mine," I growled, my voice raw. "You've always been mine. Every time you touched yourself, you were thinking of this, weren't you? My cock owning you."

"Yes!" she cried, her voice broke as she started to tremble. "Kirill, I'm gonna come!"

"Do it," I snarled, slammed into her, my own release built. "Come all over my cock, just like you did before."

She screamed, her pussy clenched so tight it pushed me over the edge. I groaned, spilled inside her, my thrusts slowed as we both rode out the aftershocks. I collapsed beside her, pulled her into my arms, both of us still fully clothed, her dress a crumpled mess, my suit wrinkled but intact.

"Fuck," I murmured, kissed her temple, my heart still raced. "You're even better than I remembered."

She laughed softly, her voice hoarse. "So are you."

When everything finally settled, I lay beside her, pulling her still-trembling body into my arms. Her head rested in the crook of my arm, her cheek against my chest. I could feel both our heartbeats beating in perfect harmony.

An unfamiliar emotion washed over my heart like a warm tide.

It was belonging. As if everything I'd done in my life—all the killing, the taking, the conquering—had been for this moment. For holding this woman in my arms.

I wanted her to stay with me forever. I wanted to hear her son Lucas call me Dad.

The thought shocked even me. But I knew it was true.

I needed a new relationship to redefine us. When I made that decision, my chest swelled with anticipation.

"Celia." I took a deep breath, confessing like some lovesick teenager. "Be my girlfriend. Stay with me."

"What did you say?" She shot up, staring at me with those beautiful eyes full of disbelief.

"Be my girlfriend." I sat up, looking straight into her eyes with complete seriousness. "You and Lucas will have me now. I'll give you everything you want."

I saw joy bloom in her eyes. So bright it nearly burned me.

But that light lasted less than a second. What followed was darkness and rejection.

"I'm sorry, Kirill. I can't accept that right now." She bit her lower lip, the words seeming to pain her.

"Don't apologize to me, Celia. But I want to know why."

Unease crawled under my skin, making my jaw tighten. God, I fucking needed to know why. I was certain Celia felt the same way about me! Just seconds ago her eyes had been so bright, making me think I could succeed, that I could give us something new and hopeful.

Celia seemed to choose her words carefully. "It's... too fast. I'm not ready."

"Fast?" I frowned.

"Kirill, I have feelings for you too, but I need time to think."

Seeing the struggle and sincerity in her eyes, the unease in my chest settled.

"Alright." I backed down, then assured her, "I mean it, Celia. Every word I said counts."

She nodded.

Just then, my phone buzzed on the nightstand. I frowned, reaching for it. Volkov's name lit up the screen. He wouldn't dare interrupt me at this hour unless it was urgent. I answered.

Volkov's voice came through immediately.

"Boss, the guys we sent to investigate reported back. That stolen cargo from the docks—we found it in one of Theodore's warehouses."

My expression went ice cold.

"He made his move?"

"Our men didn't alert him. Looks like he hasn't had time to move it yet. Boss, should we—"

"Don't do anything rash." I cut him off. "Cornering him won't help us. This isn't the time to force a confrontation."

"So... we just let it slide?" Volkov's voice carried frustration.

"Let it slide?" I laughed coldly. "In my world, there's no such thing as letting it slide. I'll make him spit up everything he swallowed."

"Yes, boss."

When I hung up, Celia was watching me with concern. "Trouble?"

"Yeah." I didn't elaborate. "Stay here and rest. I need to handle something urgent. I'll be back soon."

I got out of bed quickly. As I reached for the door, she called out.

"Kirill, be safe."

I stopped. That simple concern warmed something deep inside me.

I walked back to the bed, leaning down to kiss her forehead.

"Don't worry," I promised. "In this city, no one dares lay a finger on me."

* * *

Half an hour later, I met with Theodore.

"Kirill! Didn't expect you to ask me out this late." He personally poured me an expensive glass of red wine.

"I'm in Chicago on business. Thought I'd check on our shipping route." I leaned back in my chair casually.

"Oh, everything's running smoothly!" He patted his chest in assurance. "I've added plenty of security at the docks to prevent any more cargo losses. Everything's been safe lately."

"Is that so?" I tilted my chin, studying him. "Good. You know what I hate most—management failures with cargo."

Theodore's smile clearly stiffened. He lifted his wine glass, taking a large gulp to mask his discomfort. "Naturally. Kirill, I know the rules."

Sometimes a batch of cargo sits in a warehouse, forgotten and unregistered, then someone else mistakes it for their own. That gets complicated.

"Right, rules." I leaned forward, my voice carrying authority. "Like never touching what isn't yours. Because some things will burn your hands. Wouldn't you agree, Theodore?"

The air in the private room seemed to freeze. Theodore's face had lost all traces of his smile. His eyes darted nervously, beads of sweat forming on his forehead.

"Kirill." His voice had gone dry. "Sometimes... the guys below don't know better, security gets lax, small mistakes happen. You have to understand."

For profit's sake, I was happy to give him an out.

"I understand." I relaxed my posture. "That's why I came to remind you. Discipline the guys who need disciplining. Return what needs returning. After all, we're allies, aren't we? I wouldn't want some little misunderstanding to damage our deep friendship."

I stood up, not bothering to look at his ashen face, and walked out of the room.

I knew that before dawn, that "stolen" cargo would be back in my designated warehouse, safe and sound.

When I returned, it was already past midnight.

I thought Celia would be asleep, but when I opened the door, I found her sitting on the bed waiting for me, wearing one of my white shirts I kept here.

The shirt was oversized on her, the hem barely covering her thighs, leaving her long, straight legs exposed. That sight was more arousing than any lingerie.

She turned when she heard the door.

"You're back!" She seemed relieved.

"Why aren't you sleeping?" I sat on the bed beside her.

"Couldn't sleep." She looked at me. "Is everything handled?"

"Yeah." I nodded. "Just a minor issue."

"Get some sleep. Tomorrow's negotiation won't be easy." I watched her lie down.

The next morning, we met with those difficult local developers.

The meeting wasn't going smoothly. They kept arguing about some subsidiary clause in the land deal, claiming our community integration plan wasn't adequate and might cause local resistance, which would damage their corporate image.

"Mr. Zaitsev, we respect your business capabilities," one elderly man said, "your plan looks perfect, but it doesn't consider the actual needs of low-income families."

"We're doing business, not charity," I replied steadily.

"Chicago's government takes this development project very seriously. We have to execute it flawlessly. If there's resident resistance, the city will interfere, and our project won't proceed smoothly." Another man spoke up.

I leaned back in my chair, fingers unconsciously tapping the table. For me, all problems could be reduced to numbers and terms. If they weren't satisfied, I could increase the donation amount, or simply abandon this project and let them deal with less generous corporations.

I was about to speak, to end this negotiation my usual way, when my gaze swept to Celia sitting beside me, taking notes on the discussion. She looked thoughtful.

"Celia, what's your perspective on this?" I said slowly. The developers' eyes turned to Celia in surprise.

Celia froze too, clearly not expecting me to suddenly call on her.

I gave her an encouraging look. Celia quickly composed herself.

Then she turned her attention to the developers.

"I think we could build a community shared center to reduce residents' sense of isolation regarding community integration."

Celia's confident voice rang out. I saw the developers listening intently.

"I suggest adding a community shared center to the project plan, truly bringing new and existing community residents together." She continued outlining her vision. "The shared center could provide services like free childcare—that wouldn't cost much."

The negotiation succeeded dramatically. The developers loved the proposal and decided they would fund the community shared center construction themselves.

I watched Celia smile at successfully facilitating the deal. She always brought me unexpected surprises. She'd only been my assistant for a short time, but she could already handle situations independently. I thought I knew her well enough, but I kept discovering she was more than I'd imagined. There was so much more about her to explore.

Excitement and satisfaction filled my chest.

CHAPTER SIXTEEN

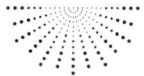

Celia

THE FIRST DAY back at work in New York, the air on the top floor of the Zaitsev Group felt thinner than anywhere else. Kirill sat behind me, focused on his work, his presence so commanding it seemed to consume every oxygen molecule in the room.

I forced myself to dive into work, staring at the endless spreadsheets on my computer screen, but I failed. My mind wasn't on these numbers at all—it kept drifting back to that boutique hotel in Chicago, back to Kirill's soulful gray-blue eyes.

"What if I offered my heart instead of money?"

"Be my girlfriend. Stay with me."

"You and Lucas will have me from now on. I'll give you everything you want."

Those words felt carved into my brain. Every time I replayed them, my heart would race uncontrollably, followed by a sweet, dizzying shiver. Kirill had actually confessed to me! It felt too surreal, like a beautiful dream I could wake up from at any moment.

Of course I was happy. I'd been so elated I wanted to scream and run through Chicago's streets. What woman could resist a man like that? He was powerful, handsome, wealthy, yet he looked at me like I was some precious treasure he'd lost and found again. That focus and longing could melt any frozen heart.

But after the joy faded, panic and unease washed over me. Too fast. Everything was happening too fast.

From our reunion when he proposed that lover contract, to his jealous transfer of Josh, to that sudden confession in Chicago—it had been only a few weeks. A man like Kirill couldn't possibly lack women. The socialites, beauties, and stunning creatures he'd encountered probably outnumbered all the clothes in my closet combined.

Why me? Just because of that one night five years ago? Or was he simply caught up in the moment, feeling some brief novelty for a Cinderella type like me? I was terrified. Terrified that his so-called sincerity had an expiration date so short I wouldn't even have time to fully surrender before it ran out.

So when he looked at me with those eyes full of expectation, I pulled back.

I really did need time to think. For Lucas, and for myself.

"Celia, there's a document that needs your attention." Kirill's voice cut through my tangled thoughts. I walked over to stand beside him as he pointed at the file, explaining the key points.

"This section here, pay attention to..." Kirill's deep voice wrapped around me. As I listened, my gaze drifted to his strong, sculpted profile, and desire coursed through my entire body.

"Kirill, darling, I brought your favorite—"

I instinctively looked up. The sultry female voice cut off abruptly when she saw me.

A stunning blonde stood in the doorway. She wore high heels, carried an expensive-looking bag, and her tight dress showcased every curve of her smoking hot figure. She'd emerged from Kirill's private elevator and strode confidently into the office, radiating an aura of self-assurance and glamour from head to toe.

She removed her sunglasses, giving me an X-ray scan from head to toe before her gaze settled on my old, faded blazer that I'd worn for years. Her lips curved into an undisguised sneer.

"Oh, sorry, am I interrupting?" She said sorry, but there wasn't a trace of apology in her tone. Instead, she sounded like a lady of the manor surveying her territory. "You're the new assistant? Your fashion sense is... truly unique. I didn't know the washed-out look was trending again."

Ice-cold water doused the heat in my veins. My face went white instantly. I wanted to step away from Kirill, but he moved first. He pulled me closer to him, his arm tightening around my waist.

"Anastasia," Kirill's voice was cold as ice, "who the fuck let you in here?"

Anastasia's smile froze for a moment when she saw Kirill's gesture, but she quickly recovered, running her fingers through her hair with practiced seduction. "Don't be so cold, darling. I brought your favorite ultra-thin ribbed condoms. Didn't we agree? Every month at this time, I come to you..."

She licked her lips as she spoke. She didn't finish, but I understood the implication.

Every month at this time she came to find Kirill. So she was his regular fuck buddy?

Just days ago, Kirill had passionately confessed to me, asking me to be his girlfriend. Now his regular hookup was at his door. So this was his idea of sincerity? A sharp pain shot through my chest. I felt like I'd been slapped in public.

Kirill's face darkened like a storm cloud. He stared coldly at Anastasia, his voice carrying undeniable authority.

"How dare you come up here without notifying my secretary? Our arrangement is canceled as of now. Get the fuck out!"

"What? Didn't we have a great time last month?" Anastasia looked at Kirill in disbelief, then shot me a venomous glare. "Kirill! You're throwing me out for this... this nobody? Have you lost your mind?"

"Get out! I won't let you talk about her that way. Get out of this building and don't let me fucking see you again!" The murderous intent in Kirill's voice seemed to drop the office temperature to freezing.

Anastasia shuddered at the viciousness in his eyes. She bit her lip resentfully but didn't dare say another word.

After Anastasia left the office, we fell into deathly silence.

Kirill's arm around my waist tightened. He turned me to face him, then lowered his head, trying to catch my eyes.

"Celia, let me explain."

I kept my head down, staring at my shoes. I felt my eyes burning. I didn't want to cry, especially not in front of him. That would make me look even more pathetic.

"She's right," I said with a bitter smile, hearing myself speak in a voice devoid of emotion. "I am a nobody. You should find someone like her."

"Don't say that!" He let out a low roar, his voice full of urgency and frustration. "That's all in the past. Celia, look at me!"

He lifted my chin, forcing me to meet his gaze. The regret in his eyes tugged at me.

"Since we reunited, I haven't touched any other woman." His tone was sincere and forceful. "Anastasia was just one of many mistakes from the past. Believe me, now the thought of touching any of them makes me sick. My body, my heart—they only want you."

His explanation sounded flawless. His expression showed no signs of deception. Logic told me I should believe him. He'd thrown that woman out in front of me, decisively, without leaving any room for sentiment. That was proof enough of how special I was to him.

But emotionally, I couldn't accept it.

Anastasia's beautiful, contemptuous face haunted my mind. She was like a mirror, reflecting the unbridgeable chasm between him and me. They were from the same world, while I was just an outsider who'd wandered in by accident.

"I understand." I pulled free from his hands and stepped back, creating distance between us. I saw something die in his eyes.

"You don't believe me?" His voice carried deep defeat and helplessness.

"I do." I was telling the truth—I believed he meant what he said right now. "It's just... give me some time and space, okay? I need to think clearly."

"Celia, what we should be doing is solving the problem, not fucking running away!" Kirill roared.

"Solve the problem? How? Your fuck buddy shows up and I'm supposed to pretend I didn't see it? Is maintaining surface calm what you call solving the damn problem?"

I challenged him right back. Did going along with him count as solving the problem?

"That's not what I meant, Celia." Kirill pinched the bridge of his nose, took a deep breath, then spoke. "I'll give you time and space, but you can't use this incident to completely dismiss my feelings."

The vulnerability on Kirill's face made me waver. I nodded.

Back at my desk, I sat down mechanically, worked mechanically. My fingers tapped on the keyboard, producing gibberish I didn't recognize. My vision blurred as Anastasia's words and Kirill's explanation battled repeatedly in my head, leaving me agitated and confused.

Anastasia's appearance reminded me what kind of women Kirill was used to. They were beautiful, confident, sophisticated. And me? I wore cheap clothes, scrambled to pay rent and my son's expenses. My world and his were so completely different.

Even if he was infatuated with me now, how long could that infatuation last? When the novelty wore off, wouldn't he get tired of my ordinariness and dullness, then return to those women who actually matched him? Just thinking about that possibility made my heart ache like it was being crushed.

I couldn't take that gamble, because I couldn't afford to lose.

For the next few hours, I buried myself in stacks of documents, using frantic work to numb myself. Kirill was a gentleman and kept his promise—though we shared the same office, he didn't disturb me.

Finally, the clock hands pointed to five. I practically shot out of my seat, grabbed my worn canvas bag, and rushed toward the elevator without looking back.

"Celia!"

Kirill's urgent voice came from behind me.

I pretended not to hear, frantically pressing the elevator's down button. Thank God the doors opened just in time. I shot inside, and in the second before the doors closed, I saw Kirill's figure rushing after me, his face full of frustration.

Escaping that suffocating building, I drove my beat-up second-hand car through New York's congested rush-hour traffic. I picked up Lucas from kindergarten first. The little guy threw himself into my arms happily, chattering about his day.

"Mommy, Ben told me his dad took him to an amusement park last week!" Lucas gestured excitedly. "He said there were flying chairs and a huge carousel. I can't wait for the weekend! We can go ride the carousel with Kirill."

My heart clenched. This weekend was indeed when Kirill had arranged to take us to the amusement park. But I'd just fought with Kirill—would he still want to go?

Looking at Lucas's expectant smile, my heart felt like it was being stabbed by countless needles.

I forced a smile, "Baby, just sleep a few more nights and it'll be here."

I didn't go home. I drove to Mia's apartment. I needed someone to talk to, or I felt like I was going to explode.

Mia opened the door with her hair in a messy bun. Seeing us, she threw her arms open with delight, "Come in, my darlings! I missed you so much!"

The three of us hugged together, and my eyes grew warm.

After we went inside, Lucas cheered and ran to his little corner, pulling out his brushes and paper to start creating. I followed Mia into the kitchen like a lost soul.

"Have you eaten? I just ordered pizza." Mia pulled two beers from the fridge, handing me one. "Looking at your zombie state, what happened? Did your CEO fire you again?"

I popped the beer tab and took a long gulp of the cold liquid, the bitter taste sliding down my throat.

"Maybe worse than that." I leaned against the counter, my voice hoarse.

Mia leaned beside me, nudging me with her elbow, "Spill."

"He confessed to me on that business trip. In Chicago."

"Isn't that good news?" Mia raised an eyebrow. "You turned him down?"

"I said I needed to think about it." I took another drink. "But today his fuck buddy showed up at the office. Some woman named Anastasia."

Mia's mouth dropped open.

"But Kirill threw her out."

Mia manually closed her mouth after exhaling.

"He said since we reunited, he hasn't touched any other women. I believed him."

She looked at my serious expression, was silent for a moment, then slowly spoke.

"If that's the case," she took a sip of beer, "a billionaire had fuck buddies before he met you. Honey, doesn't that sound—completely normal?"

"I know." I tugged at my hair in frustration. "I know it's normal, Mia. I'm not asking him to stay celibate for me. I just... I just can't accept it. This whole thing makes me feel like Kirill won't settle down with me. He's been with too many women. Someone like me is just a novelty for him."

"Bullshit!" Mia suddenly raised her voice, startling me. "What do you mean 'someone like you'? Celia, you're the bravest, strongest woman I know. You raised Lucas on your own. You'd do anything for him. You're independent, kind—you're a million times more noble than those plastic dolls who only know how to shop with men's credit cards!"

Mia's words hit my heart directly. I almost broke down crying.

"But Mia," I choked out, "I'm afraid he'll get tired of me eventually. He can walk away anytime."

Mia put down her beer can and turned to look at me seriously. "So when he threw that woman out, did he hesitate?"

I shook my head.

"When he explained to you, did you think he was lying?"

I shook my head again. "No, his eyes were sincere. I could tell."

"There you go." Mia spread her hands. "Sweetheart, you can't judge a man's current feelings based on his past mistakes. Who doesn't have a past? What matters is who he wants to share his future with. Obviously, he chose you, not that Anastasia whatever."

She paused, her tone softening. "I understand your fear. You're afraid of getting hurt, afraid of being abandoned. But Celia, you can't refuse the sunshine in front of you because you're afraid of possible storms. You need to ask your heart."

She pointed at my chest. "How do you feel when you're with him? Forget his money, forget his status, forget all those messy women. Just you and him, two people."

I froze.

Yeah, how did I feel when I was with him?

The way he encouraged me with his own painful past on the plane moved and touched me. In the restaurant, his calm composure subduing the criminals fascinated and impressed me. And in that boutique hotel, the sincerity and depth in his eyes during his confession—even now, remembering it still felt so sweet.

I felt my heartbeat, felt desire.

"If you can't make a decision," Mia's voice continued in my ear, "then feel more, experience more. Don't rush to give him an answer, and don't rush to push him away. Let time prove everything. Watch what he does now and in the future, instead of obsessing over what he did in the past. Listen to your heart—it'll tell you which way to go."

I looked at Mia, her eyes full of encouragement. The tangled mess in my heart was considerably straightened by her words.

I still didn't feel secure, but I knew Mia was right. I couldn't let fear control my decisions anymore, at least not cowardly slam the door shut on communication with Kirill.

I needed time, but this time not to escape, but to see clearly. To see him clearly, and to see myself clearly.

I picked up my beer and clinked it against Mia's can on the counter.

"Thank you, Mia."

She winked at me, flashing a brilliant smile.

"Anytime you need me, sister."

CHAPTER SEVENTEEN

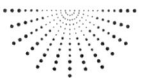

Kirill

8:59 AM.

I leaned back in my office chair, my eyes fixed on the one-way glass wall facing the door. Would she come? The question had been eating at me all night.

That idiot Anastasia—I'd already had my men throw her out last night, making sure she'd never show her face in New York again, never appear before Celia and me. But I knew perfectly well that getting rid of one Anastasia wouldn't solve anything. The problem was me—my goddamn chaotic past.

Nine o'clock sharp. Celia's silhouette appeared beyond the glass.

The tension stretched tight across my cheekbones instantly released, and I hadn't even realized I'd been holding my breath.

She came. At least that meant she hadn't completely condemned me.

She wore a light blue blouse and pale jeans—simple and beautiful.

"Morning." She nodded as she entered, then walked straight to her workstation, sat down, and powered up her computer, as naturally as if nothing had ever happened.

"Good morning, Celia." My response came out sluggish.

I wasn't naive enough to think that Celia greeting me meant she'd forgiven me. But it was significant progress, wasn't it? She wasn't as resistant to communicating with me as she'd been yesterday.

I stared at her working silhouette, unable to concentrate on a single document. Real estate projects with multinational conglomerates, arms dealer quotes from Europe—none of it could capture my full attention. My entire world seemed to have contracted to nothing but Celia's figure.

Her voice remained steady during phone calls, meticulous while handling emails. The more she acted as if nothing had happened, the hotter the fire burned inside me.

I had to communicate with her. We had to return to how things were before. This current situation of only being able to watch her back was driving me fucking insane!

"Cel—" I was about to speak when Celia stood up with her mug, heading toward the break room.

FUCK! I clutched my head in frustration. What a goddamn terrible start.

Just then, my phone vibrated. Viktor's name flashed on the screen.

I took a deep breath, suppressed my irritation, and answered the call.

"What is it?"

"Whoa, who's gotten our Tsar all riled up?" Viktor's lazy voice drifted through the speaker. "You're burning hot. Want to come to Novak so I can spar with you? We just got a new batch of Russian girls —I guarantee they'll extinguish any fire you've got."

"Not interested," I rejected him curtly.

The mere thought of other women made my stomach churn with revulsion. Since reuniting with Celia, my body seemed to have automatically activated some kind of purity mode, losing all basic desire for any woman except her.

"Seriously?" Viktor whistled exaggeratedly on the other end. "Don't tell me this is still about that one-night stand from Chicago. Take my advice—she's probably married with a houseful of kids by now. You should give up while you're ahead."

"I have a question." I ignored Viktor's stream of bullshit.

"Ah, shoot away. Let me take a sip first."

"Viktor, if you... hurt a woman's feelings, how would you win her back?" The words came out with difficulty.

A coughing fit, then laughter. Thank God Viktor didn't choke to death. After his violent coughing subsided, he answered, "Did I hear that right, Kirill? You're asking me for relationship advice?"

"Speak up or I'm hanging up."

Viktor always hid the point under a mountain of words.

"My bad." Viktor surrendered. "First tell me what exactly happened, so I can prescribe the right remedy."

I used the most concise language possible to explain my reunion with Celia, how we'd finally made some progress only to have that idiot Anastasia ruin everything.

The other end fell into prolonged silence. I could practically picture Viktor's expression—like he'd seen a ghost.

After a full thirty seconds, he spoke in a dreamlike tone, "Honestly, Kirill. I'd really like to meet the woman who can make you this miserable."

"Get to the point."

"OK, OK." Viktor cleared his throat, returning to his cynical tone. "Hurt a woman's heart? That's too easy—throw money at the problem. Give her a limitless Black Card, let her buy out everything on Fifth Avenue. Ever heard this saying? Nothing heals heartbreak like a Hermès bag—if that doesn't work, make it two."

"She's different," I immediately objected.

Celia's proud, strong image flashed through my mind. Throw money at her? That would only make her feel I was insulting her, lumping her together with women like Anastasia.

"Oh, 'she's different'—every man who falls in love says that." Viktor snorted. "No matter how different she is, all women need to be coddled, need security. You have to provide everything she wants.

Whatever she lacks, you give her. Isn't this supposed to be your greatest talent?"

Whatever she lacks, you give her—this sentence cleared my muddled thoughts.

This really should be my greatest talent. Those former booty calls wanted my money, so I could satisfy them easily.

But what Celia wanted was definitely something different from theirs.

I thought of Lucas, remembered when I drove her and Lucas home, seeing that run-down apartment building. I still remembered the indescribable stab of pain in my chest when I watched through the rearview mirror as she took Lucas's hand and walked into that darkness.

What Celia lacked was a stable home, an environment where she wouldn't have to worry about next month's rent, a space where Lucas could grow up healthy and happy.

Security.

Viktor was right. I couldn't give her ethereal promises, but I could give her tangible, touchable security.

I owned countless properties on Long Island, in the Upper East Side, in all of New York's prime locations. I could select one and make it a fortress to shelter Celia and Lucas from wind and rain. I also needed to fill her closet—seeing her in those old clothes broke my heart.

"Kirill? Are you still listening?"

"I know what to do now." I hung up the phone.

I was about to press the intercom to have my secretary contact my property manager and have all the top-tier villa materials sent over, when the office door suddenly opened.

I looked up to see Celia standing in the doorway. All color had drained from her face, those beautiful eyes filled with panic and despair, like she'd been cornered.

Her fragile appearance made my heart feel like it had been punched, aching as it beat. I asked softly, "What's wrong, Celia?"

"Kirill..." Her voice trembled uncontrollably, thick with tears. "Help me, please..."

My stomach dropped. I immediately stood from behind my desk, crossed to her in several strides, and steadied her trembling shoulders. "What happened? Celia, calm down, take it slowly."

She gripped my arm desperately, as if clutching a lifeline.

"It's Lucas..." she choked out, each word taking all her strength. "Our child... Lucas... he's missing!"

After saying this, her tears burst forth like a broken dam.

"What did you say? Our child? Lucas is our child?" I couldn't believe what I was hearing.

This information shot through my skull like a bullet, shattering all my reason and composure.

Lucas was our child.

That little boy with the same gray-blue eyes as mine, that kid so considerate at the restaurant it melted your heart, that child who looked up with his little face, hoping I'd take him to the amusement park... was my son?

Lucas was my biological son!

My brain went blank. Blood rushed to my head, then froze solid the next second.

What did Celia say? Lucas was missing!

"There's no time to explain! We have to find Lucas right now. The principal just told me Lucas disappeared. Your identity isn't simple—what if someone kidnapped him to get at you? What if they..." Celia couldn't continue, shaking like a leaf in the wind.

Celia's words ignited the fuse in my brain.

Enemies.

Theodore? Those Irish bastards? Or remnants of some family whose name I'd long forgotten, someone I'd personally sent to hell?

The thought that my son might be in the hands of those wolves sent the darkest, most violent killing intent surging through my blood. I swore that whoever it was, if they dared touch one hair on Lucas's head, I would make him and his entire family disappear completely from this earth.

But now wasn't the time for such thoughts. I forced myself to suppress all emotions.

I pulled Celia into my arms. I felt her violent trembling finally subside somewhat.

"Listen, Celia!" My voice sounded calm and strong. "They won't be stupid enough to make a move. Lucas will be fine—I promise you."

After saying this, my brain began operating at high speed, clear response plans forming in my mind.

While questioning Celia for the information I needed, I guided her to my desk, then pulled out my phone and dialed a number.

"Volkov?" I spoke into the phone, my voice cold and hard. "I don't care what you're doing right now—immediately arrange personnel to lock down Brooklyn. Tell them to look for a four or five-year-old boy, black hair, gray-blue eyes, wearing a Star Kindergarten uniform."

I hung up and dialed several more numbers.

"Immediately pull up all street surveillance footage from the past hour within a five-block radius of Brooklyn's Star Kindergarten. I want every frame, sent to my computer right now."

"Prepare as much cash as possible—I want to see it within thirty minutes."

"Have the principal and teachers from Brooklyn's Star Kindergarten wait for us at the school entrance."

...

Orders flowed systematically from my mouth.

Celia looked up at me through tear-filled eyes, but hope was now burning in her gaze.

Seeing her like this tugged hard at my heart. This woman had been raising our son alone for nearly five years—how difficult and challenging must that have been? Yet I knew nothing about any of it.

"Let's go." I gripped her ice-cold hand tightly with one hand, grabbed the car keys from the drawer with the other. "We're going to the kindergarten."

The Bentley sped along the road. I ran countless red lights, the harsh honking and cursing muffled by the heavy windows.

Soon, that colorful but aging adorable building appeared before us.

Several women with panicked expressions stood at the kindergarten entrance. Celia told me the one in the middle was the principal.

"Mr. Zaitsev..." the principal stammered. "We... we searched everywhere—classrooms, courtyard, restrooms... couldn't find Lucas anywhere. The police are on their way."

"Where was he last seen?" I pressed.

"At... at the sandbox in the back courtyard," one of the female teachers answered through tears. "After nap time was free play period. Lucas was playing hide-and-seek with several children. Then he just..."

Celia and I rushed to the back courtyard, carefully searching every corner.

Time passed mercilessly, each second like torture on my heart. My phone kept vibrating with incoming messages.

"Surveillance detected no suspicious vehicles."

"No trace of the child found at any intersection."

"No ransom calls received."

This stream of bad news pressed on my chest like boulders.

Celia was on the verge of complete collapse. Without my support, she would have collapsed to the ground at any moment.

Just as the despair in my heart was about to consume me entirely, a timid voice came from not far away.

"I... I remembered..."

The speaker was a little girl, about five or six years old, being led over by a teacher.

"Lucas seemed to run toward the laundry room."

Laundry room! Celia and I rushed frantically toward that small independent building in the back corner.

The room wasn't large—several industrial washing machines lined the walls, with several half-person-high old laundry baskets filled with clean sheets stacked in the corner.

"Lucas!" Celia called in a hoarse voice while opening washing machines to search.

From visual inspection, besides the washing machines, only those old laundry baskets could accommodate a nearly five-year-old child.

I held my breath and strode to the baskets to search. When I moved aside the top layers of sheets, I finally saw Lucas. He was curled up in the pile of sheets, sleeping soundly with a satisfied smile on his face, as if he'd had a wonderful dream.

My heart settled back into place, and all the colors of the world returned to my life.

"Lucas!" Celia let out a joyful sob and rushed over, pulling our sleeping son tightly into her arms.

The little guy was startled awake and drowsily rubbed his eyes.

"Mommy?" he asked in his sweet voice. "Did I win? Did they find me?"

"You scared Mommy to death, Lucas!" Celia could no longer hold back, sobbing as she held Lucas.

I embraced both mother and son, letting that surging emotion—the relief and gratitude of recovery after loss—envelop me completely.

CHAPTER EIGHTEEN

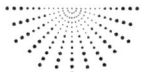

Celia

WHEN WE FOUND Lucas buried in that pile of bedsheets, the wire stretched to its breaking point in my head finally snapped.

One second I was teetering on the edge of hell, imagining every horrible thing that could have happened to my child, that fear nearly swallowing me whole.

The next second his warm, real body was in my arms, pulling me back from that endless darkness.

Kirill wrapped his arms around both of us too, the three of us clinging together like we could never be separated. Kirill's chest was broad and warm. I didn't know when this man's embrace had become my safe harbor, making me feel completely secure.

The moment I got that call about Lucas being missing today, my world collapsed. I panicked so hard I could barely stand. I forgot about the unresolved issues between Kirill and me, instinctively turning to him for help. Kirill's composure and steadiness made me lean on him—like there was nothing he couldn't handle. He was so strong, so reliable.

"Mom, you're squeezing me into french fries!" Lucas's muffled voice came from my arms.

"Sorry, baby!" I loosened my grip and kissed his forehead. "Mommy was just so worried about you."

"Sorry, Mom. My friends and I were playing hide and seek." Lucas looked up at me. "I waited here forever and nobody came to find me. Then I got bored and fell asleep."

"Quality sleep, from the looks of it." Kirill had moved to the side, watching us with that teasing voice of his as he ribbed Lucas.

"Kirill!" Lucas finally noticed Kirill was there. "I've been counting—four more days till the weekend! We promised to go to the amusement park! We're gonna ride the flying chair, and the carousel, and..."

Kirill waited patiently for Lucas to rattle off every single attraction on his wishlist before rubbing his chin and answering, "Of course. Though I remember you need to be a full 3 feet 6 inches tall for the children's flying chair. You meet that requirement now, little guy?"

"I've been tall enough since my birthday last year! Ask my mom if you don't believe me!" Lucas immediately puffed out his chest, chin raised with pride.

Kirill and Lucas's interaction finally helped me recover from that terrible false alarm.

I smiled and joined in, "Lucas is right. He's 3 feet 8 inches now—they measured him when we enrolled."

I watched Lucas's head lift even higher, his little frame straightening up more, like he'd just gotten recognition from the whole world.

"Well then, congratulations, Lucas. I have a feeling the three of us are going to have a wonderful weekend."

The second Kirill finished speaking, Lucas jumped up with joy.

When the kindergarten director learned Lucas had been found, she let out a huge sigh of relief and gave the kids the day off. Kirill told me I could skip work tomorrow too, and drove us back to the apartment.

In the car, Lucas turned into a little chatterbox, excitedly sharing every interesting thing that had happened since he started school. He still looked like he had more to say when we got out.

I took Lucas upstairs, planning to take him grocery shopping nearby in a bit. When I passed by the window and glanced down casually, I spotted Kirill's black Bentley still parked quietly downstairs.

My heart skipped a beat. I'd said I shouldn't refuse to communicate with Kirill. This morning had been a good start. This wasn't hard—we just had some issues between us. That didn't mean I'd stopped having feelings for him. Besides, I had to clear things up about Lucas.

"Baby, Mommy's going downstairs for a minute. Be good and stay inside."

After getting Lucas's response, I turned and headed downstairs.

I walked to the car window and bent down to tap gently on the driver's side. The window slowly rolled down, revealing Kirill leaning back in the driver's seat, brow hard and cold, an unlit cigarette between his fingers.

When he saw me, he seemed stunned for a moment before asking, "What brings you down here?"

"I need to talk to you."

The moment I finished speaking, he opened the driver's door and got out. We stood face to face, the air silent for an instant.

"I'm sorry." I looked down. "I shouldn't have kept Lucas from you. I didn't know you well back then. I thought once you knew Lucas was your son, you'd take him away from me. As a single mom with no power, I was scared I couldn't fight you for him. So I've been guarded about Lucas's identity around you."

"Lucas looks too much like you, so I gave you the wrong age to throw off your suspicions." I bit my lip and continued. "But his birthday is real—last month, August 16th."

I didn't dare look at Kirill. My thoughts scattered in a dozen different directions. How would he react? Would he angrily demand to know why the fuck I'd lied to him? Would he look at me with disappointment and say I didn't trust him? Would he accuse me of robbing him of his rights as a father?

My fists clenched tight. Whatever his reaction, I deserved it.

"Celia, you did great." His voice came from above my head.

My eyes went wide, staring up at him in disbelief. He told me I did great?

God, what did I just hear! That was the last thing I'd expected him to say, the last reaction I'd imagined.

His tone was full of praise and pride, like I'd done something amazing instead of fucking hiding his child's identity from him.

"You raised Lucas beautifully." His expression was moved as he continued. "He's healthy and cheerful, well-behaved and polite... He's a wonderful kid. That's all your doing."

Tears fell from my eyes without warning. That simple acknowledgment hit the softest part of my heart.

Kirill stepped forward and pulled me into his arms. His embrace was still so warm.

"I know being a single mom is hard, especially when you first got to New York—you must have been unfamiliar with everything here. You're an amazing mother, Celia." Kirill patted my back gently as he spoke.

I nearly cried myself unconscious in his arms.

When I recovered, I said into his chest, "We should tell Lucas. He has a right to know who his father is."

Like Mia said—follow your heart, experience more. After nearly a month together, my heart and experience had clearly told me Kirill would be a responsible, good father.

"No." His answer was crisp and decisive.

I looked up at him, completely confused. "Why? Don't you want to claim him?"

"I dream of acknowledging him." His gaze was deep. "But for these five years, I haven't fulfilled a single day of fatherly responsibility. I missed every important moment in his life. I can't just parachute into his life now and matter-of-factly tell him 'I'm your dad.'"

His words left my mouth hanging open.

"A title means nothing if it isn't earned through actions." He stared into my eyes. "Lucas deserves a real father—a man who'll play with him, teach him right from wrong, be there whenever he needs him. Not some identity he's suddenly told about. I'll work to earn Lucas's acceptance."

He was so serious in that moment. I truly realized his age had never been for show—he always thought about things so differently than I did.

My heart completely surrendered.

The weekend arrived as promised, with Lucas's eager anticipation, though his dinosaur had been washed off so he couldn't bring it.

The air at the amusement park was filled with the sweet scent of popcorn and cotton candy, mixed with children's laughter, like a real fairytale wonderland.

Lucas was so excited his little face turned red. He held my hand with one of his and Kirill's with the other, weaving through the crowd like a happy little bird.

Kirill dressed casually today—simple black T-shirt and jeans. It made him look less intimidating than usual, more approachable like the guy next door. But his tall frame and outstanding presence still drew plenty of female attention.

I felt somewhat annoyed by those covetous looks, but I kept it under control.

We rode Lucas's beloved flying chair. When the chair swung up into the air, I cried out with excitement.

"Mom, look! We're flying like Superman!" Lucas's voice was thrilled, his face full of joy and wonder. "It's magic!"

Kirill, sitting on his other side, smiled and responded to Lucas, "You could call it scientific magic. When the chair spins at high speed, it creates an invisible force that wants to push us outward."

"Wow! That's so amazing!"

Watching father and son—one asking wild questions, the other answering with childlike wonder—I felt my heart fill up. Kirill really was a good father, better than anything I could have imagined.

After the flying chair, we rode the carousel. With melodious music playing, the three of us rode our wooden horses, rising and falling with the rhythm. Lucas was ahead of us, turning back to laugh at us, "Mom and Kirill can't catch me!"

"Not so sure about that, baby. I feel like we're getting closer." I pretended to reach out and grab Lucas.

Lucas giggled with delight, and Kirill laughed along.

In that moment, I felt like we were a real happy family enjoying a perfect weekend.

But Anastasia's face appeared in my mind at the wrong time. The issues between Kirill and me still weren't resolved. I thought this needed the right moment, but I didn't know when that would come. Or rather—would it ever come?

The smile on my face gradually faded. The air that had seemed so sweet moments ago now felt a bit thin.

"What are you thinking about?" Kirill's voice pulled me back from my thoughts.

"Nothing." I shook my head, forcing a smile. "Just feels like I'm dreaming."

After playing in the sun all morning, the three of us were getting tired. We found an ice cream truck to refuel.

"Mom, I want that prettiest ice cream!" Lucas pointed at the picture of the cream-colored passion fruit flavored ice cream.

"No, baby." I wiped the sweat from the tip of his nose and explained, "Remember? You're allergic to passion fruit."

"Oh..." Lucas's little face immediately fell.

"That's quite a coincidence." Kirill looked at Lucas. "I can't eat it either. We're both allergic to it."

Lucas's eyes instantly lit up, like he'd discovered some earth-shattering secret. He looked at Kirill, then at me, finally grabbing Kirill's hand excitedly.

"Really? You too?"

Kirill nodded.

"Wow! So cool!" Lucas danced with joy. "Mom, Kirill and I are on the same team! We're the No Passion Fruit Alliance!"

Watching Lucas find belonging over sharing an allergy with Kirill,

I shook my head and laughed. I hadn't expected Lucas to inherit not only Kirill's gray-blue eyes but his allergies too.

We ended up choosing vanilla ice cream and found a bench to sit on.

Lucas licked his ice cream while looking up at Kirill, who had nearly finished his in a few bites, then dropped a bombshell out of nowhere.

"Kirill, do you have a girlfriend?"

I froze mid-lick, nearly choking. I looked nervously at Kirill, wondering how he'd answer this question.

Kirill obviously hadn't expected Lucas to ask this either. After a moment of stunned silence, he turned his gaze to me and said slowly, "Well... you'll have to ask your mom about that."

My face instantly burst into flames. That bastard! He actually passed the buck to me!

He leisurely finished the rest of his ice cream, tossed the wrapper in a nearby trash can, then sat down to wait for my answer.

Lucas naturally turned to look at me with curious, knowledge-seeking eyes.

I was so flustered I could only deflect vaguely, "Never mind that question for now, Lucas. Your ice cream is melting."

Lucas quickly licked his ice cream a few times until there was no more dripping liquid before stopping.

"I know—Kirill doesn't have a girlfriend," Lucas said in a grown-up tone. "Just like how I don't have a dad."

That sentence pierced through my skull. All the awkwardness and shyness in my heart vanished without a trace, replaced by sharp, stabbing pain.

I'd always thought I'd given Lucas enough love, that I'd used all my strength to hold up a sky for him so he could grow up carefree. But I'd forgotten—his father's love had always been missing. No matter how much maternal love I used to fill that gap, it would always exist.

I looked at Lucas, my little sunshine. I thought he was too young to understand these things. But I was wrong. He understood everything —he just never talked to me about it.

My nose stung, heavy guilt and heartbreak washing over me until I could barely breathe.

"Lucas, actually..." I couldn't hold back anymore. I had to tell him the truth. I couldn't let him live with such an incomplete understanding anymore. He wasn't fatherless—his father was right beside him and loved him deeply.

Just as I was about to speak, Kirill gently grasped my hand resting on my knee. I looked at him. He shook his head at me, his eyes firm and powerful, carrying a calming strength.

The words on the tip of my tongue were forcibly swallowed back.

Kirill crouched down in front of Lucas, bringing himself to eye level. He asked softly, "Lucas, do you want a dad?"

My heart instantly jumped to my throat as I watched Lucas nervously.

Lucas licked the corner of his mouth and thought seriously for a moment. Then he shook his head and said something that caught both Kirill and me completely off guard.

"No." Lucas continued with absolute certainty, "My dad is a scumbag. He abandoned me and Mom and ran away."

My brain shut down.

Scum... scumbag? When did I ever tell him that?

Kirill looked equally stunned.

I forgot about sadness and shock. I quickly crouched down, cupping Lucas's little face with my free hand, and pressed him, "Lucas, baby, who told you that? When did Mommy ever say such a thing?"

Lucas blinked his innocent big eyes and answered matter-of-factly, "That's how they show it on TV! Those dads who don't stay with moms and babies are all bad guys, scumbags."

Then he said with incredible seriousness, "My mom is the best mom in the whole world. If Dad left, it must be because he's bad!"

The softest part of my heart was completely occupied by Lucas's words. This child, so understanding it broke my heart, was using the purest, most passionate love to protect me without reservation.

I saw the man Lucas had labeled a scumbag. His Adam's apple bobbed, his expression carrying a bitterness I couldn't read.

After a moment of silence, he reached out and gently ruffled Lucas's hair.

"You're right." He confirmed Lucas's assessment. "Your mom is the best mom in the world, and you're a little hero who protects his mom."

My chest felt stuffed full, aching with tightness. I felt like I was going to cry again. Why did I have so many tears these past few days?

CHAPTER NINETEEN

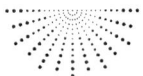

Celia

OUR TRIP to the amusement park was absolutely one of the happiest moments of my life. Even though two days had passed, the memory still filled me with joy and warmth.

Monday evening, I held Lucas's hand as we walked through the dim hallway of our apartment building. Lucas clearly hadn't come down from his amusement park high yet, excitedly telling me about how he'd shared flying chair science with Ben at kindergarten today.

"Mommy, I told Ben that flying chairs aren't magic—they're science."

"That's wonderful, baby. You remembered what Kirill said." I praised Lucas while lowering my head to dig through my canvas bag with my free hand, searching for my keys. We were almost at our door.

"Mommy, there's someone at our door."

Lucas's words sent a chill through me. I stopped searching for my keys and looked up toward our apartment.

When I saw who it was, my blood turned to ice. I desperately hoped I was seeing things. How could Rick be here? How had he found me?

I barely recognized him. His hair hung in greasy clumps, plastered to his scalp. He was skeleton-thin, his cheekbones jutting out like razors—he looked like a walking corpse.

In the few seconds I stood frozen, Rick spotted me too. He immediately crushed his cigarette underfoot and stood up, walking straight toward us.

I instinctively pulled Lucas behind me.

"Well, look who's gotten bold, Celia." Rick's raspy voice cut through the air. "Hiding in New York for five years, forgetting you even have a home, forgetting your own father?"

Only then did I take in his sunken eye sockets and deathly pale complexion.

"How did you find me?" I finally found my voice.

"I have my ways. But you—didn't that man give you any money after buying your first time? You're living in this dump?"

My stomach twisted into knots. I fought down the urge to vomit.

"Mommy." I heard Lucas's frightened voice. The little guy had never sounded so scared.

"Ha! You even popped out a little bastard?" He let out a cruel laugh, his malicious gaze shifting to Lucas. "No wonder you didn't dare come back. Got yourself knocked up and squeezed out this little mutt."

"Shut up!" I screamed, covering Lucas's ears with both hands, trying to block out those vile words. "I won't let you talk about him like that! He's my child!"

"Celia, don't think you can defy me now just because you're playing house. I'm not dead yet." His voice turned ice-cold, his face twisting into something grotesque.

"What do you want?" I forced myself to stay calm. Lucas was here —I couldn't let Rick hurt him.

"Money." He stretched out one skeletal hand toward me. "Give me money. Whatever you've got."

"I don't have any." I spoke through gritted teeth. Even if I did, I wouldn't give it to him.

"No money? You think I'm some three-year-old you can bullshit? How the hell did you raise this little bastard without money? Open the door! Let me search the place!"

He lunged for my bag. I quickly stepped back, clutching Lucas tight. I felt his small body trembling in my arms—Rick had terrified him.

"Don't be scared, baby." I kissed the top of his head.

"I'm not scared, Mommy."

Lucas's brave front broke my heart. I couldn't let this escalate. I had to keep Rick calm.

"Okay, okay. Let's go inside and talk." I took a deep breath, led Lucas to the door, pulled out my keys, and unlocked it.

Rick shoved past me, swaggering inside like he owned the place. He surveyed the tiny space with pure disgust.

I closed the door and turned on the lights.

I crouched down and spoke softly to Lucas, "Baby, why don't you go play in your room for a bit? Mommy needs to talk to him about something."

But Lucas shook his head. He gripped my shirt tightly and said with determination, "I'm not leaving. I need to stay here and protect Mommy."

Tears nearly spilled from my eyes. Lucas was so frightened, yet he still wanted to protect me.

Rick heard what Lucas said and burst into harsh, grating laughter. "Protect? With what, you little bastard? Celia, what the hell kind of job did you do raising this little shit? Kid doesn't know his place!"

While hurling insults, he began tearing apart the living room—flipping couch cushions, sweeping books and objects off tables. The sounds of destruction mixed with his heavy breathing and vicious curses, stabbing at my temples like needles.

"Where's the money? Where are you hiding it?" he roared while ransacking everything.

After destroying every possible hiding spot in the living room, his eyes locked onto the canvas bag on my shoulder.

He strode over and snatched it away. After rifling through it, he only found about fifteen dollars and my phone.

The money disappeared into his pocket. The phone and bag were tossed carelessly onto the couch.

"You're definitely hiding more cash somewhere. Hand it over!"

"That's really all I have." I stuck to my story.

Kirill's advance was nearly gone after paying overdue rent and Lucas's kindergarten fees. If I gave him what little remained, Lucas and I would starve.

Rick clearly didn't believe me. He advanced threateningly, "Looks like I need to teach you a lesson before you'll cough up the rest."

"Don't touch my Mommy!" Lucas charged forward on his little legs, spreading his arms to shield me.

"Get lost, you little bastard!" Rick raised his foot to kick Lucas.

I lunged forward, wrapping Lucas in my arms and taking the brutal kick to my back.

Pain exploded through my spine. I bit back a groan, nearly collapsing, but I held Lucas tight, refusing to loosen my protective grip.

"Mommy!" Lucas sobbed in my arms. "Mommy, are you okay?"

My defiance seemed to enrage Rick further. He grabbed my hair and yanked my head back, spitting in my face.

"You dare protect him? For this little bastard, you'll even defy your own father?" He raised his hand and slapped me viciously across the face.

The crack echoed through the room. My right ear went silent momentarily. Half my face burned with fire, and I tasted blood at the corner of my mouth.

"Stop hitting my Mommy! You bad man! Stop hitting my Mommy!" Lucas struggled frantically in my arms, pounding Rick's legs with his tiny fists.

Rick released my hair, but the beating continued. His fists rained down on me like hail, accompanied by his ragged breathing. I used every ounce of strength to shield Lucas beneath me, pain numbing my entire body. Only one thought consumed my mind, protect Lucas. I had to protect Lucas.

"Mommy... Mommy..." Lucas's cries grew shaky. "Can we... can we call Kirill? Ask him for help!"

"Kirill?"

That name made Rick freeze.

"Another sugar daddy? Sounds rich. Perfect! Call him—tell him to bring cash! As your man, shouldn't he show some respect to his future father-in-law?"

No. Impossible. I could handle this myself. I didn't want Kirill to see me like this.

"Stop," I gasped out the words. "I have some money in the bedroom. I'll get it for you."

"Should've said that from the start instead of making me beat sense into you." Rick spat and pulled back his fists.

I stumbled to my feet and led the still-crying Lucas into the bedroom.

"Mommy, can we call Kirill? Please?" Lucas was still sniffling, his small hand gripping mine desperately.

"It's okay, baby. Mommy can handle this." I crouched to face him. "I need you to stay in this room no matter what happens outside. Don't come out until I call for you, okay?" The bedroom door had no lock—I could only trust Lucas to obey.

"But Mommy—"

"Listen to me." I used a tone more serious than I'd ever used with him. "Don't come out until I call for you. Can you do that?"

Lucas was startled by my intensity. Tears streaming, he nodded solemnly. Lucas always kept his promises—I wasn't worried about him disobeying.

I opened the deepest drawer in the nightstand and pulled out one bill from my remaining hundreds.

After kissing Lucas's forehead, I left the bedroom and closed the door behind me.

The moment I emerged, Rick snatched the money from my hand. Seeing only a hundred dollars sent him into a rage.

"That's it? You think you can play me, you bitch! Call that Kirill guy right now!"

He grabbed my phone from the couch, frantically swiping at the cracked screen. The password lock that wouldn't budge made him even more violent.

"Password! What's the password? Tell me!"

"He won't give you money. Just leave."

"Want me to leave?" His eyes turned murderous. He spewed venom, "Bitch! Whore! You'll never escape me! You're my dog! When I tell you to do something, you fucking do it!"

Ice flooded my veins. This bastard would bleed me dry. He'd never let me go.

First using me to pay his debts, then nearly attacking Lucas, now trying to drag Kirill into this nightmare.

I was done! Why? Why could he destroy my life like it was his birthright?

Rage built inside me—the fury of someone pushed beyond all limits.

When his fist swung toward me, every humiliation, every degradation, every moment of pain transformed into towering hatred. I shoved him with everything I had.

What I didn't expect was how easily he lost his balance, falling straight backward.

I heard the sickening crack of skull meeting marble, then a heavy thud. Rick collapsed on the floor. His body convulsed twice, then went still. Dark red liquid began pooling beneath his head.

I stood frozen, my mind completely blank. I noticed the foam padding I'd installed on the table edge to protect Lucas—part of it had been knocked away, exposing the sharp, blood-stained corner underneath.

"Get up." I heard myself speak as if in a dream. "Stop playing dead. Get up."

He didn't move. Just lay there with vacant, staring eyes.

Trembling, I stepped closer and reached out with a shaking hand to check his pulse.

Nothing.

I jerked my hand back and collapsed to the floor as cold flooded my entire body.

I'd killed someone. I'd killed my father.

The realization lodged in my throat, cutting off my breath.

I could go to prison. Yes, I'd go to prison. They'd lock me away.

But what about Lucas?

No! I couldn't go to prison. I couldn't abandon Lucas.

That thought overwhelmed every fear. I grabbed tissues from the table and knelt on the floor, frantically scrubbing at the spreading blood. But I couldn't bring myself to look at Rick's corpse—I was terrified of those dead, staring eyes.

It was useless. The more I wiped, the more the stain spread. My hands became coated in sticky crimson.

The metallic smell and deep red color assaulted every nerve. My stomach lurched violently. I rushed to the sink and dry-heaved.

What now? What should I do? Call the police? No, I couldn't call the police. Would they believe it was self-defense?

My mind was pure chaos, thoughts crashing around with no escape.

Just as I was about to shatter completely, one face appeared in my thoughts.

Kirill!

He'd know what to do. He had Bratva connections—he wasn't ordinary.

Like grasping a lifeline, I crawled around searching for my fallen phone. The screen was cracked but functional. With trembling fingers, I dialed Kirill's number.

He answered on the first ring.

"Celia?"

Hearing Kirill's familiar voice, my emotions completely collapsed.

"Kirill..." I sobbed, unable to form coherent words. "I... I..."

"Where are you? What happened?" His voice was urgent and concerned.

"I'm... I'm at home. Can you come over?" I forced the words from my throat. "Please hurry..."

"Don't hang up. I'm coming right now."

I heard him leaving through the phone, then his voice, "I'm on my way, baby."

He talked me through every step—entering the elevator, starting his car. Even while driving, he kept speaking in the gentlest tones, telling me not to be afraid. I leaned against the couch arm, my trembling body drawing strength from his soothing words.

I don't know how he got there so quickly. When I heard the door open, I immediately looked up.

Kirill stood there with a thin sheen of sweat on his forehead, his black shirt collar slightly undone—clearly he'd rushed the entire way.

The moment his gaze fell on my face, those gray-blue eyes contracted sharply.

"Who did this?" He strode to me, gently touching my swollen cheek, his voice dark and lethal.

"My... father." My voice caught in my throat, so hoarse it was barely audible.

The air around him turned arctic, barely restrained fury radiating from every pore, "Where is he?"

Without speaking, I took his hand and led him to where Rick's body lay sprawled. Kirill looked down at the corpse like he was examining garbage.

The next second, I watched him lift his custom leather shoe and deliver a vicious kick.

The force was so brutal that the body flipped over with a dull, wet sound.

His action made me gasp, but at least with the corpse face-down, I no longer had to see those lifeless, accusing eyes.

He squeezed my hand reassuringly, then pulled out his phone. After quick movements across the screen, he made a call.

"It's me." His voice carried deadly ice. "Come to the address I'm sending. Bring a crew to dispose of some trash."

After hanging up, he cupped my face with one hand, forcing me to meet his eyes.

"Don't be afraid. It's over now."

His gaze held an almost mystical power, dissolving my terror piece by piece.

I trusted him completely. If Kirill said it was over, then it was over. My overwrought nerves finally began to relax. I threw myself into his arms, breathing in that familiar, comforting scent that belonged only to him.

Kirill held me tight, pressing a tender kiss to the crown of my head. In his embrace, I felt myself coming back to life.

CHAPTER TWENTY

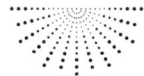

Celia

SOON ENOUGH, two burly men showed up.

Kirill barked orders at them in Russian. Then I witnessed something I'd never forget for the rest of my life.

The two men pulled on white gloves and yanked out a black bag from their gear—big enough to fit a person. They worked together like they were taking out the trash, not dealing with a corpse.

In under thirty seconds, they had Rick stuffed into that bag. After that, they broke out professional tools to scrub the blood off the floor. When they finished reporting back to Kirill and left, the floor looked spotless. Like nothing had ever happened here.

Rick Cole had been completely erased from my life.

"What did they just say?" Those men had spoken only Russian—I couldn't understand a damn word.

"They guaranteed the body would be disposed of cleanly. No one would ever know. Not even the cops."

Kirill's words made me forget how to breathe. His tone carried this absolute power that existed above all rules. Even though I'd known about his Bratva connections, his casual disregard for everything still made my skin crawl.

"Who the hell are you, Kirill?" I swallowed hard. "Your position in the Bratva has to be high up."

Kirill lowered his gaze and looked deep into my eyes. He didn't dodge, didn't lie, didn't give me any bullshit excuses.

"I'm the boss of the Bratva." He spoke slowly, watching my face like he wanted to catch every tiny reaction.

Boss.

Even though I'd suspected it, hearing that word come out of his mouth made my heart skip a beat.

The man I'd fallen in love with, the father of my child, wasn't just some billionaire with mob ties.

He was the king. The supreme ruler of the New York underworld.

That explained everything. His natural command presence, how he stayed calm no matter what hit him, his ability to make a living person vanish from the face of the earth.

That same ability had just pulled me back from the brink of hell.

"I... I need to check on Lucas." I snapped out of my thoughts. My son was the priority right now.

I didn't pay attention to Kirill's expression and rushed to my bedroom door, throwing it open.

Lucas was curled up at the foot of the bed, clutching my pillow. When he heard the door, he looked up immediately. Seeing it was me, he jumped up and ran over. I quickly crouched down and pulled him into my arms.

"Mommy!" He buried his little face against my chest. "Is the bad man gone?"

"Gone." I held him tight. "He'll never come back, baby. Never again."

"Did Mommy fight him off?" Lucas asked.

"Mommy and Kirill made him go away together," I answered.

"Mommy's so brave!" He looked up at me with bright eyes, though they were still red. "Kirill came to save us too?"

Kirill walked over and knelt down in front of him, his expression gentle, voice soft.

"Yes, he won't come back to hurt you anymore."

"I knew it." Lucas's face lit up with admiration.

Then, like he remembered something, his little brow furrowed. He reached out his small hand and gently touched the wound on my face, saying with concern, "Mommy, does it still hurt?"

"No." I shook my head, but my voice choked up.

"Kirill, that bad man kept hitting my mommy. He punched us, but mommy protected me."

When Kirill heard Lucas's words, his lips went thin. I saw him clench his fists, a dark pressure forming around him.

But he was controlling that terrifying emotion, especially in front of Lucas.

"You can't stay here anymore." He stood up. "Pack your things. Come with me."

I had no objections. Just thinking about Rick's body lying in the living room moments ago made me not want to stay another second.

We didn't have much to pack. A few changes of clothes, Lucas's toys, and that photo I'd cut out of me and my mother.

When we left the apartment building, it was already dark.

A Rolls-Royce waited by the curb. The driver opened our door, and we got in.

The car smoothly pulled away from Maple Lane, leaving that rundown apartment building and all the nightmares of my first half of life behind.

The car passed through heavily guarded gates, driving down a long driveway lined with birch trees and streetlights, finally stopping in front of a building that looked like a medieval castle. A well-dressed middle-aged man was already waiting at the entrance to greet us—Kirill's butler.

Kirill led us into this manor that was staggeringly huge. After walking through a meticulously manicured garden, we reached an ornate door. Stepping into the main hall, marble floors gleamed beneath our feet, crystal chandeliers sparkled overhead, oil paintings I couldn't understand but sensed were priceless hung on the walls, and antique vases were placed throughout for decoration.

This place was too beautiful. I'd never seen anywhere so elegant.

Kirill settled sleeping Lucas into a room that was several times bigger than my entire apartment.

Then he took me to the room next door.

"Take a shower and relax." He pointed to a button by the bed. "If you need anything, just press this. If you're tired, go straight to sleep."

We said goodnight to each other.

After he left, I showered and lay on the soft, huge bed, wide awake.

Every time I closed my eyes, I saw Rick's corpse and those eyes that couldn't close even in death.

I didn't feel much sadness. More than anything, I felt relief. My feelings for him had been worn away long ago by all the shit he'd put me through.

But I'd killed him with my own hands. I'd taken a life. That thought wouldn't leave my head. The fear and guilt of killing someone doesn't just disappear, even when the person you killed was pure evil.

I resigned myself to sitting up and let out a breath. I checked my phone—almost ten-thirty at night.

I walked out onto the balcony. The night breeze on my face cleared my chaotic mind a little.

Light footsteps sounded behind me.

"Can't sleep? Still thinking about what happened at the apartment?" Kirill was already beside me.

The simple gray silk pajamas he wore stripped away his usual edge, adding a relaxed, domestic quality.

I nodded. "Every time I close my eyes, I see his body falling and those eyes that wouldn't close. I don't know how it happened. I just pushed him, and he hit the corner of the table. I hated him, but... when he actually died in front of me, I was still scared. I really killed someone."

My voice sounded distant and strange, like I'd heard it in a nightmare.

"He wasn't even a man anymore, Celia." Kirill's hand gripped mine on the railing, his voice cutting through my confused thoughts. "He had no conscience, no bottom line. You know what I was thinking when I heard Lucas say he punched you both? I wanted to tear his fucking corpse to pieces. If you hadn't killed him, I would have. Celia, don't punish yourself for someone else's sins."

He was always so blunt, even brutal. But damn it, his words always hit the mark, chasing away my confusion.

"He wasn't always like this." I needed to talk. These suppressed emotions were driving me crazy.

Kirill didn't rush me. He watched quietly, being a patient listener.

"When I was little, when my mom was still alive, he was a good father." My voice was soft, like telling a distant story. "He'd lift me over his head so I could reach the leaves on trees. He'd buy me the sweetest cotton candy and watch me get it all over my face."

Images from years ago floated before my eyes. Afternoon sunlight streaming in, my mother humming in the kitchen, my father laughing heartily, me running around the living room.

"I don't know when everything changed. Maybe after Mom got cancer, maybe after she died. He started drinking heavily, gambling, even doing drugs later. The way he looked at me lost all warmth. He only wanted to squeeze any useful value out of me. Kirill, I really hated him."

Kirill threaded my cold fingers through his, one by one. We intertwined our hands, the warmth from his palm spreading to me.

"I hate my father, too." His voice carried ice that had been buried for years.

I stared at him in shock. His profile was hidden in shadow, but I could feel the air around him growing thin.

"He was a successful businessman and a competent boss. But he wasn't a good husband, and definitely not a good father." His gaze fell on the distant darkness, those gray-blue eyes that were always unfathomable now churning with pain.

"My mother was a noblewoman from a distinguished family. She married my father through an arranged union. When I was young, they did have a period when they loved each other. But soon, my father's heart wandered. He started bringing different mistresses home, right in front of my mother, into their marriage bed..."

My heart clenched hard.

He paused, then continued, "My mother couldn't accept this humiliation, but she couldn't leave because of family honor and her feelings for my father. She buried all her pain inside and gradually fell ill. I'll never forget how she wasted away to nothing but bones in her final days."

Kirill squeezed my hand tighter, as if drowning in painful memories. "One day, my father brought another mistress home and literally made my mother so angry she coughed up blood and died. And my father didn't even show up at her funeral. He was vacationing in France with his new lover."

In that moment, I forgot everything in my head. All my senses were captured by the bottomless grief in his words. This man who was always powerful, always in control, this boss of the Bratva—in this moment, he was just a boy who'd watched his mother die in agony while he stood helpless.

My heart ached for him.

Our eyes met in the air. We both saw similar, unhealable wounds in each other's gaze.

This profound connection linked our souls together. I even felt like everything tonight had happened so I could truly understand him in this moment.

I raised my other hand to his cheek, tracing over that sexy scar above his eyebrow. He let my fingertips linger on his skin.

"Kirill..." My voice was hoarse with sympathy. "You must have been so heartbroken then. I'm sorry I wasn't there with you."

His Adam's apple bobbed, those deep eyes locking onto mine like they wanted to pull my soul in. "Celia, I just need you with me now and always."

His voice was full of suppressed emotion. "I was affected by how my father treated my mother. Before I met you, I didn't understand love. I didn't believe in feelings at all, so I slept around with many women—just sex, never love. But I didn't know I'd meet you. If I'd known, I definitely wouldn't have touched other women. Celia, will you forgive me?"

My mouth fell open. All my fears, hesitation, and insecurity were shattered by his words. Fuck Anastasia, fuck feeling insecure—I threw all of that into the ocean.

"I love you, Celia." He brought my hand from his face to his lips and kissed it.

I love you.

Those words carried weight, full of solemnity and love. A king who'd sealed himself away emotionally was handing me the only key to his heart.

My chest filled with so much love it felt like a butterfly growing wings, ready to fly out.

"I love you too, Kirill."

I stood on my tiptoes and kissed his lips.

This kiss was gentle, lingering, yet charged with the passion of confirmed feelings. We were like two souls who'd drifted alone in darkness too long, finally finding each other.

Kirill swept me up in his arms and strode into his bedroom. Moonlight streamed through the huge floor-to-ceiling windows, bathing everything in gentle silver.

He laid me gently on that wide, soft bed. I felt like I was lying in his scent.

He leaned down and kissed me tenderly. From my forehead to my eyes, then to the handprint on my cheek.

"Does it still hurt, Celia?" His eyes were full of heartache.

I shook my head and mimicked Kirill by kissing the scar on his brow.

"How did you get this?"

"Some bastard cut me with a knife."

I didn't doubt his words. Few people would register in his mind.

He stripped away our pajamas. Our skin touched bare, his warmth spreading to every inch of my body, my lower belly burning.

Seeing the purple bruises from the beating on my body, his eyes darkened. "I really wish I could throw that piece of shit in the river to feed the fish."

Then he gently licked at those purple marks on my body, like he was healing my wounds.

"Enough, Kirill." The gentle kisses made my whole body itch. "Come inside. I want you."

"Don't rush me, sweetheart," he said, his lips curling into a wicked grin. "I haven't tasted you in too damn long." Before I could respond, he lowered himself, his broad shoulders settling between my thighs. The first swipe of his tongue against my core sent a jolt through me, my back arching off the bed. His hands gripped my hips, holding me in place as he devoured me, his tongue circling my clit with agonizing precision before plunging deeper, tasting every inch of me.

"God, Kirill," I gasped, my fingers tangling in his hair, tugging hard as waves of pleasure crashed over me. He groaned against me, the vibration making my toes curl. His tongue worked relentlessly, alternating between slow, languid licks and quick, teasing flicks that had me teetering on the edge. My thighs trembled, my breath coming in short, desperate pants as he pushed me closer and closer to oblivion.

"You're mine," he growled between licks, his voice thick with possession. "Every fucking inch of you. I'm never letting you go." His words sent a shiver down my spine, the raw intensity of his love wrapping around me as tightly as his hands. "I want you to come for me, baby. Let me feel it."

His tongue dove deeper, and when he sucked my clit into his mouth, I shattered. My orgasm hit me like a tidal wave, my body convulsing as I cried out his name, my hips bucking against his face. He didn't stop, lapping at me through every aftershock, drawing out my pleasure until I was a trembling, boneless mess beneath him.

When I finally caught my breath, I looked down to find him watching me, his eyes blazing with triumph and desire. His lips glistened with my arousal, and the sight sent a fresh wave of heat through me. "You taste like fucking heaven," he said, crawling up my body, his erection pressing against my thigh. "But I'm not done with you yet."

He positioned himself between my legs, the tip of his cock

brushing against my entrance. I whimpered, already aching for him, my body desperate to feel him inside me. "Kirill, please," I begged, my hands clutching at his shoulders. "I need you."

"You need me?" he teased, his voice low and gravelly. "Tell me how bad, baby. Tell me what you want."

"I want you inside me," I whispered, my voice trembling with want. "I want you to fuck me, Kirill. Make me yours."

His eyes darkened, and with one slow, deliberate thrust, he filled me completely. I gasped at the stretch, the delicious burn of him stretching me wide. He was big, almost too much, but the way he fit inside me felt like he was made for me. "Fuck," he groaned, his forehead resting against mine. "You're so tight, so perfect. I love you so fucking much."

He started to move, slow at first, letting me adjust to his size, but it didn't take long for his restraint to crumble. His thrusts grew harder, deeper, each one hitting that spot inside me that made stars burst behind my eyes. "You're mine," he growled, his hands gripping my hips as he pounded into me. "All mine. I want to fuck you like this forever. I want to put another baby in you, make you mine in every fucking way."

His words sent a thrill through me, the idea of carrying his child again making my heart race. "Yes," I moaned, my nails digging into his back. "I want that. I want you, Kirill. Always."

He kissed me then, hard and possessive, his tongue claiming my mouth as thoroughly as his cock claimed my body. Our bodies moved together, slick with sweat, the sound of skin slapping against skin filling the room. "I love you," he panted against my lips. "I'd die without you. I want to fucking live inside you, baby. I want to die buried in this sweet pussy."

His filthy words pushed me closer to the edge, my body tightening around him as another orgasm built. He felt it, his thrusts becoming almost brutal in their intensity. "Come for me again," he demanded. "Let me feel you milk me dry."

I shattered again, my scream muffled against his shoulder as my body clenched around him. He followed me over the edge, his hips stuttering as he spilled inside me, his groan of pleasure vibrating through my chest. "Fuck, baby," he panted, collapsing onto me, his weight grounding me as we both caught our breath.

But Kirill wasn't done. Not even close. He pulled out, his cum dripping down my thighs, and gave me a wicked grin. "Round two," he said, his voice still thick with desire. He came again not long after, his body shuddering as he filled me once more, his hands gripping my hips like he was afraid I'd disappear.

After a moment, he pulled back, his eyes glinting with mischief. "Let's try something fun," he said, his voice low and teasing. "Something new."

Before I could ask what he meant, he flipped us over, maneuvering me until I was straddling his face, his cock hard and glistening just inches from my lips. The 69 position was new, and the intimacy of it made my cheeks burn with a mix of excitement and shyness. "Kirill..." I started, but my words trailed off as his tongue found my clit again, his nose brushing against my sensitive folds in a way that made my whole body jolt.

"Fuck, you're so wet," he murmured against me, his hands gripping my ass as he pulled me closer. "Ride my face, baby. Let me taste you while you suck me off."

I hesitated for only a moment before wrapping my hand around his cock, my lips closing around the tip. He groaned against me, the vibration sending a fresh wave of pleasure through my core. I took him deeper, my tongue swirling around him as I bobbed my head, trying to match the rhythm of his tongue on me. His nose ground against my clit, the sensation so intense it made my thighs shake. Then his fingers joined in, one slipping inside me, curling just right as he sucked hard on my clit.

The dual sensations were overwhelming, my body caught between the pleasure of his mouth and the thrill of having him in mine. "Kirill," I moaned around him, my voice muffled. "God, this feels so good."

"You like this, don't you?" he growled, his fingers thrusting deeper. "You love having my cock in your mouth while I fuck you with my tongue. You're mine, baby. Every fucking part of you."

His words pushed me over the edge again, my orgasm crashing through me as I cried out, my hips grinding against his face. He came at the same time, his cock pulsing in my mouth as I swallowed every drop, the taste of him mixing with the raw intensity of my own pleasure.

When we finally pulled apart, I collapsed onto the bed, my body trembling with aftershocks. Kirill sat up, his chin glistening with my arousal. He wiped it off with the back of his hand, his eyes locked on mine as he did it, and the raw, unapologetic masculinity of the gesture made my heart skip. Then he leaned down, kissing me deeply, our mouths filled with the taste of each other. It was strange, almost primal, but it didn't disgust me—it felt like us, messy and real and perfect.

"Fuck, I love you," he whispered against my lips, his hands cupping my face. "I'm never letting you go. Not ever."

I smiled, my heart swelling as I pulled him closer. "Good," I whispered back. "Because I'm not going anywhere."

CHAPTER TWENTY-ONE

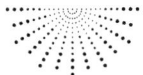

Kirill

SIX AM. My biological clock pulled me from sleep with clockwork precision. Celia was curled in my arms, her brow still furrowed even in dreams. After we'd made love yesterday, I'd carried her exhausted body to the bathroom and tended to every wound on her skin. The swelling on her face had already faded.

I stroked her hair, a dull ache settling in my chest.

Last night, seeing her hurt in that shithole apartment had triggered something savage in me—the urge to pulverize the bastard who'd touched her. Finding her father's corpse on the floor was the only thing that kept me from doing worse than a single kick. In my book, anyone who laid a finger on Celia deserved to die.

My men would clean up the mess. Celia didn't need to worry about cops sniffing around. Making scum disappear from this city? Child's play.

The Long Island house I'd prepared for her and Lucas seemed like a stupid idea now. My woman and my son belonged at my side.

Celia's lashes fluttered. She woke up rubbing her eyes, looking lost. I kissed her lips and murmured good morning.

Forget the house. But Celia's closet needed filling. Lucas had a few days off, and we both needed to unwind. When I suggested the three of us go shopping, Celia snapped awake.

"Shopping?" Her expression was priceless. "I can't picture the Bratva boss loaded down with shopping bags."

I smirked.

"I never carry my own bags." I leaned close to her ear. "But if you need me to, I'll be your personal pack mule."

After breakfast, our little family hit Fifth Avenue's flagship department store. New York's cathedral of commerce—massive brass revolving doors shut out the street noise, leaving only indoor luxury.

We started in women's wear. Every piece hung like artwork under perfect lighting that showcased the craftsmanship and fabric's gleam.

A woman in a black suit glided toward us with practiced elegance.

"Good morning, sir, madam. How may I assist you today?" Her smile was perfectly trained.

Celia waved her hands frantically, blushing. "No, we're not—"

I watched her squirm with amusement and pulled her against my waist. Her protests died.

A younger assistant crouched in front of Lucas, smiling. "If you get bored, sweetie, I can take you to our kids' zone. We have the latest LEGO sets and games."

Lucas shook his head seriously. "I need to stay here and watch. When I grow up, I'm buying Mom pretty clothes too."

The consultant blinked, then gushed. "Oh my goodness! Ma'am, how did you raise such a little gentleman? He's going to break so many hearts."

Celia laughed, bending to ruffle Lucas's hair with pure adoration. "Okay, Mom will wait for you to grow up."

Lucas's words filled me with fierce pride. My son already knew how to treasure his mother.

"Pack up everything in this lady's size for all seasons. Newest styles, best fabrics." I turned to the consultant.

The air seemed to freeze for two seconds.

The woman's professional smile cracked, replaced by shock and euphoria. "Sir, you mean—"

"I mean, wrap up everything here that's worthy of her."

"Jesus, Kirill, you've lost your mind!" Celia gasped, tugging my arm. "I can't wear that much! It's such a waste!"

Expected reaction.

The consultant recovered her composure, smiling at Celia. "Ma'am, you're so lucky. Your husband is incredibly generous."

"He's really not my husband." Celia rushed to correct her, nearly biting her tongue.

Something tickled inside my chest. I leaned to her ear, voice low enough for only us. "Not yet."

The flush spread from her cheeks to her ears. She looked up at me with those gorgeous eyes but couldn't speak.

"Mommy, your face is really red." Lucas's clear voice broke the tension.

He looked up worriedly. "Are you sick?"

Then he reached for Celia's forehead.

I could feel the air around Celia heating up. She looked like a ripe tomato.

"Mommy's fine, just a little warm." Celia caught Lucas's small hand.

Lucas's worried expression smoothed once he knew Celia was okay.

I couldn't help chuckling.

While staff efficiently packed everything, my eyes caught on a dress hanging nearby. Emerald green, body-hugging with a thigh-high slit. The fabric flowed like moonlight, cut to show off curves without looking cheap.

I could picture Celia in it. Her dark, wavy hair cascading over bare shoulders, the green making her skin glow like warm jade that begged to be touched. The slit revealing glimpses of her long, pale thighs with every step.

My throat went dry. Just imagining her in that dress sent heat shooting to my groin.

"Add that one too." My voice came out rough, pointing at the green dress.

The consultant immediately directed staff to include it.

But before they could move, Celia protested. "That's not right for me, Kirill. Too much skin. I'm not comfortable with that."

I watched her bite her lip, looking conflicted. She had no fucking clue how sexy she was.

The consultant smartly had the dress brought over. "Ma'am, you could try it on first."

Celia held the dress up against herself, face burning. "This is ridiculous!"

"Mommy looks good in it. The color matches Mommy's pretty eyes." Lucas gazed up at her earnestly.

"Trust me, Celia. You'll be beautiful in it."

Celia finally gave in to our combined persuasion and followed a staff member to the VIP fitting room.

Lucas and I waited on the couch.

Time dragged.

"Kirill, why isn't Mommy out yet?"

Just as I started to answer, the fitting room door cracked open. Celia's head peeked out, face full of embarrassment and frustration. She beckoned me over, voice barely a whisper.

"Kirill, can you help with the zipper? I can't reach it."

I had the consultant watch Lucas, then strode into the fitting room. The door clicked shut.

In the enclosed space, Celia's citrus scent hit me like an aphrodisiac.

She faced away from me, her bare back almost completely exposed. The emerald dress was only half-zipped, stuck at her narrow waist, her leg lines fully visible.

Damn. This was even better than I'd imagined.

"Arms up." My voice was rough with restraint.

She obediently raised her arms against the wall. The position tightened her back muscles and exposed more of her breasts' curves.

My cock went instantly hard.

When my fingertips touched her skin, she trembled. I didn't go for the zipper immediately—instead I traced my finger slowly up her spine, feeling every shiver under my touch.

"Kirill..." A shy moan escaped her throat, sweet poison.

"Don't move." My voice was dark as I pulled her soft body against me, my hard length pressing unmistakably against her.

She felt my arousal and her breathing quickened.

My hand finally found the small metal zipper pull hidden in the lining. But instead of pulling up, I dragged it down.

"You..." She gasped, turning to look at me through water-bright eyes.

"You have no idea what you do to me dressed like this." I lowered my head, lips against her ear. "Why didn't you call staff instead of me? Trying to seduce me?"

I pressed against her from behind, emphasizing my words.

A suppressed whimper slipped from her lips. "I just instinctively wanted your help."

I lifted her chin, commanding her to stick out her tongue. She shyly obeyed, closing her eyes, lashes trembling.

I caught her soft tongue with mine, licking and tangling, tasting her unique flavor. She made muffled sounds as saliva soon dripped from the corner of her mouth.

I wiped it away with my thumb while pushing deeper into her mouth, stealing more of her sweetness until she nearly fainted from lack of oxygen.

She opened her eyes gasping for air, melting in my arms.

I turned her whole body toward me, my fingers sliding through the dress's slit.

"No, not here, Kirill." Celia's voice was soft and pitiful, making me want to ravage her.

And I did exactly that. I ignored her plea, grabbing her tight ass with one hand and lifting her up.

"Ah!"

With her startled cry, her legs instinctively wrapped around my waist, arms clutching my shoulders, clinging to me like ivy.

This position stretched the slit to its limit, exposing Celia's legs almost to her groin. Her upper body was completely bare, fabric bunched at her waist.

Her perfect breasts stood proud, rising and falling with her breath, nipples hard as pebbles, silently declaring their owner's desire.

I lowered my head, taking her left nipple and areola into my mouth, gently biting with my teeth, grinding with my tongue.

The stimulation made her try to escape, arching backward, only pushing her chest deeper into my mouth.

My hand wasn't idle either. The one that had just slipped inside was already at her panties, where the thin lace was soaked through with her arousal. I circled her sensitive clit with my fingertip, pressing just hard enough to tease.

"Kirill, please..." Her nails dug into my shoulders, her voice breaking apart.

"Please what, baby?" My words came out muffled, my mouth busy savoring her impossibly sweet nipple. "Please stop, or please do something even naughtier to you?" I deliberately pressed harder, grinding against that tiny clit through the fabric.

She shuddered hard, letting out a sharp sob.

"No." She squirmed, eagerly offering her other full breast to my mouth, her shame and desire colliding. "This side... this side too..."

"You're fucking tempting me, Celia," I said, releasing her nipple, now red and swollen from my attention, glistening with my saliva. "Tempting me to fuck you right here in this changing room."

I gave in to her plea, taking her other nipple into my mouth, sucking and tugging with even more aggression.

"Oh, Kirill!" Celia moaned again, her voice dripping with reckless abandon. "I want you to do anything to me here."

"Not scared of getting caught?" I asked, raising an eyebrow as I let go of her slick, well-loved nipple.

"Maybe... maybe we can keep it quiet," she said, her eyes darting away but burning with anticipation.

"No chance, baby," I said, stealing a hard kiss from her lips. "I want you screaming my name."

Before she could respond, I yanked aside that flimsy lace barrier and slid two fingers into her wet, warm pussy. They glided in effortlessly, her tight walls gripping me greedily.

"Kirill, that feels so fucking good!" she cried out, unable to hold back.

I silenced her with a deeper kiss, while my fingers twisted and curled inside her dripping pussy. When I hit that spot, she came with a silent scream, her body shaking.

I pulled my fingers out, coated in her juices.

"Taste how fucking delicious you are," I said, slipping my fingers into her mouth. She obediently sucked them clean.

My gaze darkened. My cock was throbbing, painfully hard, desperate to bury itself in her tight little pussy.

My hand had just touched my belt when—

"Mommy, Kirill. Are you done? I've been waiting forever."

Lucas's childish voice came through the door.

Celia snapped awake. "Lucas is still waiting for us."

I set Celia down, roughly running my hands through my hair.

I had to fucking wait for my hard-on to calm down.

When we emerged, Celia couldn't meet anyone's eyes.

My expression remained unchanged as I calmly had staff pack the emerald dress too.

After all the clothes were wrapped, I turned to Lucas. "Your turn now, little man."

I used the same approach, having the children's department pack everything suitable for Lucas's age. This time the protests came in stereo.

"Even a hundred of me couldn't wear all these clothes!" Lucas spread his arms dramatically.

"Lucas is right at his growing stage," Celia chimed in urgently. "Buying this much is ridiculous—he'll outgrow most before wearing them."

I looked at their matching protests and compromised.

"Fine." I shrugged. "We'll listen to you. Just a few pieces of each style then."

With their strict oversight, we ended up with only dozens of outfits for Lucas. Celia insisted waiting until he outgrew them to buy more was the smart move. Watching her seriously save my money was amusing, but more than that—it brought a strange new satisfaction.

We hit the toy and stationery sections next. Kid paradise—models, LEGO, gaming consoles everywhere. I told Lucas to pick anything he wanted.

But the little guy's desires seemed as modest as his mother's. After wandering the massive toy aisles, he carefully picked up a half-sized T-Rex plush and chose a cool-looking pencil case with some pens.

"That's it?" I raised an eyebrow.

Lucas thanked me and nodded firmly, looking completely satisfied.

I sighed, telling the nearby sales associate, "Give me one of everything that's popular for his age group."

Before Celia could protest again, I stopped her with a look. This was the least I could do as a father.

After outfitting both mother and son, Celia let out a long breath like she'd just finished a hard battle. Lucas excitedly hugged his new dinosaur, saying he'd sleep with it tonight.

We walked out empty-handed—these things didn't need carrying. Celia was a bit disappointed not to see me loaded with shopping bags.

That afternoon, car after car pulled up to my mansion. My men carried in boxes of clothing and toys, quickly filling an entire empty room.

Celia stood in the doorway staring at the mountain of shopping bags and packages, mouth forming a perfect "O" that wouldn't close.

"Kirill, did we... did we buy the entire store?" Her eyes were full of disbelief.

"Celia, you and Lucas deserve the best." I pulled her into my arms.

She leaned against my chest, silent for a long time before whispering almost inaudibly, "Thank you."

The next few days brought a life I'd never imagined—I had a family, and the atmosphere was always warm and dreamlike.

Celia and I made pizza together in the kitchen. I'd thought it would be simple, but wrestling with dough proved harder than negotiating with Italian mobsters.

Flour covered my black shirt and face while Celia and Lucas laughed themselves silly at my mess. Watching Celia's bright laughter, I just wanted to kiss her.

We also baked cookies together. Lucas used various molds to press the dough into dinosaur shapes while Celia patiently guided him. I stood watching the sweet scene, grateful Lucas didn't ask me to identify which was his friend Dino.

When Celia showered, I took over bedtime story duty for Lucas.

But after I finished, Lucas's eyes were still bright and alert, no trace of sleepiness.

He mysteriously pulled out a drawing from behind his back and gave it to me.

The picture showed three green dinosaurs—a small one being led by two larger ones, with a bright red sun overhead.

"This is Kirill, this is Mommy." He pointed at the drawing. "The one in the middle is me."

Lucas's artwork was colorful and artistic. I genuinely thought he'd make a great painter someday.

"Thank you, Lucas. This is the best gift I've ever received. I'll treasure it." My heart felt full—this was my first gift from my son.

Lucas shyly buried his face in the blanket. After a moment, he asked a question that caught me off guard.

"Kirill, are you pursuing my mommy?" Lucas's curious voice reached my ears.

I paused. These past few days, the three of us had been inseparable, but I'd avoided too much intimacy with Celia in front of Lucas, afraid he wasn't ready to accept me.

But his next words bounced in my chest, making my heart feel light.

"If Mommy and Kirill got together, I'd be really happy. I know Mommy really likes Kirill, and you like my mommy too, right?"

"You're right, I am pursuing your mommy. I love her, and I want to take good care of you too." I pinched Lucas's cheek.

The next second, I saw Celia standing in the doorway. I didn't know how long she'd been there, but her eyes were bright with tears.

CHAPTER TWENTY-TWO

Kirill

THE PAINTING LUCAS gave me now held pride of place in my study. I'd had it framed with the finest bulletproof glass and climate-controlled housing. With Lucas's artwork there, the study was no longer just a sterile office for conducting business.

That afternoon, I'd just finished an international video conference when Celia walked in carrying a cup of tea.

She set the cup beside me and naturally leaned down to kiss my cheek.

"Still busy?" Her voice carried that gentle warmth of home.

"Almost done." I caught her hand and pulled her onto my lap. She let out a soft gasp, shyly wrapping her arms around my neck. I lifted her chin and gave her a deep kiss.

"Where's Lucas?"

"In the garden with the butler, learning to identify plants. He's been really into nature lately."

I couldn't help but chuckle. I could picture it perfectly.

"I'm going to join them." Celia stood up from my lap.

"Wish I could ditch this damn paperwork." I sipped the tea. Perfect temperature.

"You'd better hurry up." Celia teased with a smile. "Or you might end up being dead last at plant identification in this house."

She walked out, leaving me grinning.

My smile barely had time to fade before my phone buzzed. Volkov. "Talk."

"Boss. That shipment we were running through the Chicago route to Montreal—Theodore grabbed it."

My smile vanished. This wasn't ordinary cargo. Twelve state-of-the-art electromagnetic sniper rifles with a five-kilometer range, capable of silently punching through most armored vehicles on the market. They were my key to opening doors with a new Canadian arms dealer. Their strategic value went way beyond money.

"He wants to tear everything up?" I sneered.

"Not exactly. He wants to renegotiate the shipping route profits."

My eyes narrowed. Last time's warning clearly hadn't sunk in.

"Let him dream. I'm not budging on profit margins. But I am going to see him—I want our fucking cargo back!"

I mapped it out in my head.

"Contact Theodore. Tell him we're meeting tonight at eight, Fairmont Hotel in Pittsburgh, penthouse suite. Neutral ground—he'll bite."

"Yes, boss. I'll book the right suite."

"You're coming with me. Bring a dozen of our best."

"Understood."

After explaining the situation to Celia, I prepared to fly to Pittsburgh.

The private jet's engines drowned out New York's chaos. Just over an hour later, we touched down in Pittsburgh.

The moment the cabin door opened, icy air rushed in. It stripped away the last traces of Celia's warmth still clinging to me, sharpening my edge to cold steel.

Cadillac One waited at the bottom of the stairs. Volkov and I settled in, him across from me.

Volkov was a few years older, had served my father before I took over. When I claimed the boss chair, he became my right hand. My sharpest blade, earned through absolute trust. Fifteen years ago, during a pier shootout, he caught a bullet meant for my chest. The scar still marked his left shoulder.

"All set." He handed me bourbon, voice steady. "Penthouse suite, top floor, clear sightlines, single entry point. Our people control the floors above and below, plus all fire exits. We're locked down tight."

I sipped the bourbon and nodded.

When we arrived with our crew, Theodore was already sprawled on the couch with a dozen of his own men behind him.

Seeing I'd matched his numbers, his expression darkened briefly. Then he stood up, all fake smiles.

"Kirill! Been too long!" He seemed genuinely excited about this negotiation.

I ignored his bullshit and walked straight to the opposite couch, tossing my coat aside. My men took positions behind me, hands clasped behind their backs.

"Theodore," I cut to the chase, "my cargo. I want it in Montreal before sunrise tomorrow."

Theodore's fake grin froze for a moment, then reassembled itself. "Well, Kirill, since you put it that way. Let's cut the crap. Your cargo's safe with me."

"Good to hear." I pulled out a cigar. Volkov stepped forward to light it. "So when are you planning to cough it up?"

Theodore dropped the act entirely.

"That depends on our cooperation." Theodore leaned forward, shoving his greasy face closer. "Kirill, times have changed. Great Lakes business is booming, but so are the risks. My people bleed every day protecting your shipping routes. Thirty percent... honestly, it doesn't go far enough among the boys."

"And?" I blew smoke directly into his face. Theodore coughed and sputtered.

"I want a new deal." He held up five thick fingers. "Fifty-fifty. Fair, right?"

I looked at him and laughed.

"Fair?" My voice dripped mockery. "Theodore, let me refresh your memory. This shipping route—the startup capital, the transport vehicles, the supply chains, the buyer connections—all Zaitsev Group. What the fuck have you done besides having your losers collect protection money at the docks?"

My words hit him like a slap. His thugs reached for their pieces. My men responded in kind, hands moving to their waistbands.

The air turned to ice.

That's when Volkov stepped forward, trying to play peacemaker.

"Boss, Mr. Moretti," his voice stayed smooth and diplomatic, "we're allies here. Nobody wants bloodshed. Mr. Moretti's people have put in work too. Maybe... we could consider a small concession on the original terms? Benefits everyone."

I didn't look back at Volkov, but my stare turned arctic.

Volkov was questioning my call. In front of outsiders.

Theodore pounced on the opening. He burst out laughing, but directed it at Volkov. "See that, Kirill! Look at your guy! Now that's someone who knows business!"

I felt Volkov's breathing hitch behind me.

"Volkov." My voice stayed level but carried absolute authority.

"Yes, boss."

"Stand down."

"...Yes." Two seconds of silence, then he stepped back to his original position.

I crushed the cigar in the ashtray.

"Seventy-thirty. That's my price and what you're worth." I leaned back into the couch, returning to casual indifference. "Spit up what you swallowed, intact, and I'll pretend this never happened. Last chance, Theodore. I don't mind going to war—my boys haven't had practice in weeks, and I've got hardware gathering dust in storage."

Theodore's face twitched. I could feel his internal battle—greed wrestling with fear. His dozen men weren't nearly enough.

But he couldn't let go. Nobody wants to give up meat already in their mouth.

Finally, he forced out a smile uglier than crying. "Kirill, why so worked up? We're allies, right? Business is about negotiation. If fifty-fifty doesn't work, we can talk. How about sixty-forty?"

"You still don't get it." I stood up, grabbing my coat. "I never repeat myself. You've got half a day."

I headed for the door, my men falling in behind me.

Theodore could only watch us leave through gritted teeth. When his muscles tried to move, he held them back.

"You talked too much today, Volkov." I studied the mirror's reflection, voice flat.

"I'm sorry, boss." His voice carried regret, but that meant nothing. "I just didn't want to see our relationship with the Moretti Family completely implode. That would bring unnecessary complications."

"Complications?" I turned to face him directly. "When have I ever been afraid of complications? Your job is executing my orders, Volkov. Not thinking for me. And definitely not teaching me business in front of outsiders."

Each word hit him like a stone to the face. His face went white, lips moving soundlessly.

"I eliminate troublemakers," I added coldly. "Outsiders and insiders alike."

The elevator dinged open. I walked out without another glance.

The ride from hotel to airport passed in suffocating silence. I closed my eyes, pretending to rest while figuring out how to handle Volkov.

He'd been my most loyal, reliable lieutenant. But today he'd tried to think for himself, overrule me.

Most dangerous sign there is.

The private jet lifted off again, leaving Pittsburgh's gray industrial sprawl behind.

Volkov stood like a statue by the bar. Didn't dare sit, didn't dare speak. Waiting for judgment.

"What the hell did you think you were doing back there, Volkov?" I finally spoke, voice ice-cold. "Showing off your diplomatic skills? Or think I'm too fucking hotheaded and need you to pump the brakes?"

"I wouldn't dare, boss." His immediate response came out hoarse. "I just... I was wrong."

"Wrong how?" I pressed, giving him no breathing room.

"I shouldn't have questioned your authority in front of enemies. Shouldn't have acted on my own."

"Good. You're not completely brain-dead." My stare softened slightly. "Remember this mistake. Don't let there be a next time."

"Go sit down." I waved him off.

When the plane touched down, New York's night skyline spread before us. The warmth of coming home tried to chase away the violence in my chest.

A good lieutenant shouldn't think for himself. But Volkov had served faithfully as my right hand for over a decade.

Every international negotiation, he was there at peak performance. Every firefight and shootout, he had my back. He'd devoted almost every waking hour to the Zaitsev family.

So I wasn't planning anything permanent. Everyone makes mistakes and acts foolishly sometimes. What mattered was how to make it right.

The car pulled into the manor grounds. I walked into the main house, Volkov following like a silent shadow.

I stopped without turning around.

"Theodore might not let this go," I commanded. "Raise manor security to maximum. And assign our most reliable team to shadow Celia and Lucas around the clock. I don't want them losing a single hair."

"Yes, boss." Volkov's response came crisp and clear. "I'll handle it personally."

"This is your chance to make up for your fuck-up. Don't disappoint me."

"Yes, boss." His answer rang firm and solid.

CHAPTER TWENTY-THREE

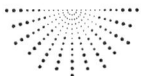

Celia

Sunlight streaming through the car windows bathed everything in warm gold as Kirill's Bentley glided smoothly down the road.

One hand rested on the steering wheel while the other reached over to envelop my hand resting on my lap. His thumb traced gentle circles across my knuckles—such a simple gesture, yet it sent electricity coursing through my entire body.

We'd just left the manor. Lucas slept peacefully in his car seat behind us, completely exhausted from staying up until midnight last night, too excited about seeing his friends again to sleep.

I'd been awake at midnight too, but for entirely different reasons.

The hours Kirill spent in Pittsburgh negotiating with Theodore, that Chicago gang boss, felt longer than any month I'd spent struggling to survive alone with Lucas.

After he left, that magnificent manor—the place that should have been the safest in the world—couldn't give me peace.

I kept telling myself over and over that he was Kirill Zaitsev, head of the Bratva, that he'd handled situations I couldn't even imagine, that nothing would happen to him. But my heart wouldn't listen to reason. It kept conjuring up countless terrifying possibilities.

Only when he appeared safely in the foyer did my suspended heart finally settle back into my chest. I'd rushed into his arms, breathing in his familiar scent.

"What are you thinking about?" Kirill's low voice broke the quiet. His gaze remained fixed on the road ahead, but I could feel his complete attention on me. This man had a terrifying ability to make you feel exposed under a microscope even when he wasn't looking directly at you.

I smiled, turning to look at him. Morning light outlined his sharp jawline, that scar cutting through his eyebrow giving him a perpetually wild edge. But right now, his gray-blue eyes were soft with tenderness.

"Just thinking about how surreal this all feels," I admitted. "A few months ago, I was worried about my next meal and rent I couldn't pay. Now... I'm sitting in your car, our son's sleeping in the back. We're dropping Lucas off at kindergarten together, then I'm going to work at Zaitsev Group as your personal assistant. It feels like I've stolen someone else's life."

The light turned red and we stopped. Kirill turned to look at me, his gaze intense. "This isn't someone else's life, Celia." He lifted our joined hands, pressing my knuckles to his lips for a burning kiss. "This is your life. Our life. This is what we deserve."

My heart skipped a beat. God, this man could always soothe every anxiety in my soul with the simplest words.

The car started moving again, and soon we reached Star Kindergarten. We woke Lucas and walked him to the entrance.

Lucas greeted the teacher at the door politely, said goodbye until this afternoon, then immediately started chatting with another little friend. We watched him go inside, and even back in the car I was still replaying the image of Lucas's cheerful little figure.

"We should transfer Lucas to a different kindergarten."

I froze, turning to stare at him. "Why? He has so many good friends here. He's happy."

"Celia." Kirill started the car, the Bentley smoothly merging into traffic. "I understand your thinking, but Lucas needs better education now. Star Kindergarten can't compete with elite private academies in any respect. They have extensive programs. Lucas could learn violin and horseback riding, naturally pick up multiple languages in that environment. Lucas is a bright kid—he might love everything they offer."

He continued, "As for Lucas's friends, we can stay in touch through phones. Whenever Lucas wants to see them, we'll bring him back for visits."

I knew Kirill was right. The programs he described were things I'd never dared dream of. What mother wouldn't want the best future for her child? And Kirill had considered every factor.

But I still worried Lucas wouldn't adapt to the new environment.

"I'm worried Lucas won't fit in at a private kindergarten. Those kids come from completely different backgrounds."

"Don't worry, I won't let anyone bully him. And I have faith in Lucas. His personality will help him make friends anywhere." Kirill's voice carried certainty and pride.

I smiled. True—so far, nobody disliked Lucas. Even Kirill's lieutenant, that man who always wore black suits—Volkov—brought Lucas age-appropriate gifts whenever he visited.

"But we have to ask Lucas first. As long as he's willing, I'm fine with it."

"Of course. I'll talk to Lucas."

This was another thing I appreciated about Kirill—he always treated Lucas as an equal in conversations.

Finally, we reached the company.

"All right, my capable assistant." Kirill leaned over and kissed my lips softly. "Go to work. I have a meeting this afternoon, outside the city, with a new arms dealer. Might be tricky."

"Is it safe?" I asked instinctively. Since learning his true identity, my nerves went on high alert every time he mentioned business. He occupied the boss's position—God knew how many people had targets on him.

"Don't worry, just business negotiations. I'll handle it. Volkov will stay to handle internal company matters. You can go to him if you need anything."

I nodded.

He watched me get out of the car, and I could still feel his gaze on my back as I walked into the building.

Entering the office, I sat at my desk. Taking a breath, I prepared to dive into work. I needed to organize a quarterly report on Zaitsev Group's cooperation project with NTIA—Kirill would need it next week.

Time passed in the sound of keyboard clicks and rustling papers. The office was quiet except for the occasional hum of the printer. I was completely absorbed in work until a shadow blocked the light above my head. I looked up—it was Volkov.

"Hi, Volkov. What's up?" I smiled politely.

But he didn't return my smile. His face was unusually serious, almost pale. His expression was tense and anxious.

"Yes, ma'am," his voice was low with urgent undertones. "We have a problem."

My heart plummeted, the pen dropping from my hand to clatter on the desk. "What? Is it Kirill?"

Fear coiled around my breath like a serpent.

"We received word that the Moretti Family is making moves in New York. Their target is you and Lucas."

The Moretti Family. Kirill had mentioned them—that greedy Theodore from Chicago was the Moretti Family boss. He'd threatened Kirill about redistributing profits last time.

My face went rigid.

"The boss is dealing with them now, can't break away. He ordered me to immediately move you and Lucas somewhere safe." Volkov's tone was urgent. "We need to leave now. To Kolomna Estate—it has the most advanced security system. Nobody can break in."

When did this happen? Wasn't Kirill supposed to be negotiating with arms dealers? Had the negotiations ended already? Then why hadn't he contacted me?

My brain was in chaos. My first instinct was to call Kirill—I needed to hear his voice.

"I'm calling Kirill."

"No!" Volkov immediately stopped me, his hand slamming down on my phone with shocking force. "Ma'am, listen! He's facing off with an extremely dangerous opponent right now. Any call or message could distract him, expose his location—that would get him killed! This is his direct order, take you away immediately, don't contact him. He'll come to the manor to meet you once he's handled things."

His words struck my nerves like a sledgehammer. He was right—Kirill's world was full of dangers ordinary people couldn't imagine. At a critical moment like this, any impulsive action from me could become his fatal weakness. I couldn't be that selfish.

Anxiety and doubt knotted my stomach. My palms were clammy with cold sweat. I trusted Kirill, and Volkov was Kirill's most trusted man. I had no reason to doubt him.

"Better not bring your phone—it could expose our location. Don't take your bag either, might draw attention." Volkov spoke again.

I could only follow his instructions. One more possibility of exposure meant one more danger.

"...Okay." I heard myself speak in a voice that barely sounded like mine. Logic told me this was the only choice. But my instincts were screaming warnings deep in my mind.

I followed Volkov into the presidential private elevator. The moment the doors closed, I felt trapped in an airtight metal box.

"Lucas..." My voice was hoarse.

"Don't worry, we're picking him up first. I already called the kindergarten, said there was a family emergency." Volkov's response was quick and smooth—clearly he'd planned everything.

This actually suppressed that ominous feeling in my heart. He'd thought of everything so thoroughly—this had to be Kirill's arrangement.

The elevator went straight to the underground garage. A black bulletproof SUV was waiting, engine running. The windows were dark tinted—nothing visible from outside. Volkov opened the door for me and I got in. An unfamiliar driver sat behind the wheel.

The car smoothly exited the garage and merged into traffic.

How was Kirill doing? Was he safe? I twisted my fingers together, nails digging deep into flesh. I forced myself to calm down, repeating over and over, Kirill will handle everything. He's invincible.

We quickly reached Lucas's kindergarten. Volkov got out, returning minutes later carrying Lucas.

"Mommy!" Lucas saw me and opened his arms happily.

I held him tight, breathing in his familiar scent. My suspended heart settled just a little.

"Volkov said we're going somewhere mysterious, and Kirill will come too!" Lucas said excitedly.

I looked at Volkov. He nodded reassuringly, forcing a smile that didn't reach his eyes.

"Yes, baby." I kissed Lucas's forehead.

The car started again. Lucas looked out the window curiously from my lap. I held him, my racing pulse making me dizzy. I tried to judge if we were heading toward the manor by watching the street scenes outside. At first, the route seemed correct—we were heading toward the Upper East Side.

But after a few blocks, my heart began to sink.

The driver put on his turn signal and turned onto a road leading to Brooklyn Bridge.

Wrong. Going to Kolomna Estate, we wouldn't take this route at all.

"Volkov," I tried to keep my voice steady, but that damn tremor betrayed me anyway. "I think we're going the wrong way. To get to the manor, we should take FDR Drive."

Volkov sat in the passenger seat, glancing at me through the rearview mirror. That look held no warmth. The tight, anxious expression disappeared from his face, leaving only chilling calm.

"We're not going to the manor, ma'am."

In that instant, all the blood in my body froze. The unease that had lurked in my heart from the beginning now erupted to devour me.

"Where are you taking us?" My voice shot up, filled with terror. I instinctively grabbed for the door handle, only to find it was locked.

"Stop the car! Volkov, what the hell do you think you're doing?" I screamed. Lucas was frightened by my reaction, clinging tightly to my clothes, his little face pale.

"Mommy, what's wrong? Don't be scared." He patted my arm with his small hands, trying to comfort me even though his own voice was shaking.

"I'm fine, baby. I'm fine." I held him tighter, my throat constricting painfully.

Volkov didn't answer me. The car crossed Brooklyn Bridge and entered a completely unfamiliar, desolate area.

Finally, the car stopped in front of an abandoned pier.

We're fucked. The thought stabbed into my heart like an ice blade.

Volkov turned around, his face now utterly strange and menacing.

"Get out," he commanded.

I stared at him hard. "You betrayed Kirill."

He twisted his mouth into a sneer full of mockery. "Betrayal? No, I'm just choosing a more promising future."

Car doors opened from outside. Two burly men in black jackets stood there, forcing us out.

My brain raced, searching for any possibility of escape. But this place was too open—just them, no one else.

"Mommy..." Lucas's voice was small. "Kirill will come save us, right?"

"Yes, baby." I kissed the top of his head. "He will."

I took a deep breath and got out carrying Lucas. Sea wind blew over us, bringing the smell of salt and brine. The two men flanked us on either side. Volkov got out and retrieved rope from the trunk, walking toward us.

I immediately shielded Lucas. "You can't do this! He's just a child!"

"Shut up!" Volkov barked, his patience completely gone. He grabbed my arm with crushing force, nearly making me drop Lucas.

To avoid hurting Lucas, I had to set him down and keep him behind me.

Just as Volkov was about to tie me up, Lucas suddenly stepped out from behind me. He looked up, meeting Volkov's eyes directly with his clear gaze.

"Volkov." His voice wasn't loud but was unusually clear. "Why are you being mean to my mommy? Last week when you came to the manor, you brought me a red toy car. Aren't we good friends?"

Volkov froze. He looked down at Lucas, complex emotions flashing in his eyes.

I saw his Adam's apple bob.

"I don't have a choice," Volkov's voice was hoarse, as if explaining to himself.

"I don't understand," Lucas said, his words making him sound like a little adult. "You look like a bad guy now, not my friend."

In that moment, I saw the struggle in Volkov's eyes reach its peak. The two men went on alert, as if they'd eliminate him the moment he changed his mind.

But after just a few seconds, he closed his eyes. When he opened them again, all hesitation was gone.

"Innocence is a child's privilege." He spat out those cold words, then refused to look at Lucas again, roughly twisting my hands behind my back and tying them tightly with rope.

I looked at him desperately while Lucas stood nearby, small fists clenched. His expression was heartbroken—maybe he felt his friend had betrayed him.

They tied Lucas's hands with another rope, then shoved us across the dock into a musty-smelling warehouse.

The two men gripped us on either side.

A man stood in the center of the warehouse. He wore an Italian suit and was slightly overweight.

His gaze swept over us, then returned.

"Well done, Volkov." The man spoke with an oily tone. "We've got the hostages."

"Yes, Mr. Moretti," Volkov answered respectfully.

This was Theodore that Kirill had mentioned! How could Volkov be working for him?

"Now that we've got Kirill's woman and kid, we can make him crawl like a dog to call a family meeting and pass the boss position to you." Theodore seemed to already envision their success, his tone growing lighter. "Then New York will be yours. I'm sure our future cooperation will be very pleasant—no more fighting over damn profit splits."

"Of course, we need to get Kirill to sign that fifty-fifty profit agreement first, to prevent any upheaval within the Bratva from leadership changes and major policy shifts. After that, our cooperation will only get smoother." Volkov's tone was confident of victory.

"And once everything's in place, the hostages are still in our hands—Kirill will be at our mercy. I'm so fucking sick of him!"

I stared at them in disbelief, barely able to breathe. These two men—one for power, one for money—had woven a web targeting Kirill, and me and our son were trapped inside it.

Suddenly, Theodore walked up to me as if remembering something.

"This woman looks familiar."

He grabbed my chin roughly, forcing me to look up. I tried to shake my head away, but his grip was too strong. Pain shot through my jaw.

"Don't touch my mommy!" Lucas struggled and shouted at Theodore, but Theodore didn't care about the young child restrained by the men.

Theodore studied my face carefully, frowning in thought. After a long moment, realization dawned. "Oh! I remember now! Isn't this the fucking virgin from that auction stage five years ago?"

I was too shocked to care how he knew about the auction—I only felt humiliation that he'd say such things in front of my son...

"My God! Who would've thought, Kirill Zaitsev!" He laughed hysterically, pointing at me and Lucas. "He not only bought her, he fucking knocked her up! Had a kid that looks exactly like him!"

Volkov approached too, surprise on his face. "Five years ago? When he came back from Chicago, he was definitely troubled for a while. Had me go to Chicago looking for some woman. Never thought it was the same person? He really is... devoted."

"Devoted?" Theodore laughed until tears came. "Maybe. But his son he's hidden for five years and the woman he's pined for are both in our hands—these hostages pack some serious weight. I bet now, forget fifty-fifty—if I told him to kneel down and die for them, he'd do it willingly."

Die? That word crushed every inch of my body. Just thinking of it applied to Kirill made every nerve in my body scream with pain.

My eyes bored into Theodore as if that could make him take back his damned words.

"Don't look at me like that, sweetheart," Theodore said leisurely. "Your only purpose now is to be proper bait. Think about when you see your man—what kind of crying will make him sign that agreement faster."

CHAPTER TWENTY-FOUR

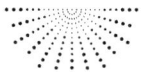

Kirill

"Perfect craftsmanship, Kirill." My business partner, a man known as Mr. K, picked up a modified Kalashnikov and evaluated it with his thick accent.

"Of course. My clients only accept the best. These babies perform better in urban warfare than any official gear."

I answered curtly, leaning back in my chair with my arms crossed over my chest.

Mr. K was a dealer cautious to the point of paranoia. This meeting took place in a suburban warehouse far from the city. According to his rules, during negotiations, everyone's phones had to be turned off and locked together in a Faraday box. This was the secret to him living this long. In our business, one ill-timed signal could bring a lethal bullet.

"My money will be transferred in full to your Swiss account before the first shipment loads." Mr. K set down the gun and extended his hand toward me.

I reached out and shook it.

After the deal was done, he quickly left with his men.

The negotiations had gone through several rounds and lasted nearly five hours. By now it was getting dark. I retrieved my phone from the iron box and powered it on. The screen lit up, the notification bar completely blank.

No messages from Celia. A strong sense of unease settled in my chest. This wasn't right. Given my relationship with Celia now, there was no way she wouldn't send a single message after being apart this long.

I immediately dialed her number. The phone rang four times, then went straight to voicemail. That artificially synthesized female voice sounded unbearably cold, and an ominous feeling gripped my heart.

I hung up, my fingers flying across the screen to find Volkov's number. He was the highest-ranking person left at the company today. If anything happened to Celia, he should know.

But what came through the earpiece was that same damn voice, "The number you have dialed is turned off..."

Turned off?

Unease spread rapidly under my skin. In the Zaitsev family rules, unless the person was dead, core members' phones had to stay on twenty-four hours a day. This was an iron law paid for in blood.

I dialed Celia's number again. Still voicemail.

Shit!

I bolted from the warehouse, my temples pounding from my spiking blood pressure. My men had already brought the bulletproof Cadillac over. I yanked open the door and got in.

"Get back to the city, as fast as possible!" I growled out each word.

Celia and Volkov going dark at the same time was no fucking coincidence. I was already preparing for the worst.

The car sped along while my chest felt like it was being strangled by an iron band, wound tight as hell. I was about to call my third-in-command Dmitri when my phone vibrated.

It was a text from an anonymous number.

My fingers trembled from the force I was using as I opened the message.

"Bring a new shipping route agreement with fifty-fifty profit split. Come alone to Brooklyn Pier 3. You have three hours. One minute late, and I'll start with your son, cutting off their fingers one by one and mailing them to you."

Below was an attached photo. My gaze locked onto it like a death grip.

The background was a dim warehouse. Celia was tied to a chair, her mouth taped shut, those eyes that always held gentle laughter now filled with fear. And sitting on the floor beside her was Lucas. His hands were also bound behind his back, his small face pale and bewildered, lips pressed tight, trying hard not to cry.

BOOM—

I was struck like lightning. Devastating rage erupted from my chest cavity, the edges of my vision starting to turn red. That fucking Theodore! I wanted to tear him limb from limb!

I punched the connection between the car window and door frame. The hardness of the bulletproof material sent sharp pain through my knuckles, and the pain cleared some of the chaos in my fury-burned brain.

Calm down. Kirill, you fucking calm down.

Celia and Lucas were still alive. They needed a boss who would save them, not a madman blinded by rage. Their lives now hung on every decision I made next. My mind raced, and soon I had a detailed rescue plan.

I took a deep breath. That breath tasted of blood.

Then I called Dmitri.

"Dmitri, gather all the brothers in New York. Full combat gear, assembly in the headquarters underground garage in fifteen minutes."

"Pull up the most accurate satellite maps and structural diagrams of Brooklyn Pier 3. I need to know every entrance, every exit, and all the high points."

"Prepare a Chicago route agreement with fifty-fifty profit distribution. Stamp it with the family seal."

"Also, prepare several sets of micro encrypted earpieces."

I gave Dmitri orders one by one. Dmitri never asked questions.

"Copy, boss."

The second call went to Viktor.

The phone rang twice before being answered.

"Well, Kirill, you coming to me for relationship counseling again?" Viktor's flippant tone came through.

"Viktor," my voice was squeezed from my throat, "I need you to do me a favor."

The laughing on the other end stopped dead.

"Fuck. Kirill, who is it?" Viktor's voice turned serious and deadly.

"Theodore Moretti."

"That Chicago moron? He's got a death wish." Viktor's voice took on cruel pleasure. "My .50 sniper rifle hasn't seen blood in a long time. Blowing his brains out won't be a problem."

"Get to the underground garage at my headquarters first. I already have a solid plan. The main objective this time is rescue, so I need you to be extra careful."

"No problem."

Over an hour later, the car reached headquarters' basement at an incredible speed.

The sight before me would make any regular army break out in cold sweat. Hundreds of men in black combat gear, faces marked with deadly intent, had assembled here. They were Bratva's most capable brothers, my most loyal and lethal force in this city.

I pushed open the car door and stepped out.

Viktor was already waiting there, wearing dark clothes suitable for action, his sniper rifle on his back. We didn't waste words, just bumped each other's shoulders hard with our fists. Everything was understood.

I walked to the front of the formation. Dmitri handed me a state-of-the-art bulletproof vest. I took off my suit jacket and put it on under my shirt.

Then from the weapons case Dmitri had opened, I took two modified Makarov pistols, checked the magazines, loaded them, holstered one at my back, and strapped the other in a holster on the inside of my left calf.

A dock structural diagram was spread out on a car's hood.

"You'll split into three teams, coordinate with each other."

"Viktor," I pointed to a spot circled in red on the map, "this is the best sniper position. I want you in place within twenty minutes. Your primary target is Theodore Moretti. I want his head."

"Piece of cake." Viktor patted his baby.

"Dmitri, you take Alpha team," I pointed to the water area of the dock on the map, "infiltrate secretly by water. I don't want to hear a sound before the action begins."

"Yes, boss."

"Ivan, you take Beta team," I pointed to the land entrance, "perimeter control, eliminate their defenses with maximum firepower."

"Understood, boss."

I distributed earpieces to the three of them. After putting on a micro earpiece myself, I connected the signal to their channel, "I'll go in alone. Nobody moves until I give the order. All actions follow my commands."

"Listen up," my gaze swept over everyone, "Location is Brooklyn Pier 3, target is Theodore Moretti. We have two objectives, First, rescue. Second, take out the trash. Remember, hostage safety is top priority."

I took one last look at my watch. Forty minutes left until the three-hour deadline.

"Move out." I gave the final command and took the agreement Dmitri had prepared.

CHAPTER TWENTY-FIVE

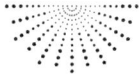

Kirill

I DROVE ALONE toward Brooklyn Pier 3, watching the city's glittering skyline fade into industrial wasteland through my window.

Viktor, Dmitri, and Ivan were already in position, waiting for my signal.

I parked a few dozen meters from the pier entrance. Killed the engine, pushed open the door. Salt air hit my lungs like a slap.

I grabbed the paper bag containing the agreement and walked toward them.

The guards at the entrance tensed immediately, assault rifles swinging toward me in perfect unison.

"Is Theodore that scared of me?" I stopped walking, voice dripping with mockery.

A guy who looked like the leader stepped forward. His eyes were steady, but his clenched jaw betrayed his nerves.

"Our boss said you can never be too careful when dealing with you. This is procedure. Please cooperate."

He nodded to his men. Two heavies moved in to pat me down.

They searched thoroughly, quickly finding the two Makarov pistols I had tucked behind my back and strapped to my calf.

They kept going, checking me over repeatedly.

But they didn't find anything else. One of the guards stepped back.

The other guard's hand hit my chest and paused.

His eyes shot to the leader, seeking orders.

The leader's face showed no surprise, as if he'd been expecting this.

"Jacket. Please."

I smirked and slowly peeled off the bulletproof vest, tossing it aside.

"Our boss was right," he said, studying me with complex eyes. "Negotiations with you are never just about talking."

I said nothing, just stared at him coldly.

"What's this?" The guard's hand moved up my neck toward my ear. My heart nearly stopped.

The micro encrypted earpiece was buried deep in my right ear canal. It was the cornerstone of the entire plan.

Every muscle in my body screamed danger. His hand was almost at my ear.

I immediately turned my head toward the leader, left side facing him, pulling my right ear out of the guard's line of sight.

"You deal with people the way they deserve to be dealt with," I said, voice full of arrogance. "Theodore's a piece of shit who can't even make it to the big leagues. You expect me to show him fucking respect?"

My words hit their mark. The leader's face darkened. The guard searching me bristled at my attitude, his movements faltering. He was about to say something when the leader cut him off.

"Hurry the fuck up! Don't waste time! The boss is getting impatient!"

The guard got flustered by the pressure. He gave my ear a quick, careless pat-down, found nothing, and pulled his hand back with a grunt.

"He's clean," he muttered.

"Dodged a bullet," Viktor's voice whispered through my earpiece.

I could barely fucking breathe until that moment.

"Bring him in," the leader ordered.

Two guards flanked me as we walked inside. The deck was dimly lit, just a few old industrial lights casting harsh circles of illumination.

Theodore stood in the center of the deck with a dozen armed men behind him.

"Welcome, Kirill." He spread his arms wide. "So glad you could make it on time."

"Where are my people?" My eyes swept past him into the shadows beyond. "I don't see them, you get nothing."

"Easy there," Theodore smiled. "Let me give you a surprise first."

He clapped his hands. Someone I never expected stepped out of the shadows.

When I saw his face, my pupils contracted sharply. Volkov!

"Let me introduce my new business partner," Theodore said smugly.

My gaze cut into the man I'd once called brother like a blade. "Why?"

Something unnatural flashed across Volkov's face, then was replaced by pure hatred.

"Why? You're fucking asking me why?" He stepped forward, voice rising with rage. "Ten years, Kirill. I've been following you around for ten fucking years! Every street fight, every shootout—who was standing in front of you? And what did I get? I'm always number two, always your fucking shadow!"

"Why should the position only be yours? Just because your last name is Zaitsev? I've bled for this family just as much as you have!" His emotions spiraled, his face twisting into something manic and vicious.

"I treated you like a brother!" The words came through my clenched teeth.

"Brother?" He laughed like he'd heard the world's greatest joke. "Would a brother dump all the dangerous jobs on me while he sits pretty in his penthouse office? Would a brother use loyalty to lock away all my ambition and ability? No, Kirill. You never wanted a brother. You just wanted an obedient fucking dog!"

"So that's your answer?" I stared at him coldly. "For a position you'll never be able to hold, you kidnap a woman and a child?"

"They're just tools!" Volkov's eyes showed no remorse. "Tools to make you submit!"

I looked at his face, twisted by ambition, and felt nothing but ice-cold rage and bloodlust.

"Alright, alright!" Theodore interrupted with fake peacemaking. "The main event hasn't even started yet!"

He clapped again. Two guards dragged Celia and Lucas forward.

My heart took a brutal hit. The pain made me clench my fists.

Celia's mouth was taped shut, hands bound behind her back, face white as paper. When she saw me, her eyes lit up, then filled with worry. Volkov moved behind her and pressed a gun to her temple.

My guts twisted into a knot of agony. I couldn't bear the thought of losing Celia.

Lucas was tied up the same way, his small body shaking with fear. When he saw me, his expression barely changed—probably scared out of his mind.

Every nerve in my body screamed. Pure rage burned under my skin, scorching every inch of me.

I was going to make them fucking pay!

"Give me the agreement," Theodore held out his hand. "And tonight, call a family meeting. Publicly announce you're passing the boss position to Volkov. Your woman and son will stay here as my guests. Once you've done all that, I'll let them leave safely."

Zero chance that was true. Once he had everything, he'd wipe us all out.

I looked past Theodore to Celia. She was shaking her head frantically, eyes pleading with me not to agree. I gave her a reassuring look. Her eyes instantly went red. Then I looked at Lucas, my son. Seeing him so scared and fragile felt like my chest was being crushed.

"Stop fucking stalling, Kirill!" Volkov jabbed the gun barrel against Celia's temple impatiently.

I ran through my options.

This was worse than I'd planned. Viktor and I had targeted Theodore—take him out first, his men would panic and focus on the armed threats, giving Celia and Lucas a better chance to escape.

But now there was the wild card of Volkov. Once he saw Theodore was dead and knew it was over, with all his hatred for me, he'd never let Celia and Lucas go.

Having Viktor snipe Volkov directly wouldn't work either. I had no way to communicate with Viktor now.

I needed to create an opportunity—something that would focus everyone's attention on one point.

I raised the paper bag.

"The agreement's in here." My voice was terrifyingly calm.

Theodore's face lit up with greed. The agreement had his complete attention. He reached out to take it. Volkov was watching closely too.

Just as Theodore was about to touch the bag, I suddenly let go, letting it drop toward the ground. Theodore instinctively bent to catch it while I dove left.

"Do it!" I barked into my earpiece.

"Party time, assholes," Viktor's voice crackled in my ear.

Thunk—Theodore's head exploded. He dropped like a stone.

Almost instantly, gunfire erupted from all sides! Dmitri and Ivan launched their coordinated assault from land and water. Theodore's men, caught off guard, went down like wheat before a scythe.

In the chaos, Dmitri shot toward Lucas like lightning, scooped him up, and retreated to safety.

Volkov was stunned by the sudden turn for exactly one second.

That was all I needed! I lunged toward him at full speed, trying to tackle him and save Celia.

But Celia's eyes flashed with determination. She lifted her high-heeled foot and drove it back into Volkov's shin with everything she had!

Volkov yelped in pain, his body lurching sideways. His grip on Celia loosened instinctively. But the pain enraged him completely.

Face twisted with fury, he swung his gun toward Celia as she broke free.

"Die, bitch!"

"Celia!" I roared.

I threw myself through the air toward her.

BANG! The bullet tore through my chest instantly. The force slammed me to the ground. Fighting through the agony, I pulled Celia close and shielded her with my body.

"Kirill!" I heard her scream, the sound tearing her throat raw.

Pain shot through me, cold sweat beading on my forehead. But I knew it wasn't over. Shaking, I grabbed a gun from the ground beside me.

My brothers had Volkov in their sights, but we were too close. They were afraid of hitting us and couldn't take the shot.

Volkov was lining up his second shot.

I used my last bit of strength to raise my arm. My vision was blurring, but on pure instinct, I aimed at Volkov and pulled the trigger.

BANG! BANG! BANG!

Volkov finally went down in a pool of blood.

The threat was over.

I couldn't hold on anymore. My arm dropped. I could hear my brothers shouting, Celia crying, but it all sounded farther and farther away.

The last thing I saw was Celia's face, streaked with tears and terror. Then my consciousness sank into endless darkness.

CHAPTER TWENTY-SIX

Celia

THE SMELL of disinfectant pierced my nostrils, overwhelming all my senses.

My memories were fragmented, chaotic.

One moment it was Kirill standing before me, that broad, solid silhouette; the next, the deafening crack of gunfire and Kirill's eyes falling closed. I remembered screaming, my voice so raw it didn't sound like my own.

How we got to the hospital, I had no idea. Viktor, maybe, or Dmitri—they'd pulled me away from Kirill's side and shoved me into a car. All I could recall was that vehicle tearing through New York's midnight streets while I learned their names and positions through my daze.

Now medical staff rushed past with the gurney, shouting terms I couldn't comprehend, their footsteps urgent and chaotic—each one striking the floor like a blow to my heart.

I could only stare at the man lying on that stretcher, his face that always commanded absolute authority now pale as parchment. His eyes were sealed shut, his usually immaculate black hair disheveled and matted to his forehead with cold sweat and blood.

"No, Kirill. Please..." A broken whimper escaped my throat.

The medical team had wheeled Kirill to the emergency room entrance. I wanted nothing more than to rush forward and stay by his side.

But a powerful arm locked around me like steel.

"Celia, get it together! You can't go in there! You'll only interfere!" Viktor.

"Let me go!" I sobbed. "He needs me! Let me through!"

But that door still slammed shut before me, severing Kirill's world from mine.

The red light above the emergency room blazed to life like a malevolent eye.

All my strength drained away with the closing of that door. I slumped against the cold wall and crumpled to the floor, burying my face in my knees as sobs wracked my body.

Time became meaningless—every second stretched into eternity.

"He'll pull through." Viktor's voice drifted down from above. "That bastard Kirill—even the Grim Reaper gives him a wide berth."

I didn't respond. I was drowning in my own anguish.

"Look," he seemed to realize his comfort wasn't working, so he cleared his throat and pressed on, "I remember this one time—he and I got cornered by Irish thugs in the street. Just the two of us against thirty goddamn Irishmen. He fought his way out of that circle with nothing but his fists, dragging me along. Point is, men like him don't go down easy."

He finished his story, convinced it proved Kirill's invincibility, that it would kindle hope in me.

He was wrong.

I lifted my head, tears blurring my vision as I looked at him. His words only made me realize with crystal clarity that tonight's violence wasn't some terrible accident—it was Kirill's everyday reality.

Viktor's mouth opened as if to say more, but he ultimately clamped it shut in frustration, raking fingers through his hair.

Dmitri stood in silent vigil nearby, cradling Lucas. The boy's face was ghostly pale, tears pooling in his eyes. He wriggled free from Dmitri's embrace and ran to me, using his small, warm hands to clumsily brush away my tears.

"Mommy, don't cry..." he hiccupped. "Kirill's going to be okay—he's really strong, isn't he?"

I gathered him into my arms, but I couldn't give him the certainty he craved. Would Kirill be okay? I honestly didn't know.

"Ma'am, you need to pull yourself together. The boy's frightened too." Dmitri approached us. "Perhaps you should contact family or friends. Having loved ones here would help you both."

My circle of family and friends consisted of exactly three people, Kirill, Lucas, and Mia.

"After being out of touch this long, they're probably worried sick." Dmitri added gently.

His words cut through my grief. I'd been missing for an entire day. If Mia couldn't reach me, she'd be frantic with worry. I couldn't be so selfish.

I instinctively reached for my phone, then remembered I'd left with Volkov empty-handed.

"There are payphones in the hospital. I'll show you." Dmitri recognized my dilemma and offered assistance.

I drew a shaky breath and stood, taking Lucas's hand as we followed Dmitri.

The phone area was deserted at this late hour. I managed to dial Mia's number without difficulty.

Mia didn't pick up initially. Hospital calls typically screamed spam or scam to most people.

Just as I was about to abandon hope, Mia's voice crackled through the receiver.

"This is Mia."

"Mia, it's Celia..." The instant I heard her voice, fresh tears spilled down my cheeks.

"Honey, why are you calling from a hospital? Are you there? What's wrong?" Panic sharpened Mia's tone when she recognized me.

"I've been texting you all day with no response. I was ready to call the cops."

"We were..." I choked out between sobs, words fragmenting, "Lucas and I were kidnapped this morning..."

"What?" Mia's voice spiked with shock and disbelief. "Are you hurt? Is Lucas okay?"

"We're both fine." I shook my head desperately. "But Kirill... Kirill took a bullet saving us. Mia, he's... he's still in surgery."

Silence stretched across the line for several heartbeats. I could actually hear Mia's sharp intake of breath. When she spoke again, her voice was rock-steady.

"Which hospital? What floor? Give me everything."

I relayed all the details to Mia.

"Got it." Strength radiated through her words, anchoring me. "Listen carefully, Celia—I need you to breathe deeply right now. Stop crying, you hear me? Kirill's going to be fine. Men like him don't just roll over and die. Hell, Death himself probably crosses the street to avoid that man. Plus he's got you and your boy to live for—no way he's checking out now."

Mia's trademark brand of comfort settled my racing pulse slightly.

"Don't think about anything except staying put with Lucas. I'm coming to you."

The line went dead. Her decisive confidence infected me, and I wiped my face clean.

"Is Mia coming, Mommy?" Lucas noticed my tears had stopped and dried his own.

"Yes, sweetheart."

I took Lucas's hand and we returned to the emergency wing corridor. Dmitri had somehow reappeared and now sat on a bench with Viktor.

Lucas and I claimed another bench.

Mia arrived with supernatural speed, clutching a bag as she swept down the hallway like a force of nature. She spotted us immediately and charged over, enveloping us both in fierce embraces.

"Everything's going to be alright, my precious ones." She released us and produced two wax-paper-wrapped sandwiches from her bag. "Made these before I left—threw in some avocado. Eat."

I shook my head. My stomach felt packed with frozen cotton. Food was the last thing I wanted.

"I can't, Mia. Every time I think about Kirill lying in there, I feel sick."

"You absolutely will eat." Her tone brooked zero argument as she pressed the sandwich into my reluctant hands. "Sweetheart, you need to maintain your strength. Want him waking up to find you've wasted away? Want him agonizing over your condition when he should be healing?"

She glanced at Lucas meaningfully. "Besides, what happens to this little guy if you collapse? Look—he's been watching your every move. If you don't eat, how can you expect him to? You've both been starving all day, and Lucas is still growing. God knows how this tough little soldier has managed not to complain about being hungry."

I looked down to find Lucas gazing up at me with naked concern etched across his features. We'd both barely eaten since morning. He had to be famished.

"I'm sorry, baby." I pressed a kiss to Lucas's forehead. "Mommy's been a terrible mother, letting you go hungry all day."

"I'm not really hungry yet, Mommy," Lucas replied with heartbreaking sweetness.

His stomach chose that moment to rumble audibly.

Mia shook her head and unwrapped Lucas's sandwich.

"Dig in, little man. Mommy's eating too." I accepted Mia's offering while addressing Lucas.

Mia was absolutely right. I couldn't afford to fall apart—not for Kirill's sake, not for Lucas's.

Lucas attacked his sandwich with enthusiasm while Mia twisted open a water bottle for him.

"Easy there, baby. Don't choke." I rubbed gentle circles on Lucas's back.

I mechanically bit into my own sandwich. The food was flavorless on my tongue, but I forced myself to swallow. Gradually, warmth began spreading from my stomach outward.

Mia's attention shifted past me to Viktor and Dmitri on their bench. The two men sat like granite monuments, radiating barely contained tension.

"Those your guy's lieutenants?" Mia murmured.

"Something like that." I nodded.

I watched Mia steel herself, grab the remaining sandwiches, and saunter over on those endless legs.

"Evening, gentlemen." Her voice carried breezy confidence. "You've been holding vigil for hours. Hungry? These are homemade—just a little something to keep your energy up. Might be a long night ahead, am I right?"

Viktor and Dmitri both looked genuinely startled. They studied this woman whose entire energy clashed with their grim surroundings. Viktor gave Mia a once-over, then actually accepted the sandwich with a gruff "Appreciate it."

Dmitri wordlessly took his portion.

What happened next left Mia and me gaping, both men devoured their entire sandwiches in precisely two bites.

Mia returned to my side, whispering, "Holy hell—real gangsters don't mess around. Even eating's a tactical operation. But honestly, Celia, your man's people seem solid."

Her theatrical yet sincere expression finally coaxed the tiniest smile from my lips after hours of anguish.

Though that crimson light still loomed like a sword over my head, Mia's presence had made this suffocating vigil marginally more endurable.

Time crawled past—perhaps an hour, perhaps eons.

Finally, mercifully, that red light died.

I launched myself forward. Mia guided Lucas by the hand while Viktor and Dmitri materialized behind us.

A surgeon in jade scrubs emerged, stripping away his mask to reveal exhaustion and perspiration.

His words rang like celestial music, "Your husband was extraordinarily fortunate. The bullet grazed his heart by millimeters. Any closer and divine intervention couldn't have saved him. Surgery was successful—we extracted the bullet completely."

My knees buckled and I nearly hit the floor, but Mia's steady grip kept me upright. This miraculous news cracked open the dam I'd built around my emotions all night. Pure relief flooded through me.

"However," the doctor's tone shifted ominously, extinguishing my newfound hope, "massive blood loss has induced a profound coma. Vital signs remain stable, but his awakening timeline is uncertain. That depends largely on his personal will to survive."

I stood frozen—paradise one instant, purgatory the next.

Mia's arm settled around my shoulders. "This is tremendous news, Celia. Your man's out of immediate danger. I guarantee he'll fight his way back to you two."

I managed a nod. While not the miracle I'd prayed for, this outcome was infinitely better than the life-or-death uncertainty we'd endured.

Kirill was transferred to a private VIP Ward on the top floor. Hospital protocol barred non-essential visitors—Mia, Viktor, and Dmitri were all refused entry.

Only Lucas and I gained admittance after donning Isolation Gowns.

The room was tomb-quiet save for the cardiac monitor's rhythmic beeping. Kirill lay motionless beneath a web of tubes and wires, oxygen mask obscuring half his face. His complexion remained ashen, his unconscious vulnerability absolutely devastating.

I guided Lucas to bedside chairs and carefully claimed Kirill's IV-free hand. His skin felt ice-cold.

The sight of thick bandages swathing his chest nearly broke my composure again. This was entirely my fault—Kirill lay here because he'd saved me. But I refused to cry in his presence. He wouldn't want to see my tears.

I inhaled deeply and wrestled my emotions under control.

"Lucas," I turned to face my son, "there's something Mommy needs to tell you. Kirill is your biological father. He's your daddy."

I braced for shock, confusion, denial.

Instead, Lucas simply studied Kirill's sleeping form and responded with preternatural calm, "I already knew, Mommy."

I stared at him in absolute bewilderment, as if meeting my child for the first time.

"I could sense it," he explained quietly. "You're different with him than anyone else. And I love his smell, how safe I feel when he holds me—like I've always known him."

Tenderness overwhelmed me. I'd underestimated the mysterious power of blood ties and my son's intuitive wisdom. He'd assembled this truth through pure instinct.

"Mommy, he's going to wake up, right? Daddy's going to wake up."

Hearing "Daddy" from Lucas's lips nearly shattered my resolve.

"He will." I nodded with fierce conviction.

I squeezed Kirill's hand tighter and clasped Lucas's small fingers. Our family formed an unbreakable chain.

Leaning close to Kirill's ear, I whispered with quiet determination, "Kirill, can you hear me? Your son is calling for you. Lucas is calling you Daddy. You can't keep sleeping."

I began weaving stories for unconscious Kirill, desperate to reach his submerged consciousness. I recounted our Chicago business trip, those magical hours at the amusement park—the three of us together on the flying chair and carousel.

I shared Lucas's entire history with his father.

"When Lucas was born, he looked like a wrinkled little monkey—nothing like either of us."

"But his eyes were identical to yours. Every single time I looked at him, I thought of you."

...

Lucas listened raptly, learning details about his own early life.

My voice drifted through the sterile silence like an endless lullaby that might never reach its destination.

But I would continue.

One day. One week.

However long it took for Kirill to open his eyes and see me again.

CHAPTER TWENTY-SEVEN

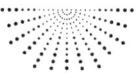

Kirill

DARKNESS. It was a tangible, weighted darkness, like a thick blanket soaked in seawater, wrapping around me layer by layer, crushing my ability to breathe, to think. I couldn't feel my body—I was just a wisp of consciousness trapped in this endless void.

Time meant nothing here. I had no idea how long I'd been floating. Then, without warning, an image split through the chaos.

My mother lying in her hospital bed. Her face pale as paper, her once-bright eyes now dull and lifeless. Every breath came with a painful, suppressed cough.

I sat beside her, gripping her skeletal hand. It was cold—ice cold—and that chill crept up my arm straight to my heart.

I saw the framed photo on her nightstand—her and my father when they were young. Back then, their eyes held real love. Father had been cold, yes, but he'd had tender moments with her. That tenderness made his current betrayal all the more brutal.

"Kirill." She looked at me, lips trembling. "My child, you're what I'll miss most. Promise me—after I'm gone, you'll take care of yourself."

"Don't say that, Mother." My voice cracked as I pressed her hand to my cheek. "You're just sick. When you get better—you will get better."

That's when we heard the car engine downstairs. Every nerve in my body went rigid.

A woman's sultry laugh drifted up to us. I watched my mother's dim eyes fill with pain, despair, and fury.

Two sets of footsteps climbed the stairs. I stood, blocking my mother's bed.

The bedroom door swung open.

My father—the man I'd once feared and now hated—walked in with a young, beautiful woman behind him. She wore a tight black dress, her aggressive perfume instantly polluting the entire room.

"What the hell are you doing here?" My voice was dangerous as I shouted at my bastard father. "Get out."

"Kirill, this is my house. I don't need your permission to come home."

"Your house?" I let out a cold laugh, stepping closer. "The woman of this house is lying right there, and you bring your whore home? What the fuck is wrong with you?"

"She's too fragile, Kirill." His voice was steady, emotionless. "In this world, fragility is a sin. Love? It's like milk—it always expires. It was beautiful once, but now it's spoiled, rotten. Time to throw it out. You understand?"

"So you just betray her without a second thought?" My fists clenched.

He didn't answer. His gaze moved past me to my mother. "You've made my son as weak as you are."

I heard my mother's violent coughing fit. I spun around, helping her sit up, trying to ease her breathing.

Her coughing gradually subsided, but tears streamed down her face. Her lips trembled like she wanted to say something.

Father didn't wait. He turned and left with that woman, like nothing had happened. I heard him telling her he'd take her to some hotel, making her giggle.

Mother's eyes stayed fixed on the doorway. Suddenly, she doubled over in the most gut-wrenching cough I'd ever heard. I rubbed her back, but nothing helped. She was coughing like her lungs would tear apart, getting worse and worse. Then I saw blood gush from her mouth, staining her chin.

Those eyes that had once looked at me with such tenderness lost their light forever in that moment of absolute pain and despair.

That scene played like an eternal curse, over and over in my mind. The blood on Mother's lips, Father's cold face, that woman's smug smile—they trapped me inside.

From that day on, I stopped believing in anything. Especially that damned thing called love.

I thought I'd stay that way forever, until Celia appeared.

This woman—she was like light breaking into the fortress I'd spent years building.

She was fragile yet resilient. Like wild grass growing on a cliff face, battered by wind and rain but never bowing her head. She wanted nothing from me—hell, she tried everything to get away from me. But the more she resisted, the more helplessly I was drawn to her. She made my dead heart feel pain for the first time, then longing.

I needed her. That thought spread like wildfire through my chaotic consciousness.

I needed to see Celia.

The darkness began to retreat. Those painful, cyclical memory fragments were washed away by this overwhelming need.

I started fighting, like a drowning man desperate to surface.

That's when I heard a voice. It cut through layers of darkness like a warm thread, wrapping around my falling soul.

Celia.

"Kirill, can you hear me? Your son is calling you. Lucas is calling you daddy. You can't keep sleeping."

Her voice was gentle but firm, guiding me toward the light filtering down through the depths.

She took me through memories of our Chicago trip—the first time I'd opened my heart to her, clumsily trying to comfort her with my own experiences. The first time I truly understood my feelings and confessed them.

Her voice flowed like a fairy tale.

She talked about our trip to the amusement park—the first time since Mother's death that I'd felt the warmth of family.

"I love you, Kirill." Her voice started breaking. "Lucas and I both need you. What would we do without you?"

Every word hit my nerves. She was scared—scared of losing me. I needed to wake up right now. I wanted to hold her.

"Please, just wake up, okay?"

Her crying pierced every corner of my consciousness. I could feel her pain, her despair. I wanted to respond, tell her I was here, wipe away her tears.

But my body felt like it was filled with lead. I fought with everything I had, but I couldn't even move a finger.

Then I heard another voice. Young, crying, childlike.

"Daddy, wake up! Mommy's been crying for two days. You promised you'd teach me to race cars. You can't break your promise..."

Daddy. Lucas was calling me daddy.

I had to go back. I used every ounce of strength I had, swimming toward that light where their voices waited.

My eyelids felt like they weighed a thousand pounds. I forced them open just a crack.

Blurry light stabbed in. I saw two fuzzy figures—Celia and Lucas. Celia was collapsed over my bed, shoulders shaking with sobs. Lucas sat beside her, wiping his own tears.

I tried to speak, but only a hoarse whisper came from my throat.

But Celia heard it. Her head snapped up, her tear-stained face instantly transformed by disbelieving joy.

"Kirill, you're awake? Oh God! You're really awake!"

She called frantically for the doctor.

I focused all my strength on her face. I tried to lift my hand to touch her, but my arm was too weak to obey.

She immediately grabbed my hand, pressing it against her warm cheek.

"I'm here. I'm here."

I looked at her, forcing words from my dry throat.

"I... love you."

Then I turned to the little boy beside her, too shocked to keep crying.

"...love Lucas too."

A few days later, in the hospital room.

I could sit up against the pillows now. My chest still ached, but having control of my body again felt incredible.

Celia was peeling an apple for me, working carefully to keep the peel in one long strip. Lucas sat on the carpet beside the bed, absorbed in his blocks.

Sunlight filtered through the blinds, casting warm patches around the room. Everything was quiet and perfect—so perfect it felt like an impossible dream.

The door burst open.

"I knew you were too stubborn to die!"

Viktor strode in carrying flowers.

I tried to grin, but the movement pulled at my chest wound. I winced. "Hell's management team said they weren't ready for me yet. Told me to wait a few more years."

"Seriously, those two days you were out, I almost dug Theodore's corpse up just to beat the shit out of it."

I looked at his earnest face and couldn't help laughing.

"Better than watching you lie there like a vegetable." He made a face. "But I knew you were too tough to die."

Celia cut the peeled apple into pieces, spearing one with a toothpick and holding it to my lips. I opened my mouth, tasting the sweet juice.

Viktor watched us, waggling his eyebrows. "Look at our great boss. Love really is a terrifying thing."

"When you find a woman willing to cut apples for you, then we'll discuss it." I shot back without mercy.

He rolled his eyes but didn't dare say more, turning his attention to Lucas instead.

"Hey, little guy, come here."

Viktor crouched down and pulled a sleek toy racecar from his pocket. "Check out what I got you, buddy. This is a limited edition—way cooler than your dad's real car."

Lucas's eyes lit up, and he ran over, grabbing the toy with a loud, "Thanks, Viktor!"

"Such a polite little gentleman, just like me," Viktor said, ruffling Lucas's hair before standing up and turning to me. "When you get out of the hospital, we have to celebrate big time. Surviving that close call? We have to let whoever up there know we're still kicking."

I nodded.

* * *

To celebrate my recovery and sweep away all the shadows, Celia and her friend Mia organized a pool party at the manor.

The late summer sun was still warm but had lost its scorching edge, becoming gentle and pleasant. The pool water sparkled, the grill gave off tempting aromas, and our friends' laughter was like background music.

I wore loose shorts, shirtless. My wound had healed enough for water contact, but I didn't swim. I just lay on a lounge chair under the umbrella, savoring this hard-won peace.

Lucas wore a little duck float, wielding an oversized blue water gun like a happy dolphin, "pew-pew-pewing" and splashing water everywhere.

Viktor, that damn warmonger, clearly found this peaceful game too boring. He waved Lucas over.

"Hey, little guy, come here!" He crouched by the pool edge, dead serious. "That's not how you use a water gun. Come on, I will teach you to be a top sniper. First, you need to learn three-point alignment—target, sight, and your eye..."

Mia walked past holding a cocktail. Hearing Viktor, she rolled her eyes dramatically. "Please, Viktor, did you even piss on specific trees as a kid after calculating wind speed and trajectory?"

Viktor's face froze instantly.

Celia panicked, running over to cover Lucas's ears, blushing as she scolded Mia. "Mia! There's a child here!"

Too late.

Lucas squirmed free from Celia's hands, looking up with innocent curiosity and asking loudly, "Mommy, what's wrong? Is it because Viktor peeing like a doggy on trees is a secret kids can't hear?"

Mia spit out her cocktail and burst into laughter. "Oh my God! Lucas, brilliant! You're a genius!"

Viktor's face went from frozen to purple—a masterpiece of expression.

I couldn't help laughing either. Looking at embarrassed Viktor, I decided to twist the knife.

"Lucas, that's not the only weird thing Viktor's done." I spoke slowly, drawing everyone's attention. "When he first came to America and couldn't speak English, there was this one time he—"

Before I could finish, a black shadow lunged at me.

"Kirill Zaitsev, shut the fuck up!"

Viktor locked me in a standard chokehold. I laughed and fought back. Clearly mindful of my injury, he didn't use full force, and I enjoyed this brotherly roughhousing. Finally, amid shouts, I dragged him down with me, and we both tumbled into the cool pool.

"Yeah! Water fight!" Lucas yelled excitedly, charging at us with his water gun like a little cannonball, jumping in to join the battle.

On shore, the two women stood side by side, watching us with exasperated amusement.

I retreated from the "battlefield," swimming to the edge and letting Viktor face Lucas one-on-one.

Then I focused on Celia on shore. Her expression was peaceful and relaxed—exactly how I wanted to keep her.

"Honestly, Celia," Mia sipped her cocktail thoughtfully, "sometimes I think this life is pretty damn good."

"Yeah." Celia's face glowed with pure happiness.

"Though," Mia continued, pointing her chin at Viktor, who was shouting for them to "get in," "there's always one or two weirdos in every friend group."

She flipped Viktor off with perfect form.

Celia doubled over laughing.

I watched it all—Celia chatting happily with Mia, Lucas playing joyfully with Viktor.

My heart felt completely full. So this was what being alive felt like.

Damn good.

CHAPTER TWENTY-EIGHT

Celia

KIRILL FINALLY WOKE UP, and his wound was healing well. Soon he'd be able to get it wet, leaving only an irregular raised scar.

So he suggested taking Lucas and me to Iceland. Honestly, I was thrilled—this would be Lucas's and my first international trip.

When our private jet landed at Keflavik Airport, the cabin door opened and a blast of frigid air rushed in.

I held Lucas's hand while Kirill carried our luggage down the stairs. Looking around, it felt like standing at the edge of the world. The sky stretched endlessly above us—that high, crystalline blue like a massive sapphire. No skyscrapers, no traffic, just infinite horizon and profound silence.

My heart somehow found peace the moment I stepped onto this land.

"Cold?" Kirill came to my side, wrapping his cashmere coat around both Lucas and me.

I shook my head, pressing my cheek against his solid chest. "Not cold. This place is beautiful."

Our hotel nestled in the open wilderness not far from Reykjavik—individual modern cabins scattered across the snow like black gems. Our room overlooked a frozen lake with snow-capped mountains stretching toward the horizon.

Lucas burst through the door and rushed to the enormous floor-to-ceiling window, pressing his little face against the glass. "Mommy! Look! There's ice outside! Can we go skating?"

"Of course, little guy." Kirill ruffled his hair. "But first, we have something even more special to do."

"What?" Lucas looked up with wide, curious eyes.

Kirill winked at me. "We're going to see the Aurora Borealis."

After nightfall, we bundled into our heaviest winter gear and climbed into a modified super jeep. Our driver was an experienced local guide who took us deep into the inland wilderness.

Outside stretched pure darkness—no streetlights, no buildings, just the small patch of rough terrain illuminated by our headlights. Lucas started out excited but soon fell asleep in my arms, lulled by the steady rocking.

I held him close, resting my head against Kirill's shoulder.

"Have you seen the northern lights before?" I whispered.

"Once." His voice sounded especially deep in the darkness. "In Murmansk, on business. Back then, I thought it was just another astronomical phenomenon. Spectacular, but meaningless."

"And now?" I asked.

He was quiet for a moment, then tightened his arm around my shoulders. "Now I hope it means something."

The guide stopped in an open valley, explaining this was tonight's optimal viewing location. All we had to do was wait.

We stepped out into air so cold it stole our breath.

Above us stretched a vast black canvas studded with countless brilliant stars—the most magnificent night sky I'd ever witnessed.

Lucas stirred awake from the cold but remained excited, pointing at the Milky Way from Kirill's arms. "Wow, Mommy, look! There are so many stars I can't count them all!"

We waited. Time crawled by in the extreme cold and absolute silence. I began to wonder if we'd see any aurora tonight at all.

Just as doubt crept in, Lucas suddenly gasped.

"Look! Over there!"

I followed his pointing finger. On the distant horizon, a faint green glow appeared, almost tentatively.

Then that emerald light began to expand rapidly, spreading across the sky. It transformed from a thin line to flowing silk to a massive river of light dancing overhead.

My breath caught. My entire being was captivated by those shifting, ethereal ribbons. They moved with elegant grace one moment, then rolled with wild abandon the next. Green gave way to purple and pink, the colors weaving together in an otherworldly tapestry.

Beneath this magnificent, humbling spectacle, human language felt utterly inadequate. I could only stare in speechless wonder.

"Mommy, it really is dancing..." Lucas breathed beside me.

Just as I became completely lost in the breathtaking display, I felt Kirill gently touch my arm.

I turned around and froze completely.

Kirill—that man who bowed to no one—knelt on one knee before me.

In his hands lay an open velvet box containing the most extraordinary ring I'd ever seen.

The centerpiece was a perfectly cut color-change diamond displaying both blue and green, surrounded by brilliant white diamonds in an intricate platinum setting.

The stone's emerald and ice-blue hues perfectly mirrored our eye colors—mysterious and beautiful.

Under the aurora's ethereal glow, the ring sparkled more brilliantly than any constellation above.

My heart stopped completely.

"Celia," Kirill's voice carried an almost reverent tenderness touched with barely concealed nervousness. "I spent the first half of my life living in my father's shadow. I believed love was an illusion—until I met you."

He looked up, those deep eyes reflecting both my face and the dancing lights overhead.

"You and Lucas came into my life like an accident—the most beautiful accident I could have imagined. You taught me what it means for a heart to beat wildly for someone else. You showed me that home isn't a place—it's wherever you two are."

"I made so many mistakes. I started everything wrong because I didn't understand my own feelings yet. Thank you for forgiving me, for choosing to stay."

"I promise you here," every word rang with absolute clarity and conviction, "from this moment forward, my life, my loyalty, everything I am belongs only to you and Lucas. I will protect you both with everything I have until my last breath."

"So, Celia Cole." He drew a deep breath and asked the question that would change everything. "Will you marry me? Will you be my wife and let me spend the rest of my life loving you?"

The world fell silent around us. I could see nothing but the overwhelming love shining in his eyes.

The moment was so perfect I couldn't find words—I could only nod frantically, tears streaming down my face.

"Mommy! Say yes!" Lucas was more anxious than I was, tugging at my sleeve. "Let Daddy put the ring on you!"

His excitement broke through my speechless wonder.

"Yes." The words finally escaped my throat, filled with absolute certainty. "Yes, I'll marry you, Kirill."

His smile transformed his entire face—radiant and unguarded. He carefully lifted the ring from its velvet nest, took my trembling hand, and slowly slid the precious band onto my ring finger.

It fit perfectly, as if crafted specifically for me.

He rose and swept me into his arms. Under the dancing aurora, with our son cheering beside us, we shared a kiss that felt like sealing our souls together.

"Yay! Mommy and Daddy are getting married!" Lucas clapped with pure joy, like a little angel witnessing magic.

In that moment, I knew I was the luckiest woman alive.

We returned to the hotel near midnight.

Lucas had exhausted himself completely and slept soundly during the drive back. Kirill carried him like precious cargo, gently settling him in his own room. He carefully removed Lucas's heavy winter gear, tucked him under warm blankets, and pressed a tender goodnight kiss to his forehead.

Then we retreated to our master bedroom.

A fireplace crackled warmly, casting dancing orange light throughout the room. I shed my heavy parka, wearing only a fitted cashmere sweater, and settled on the plush rug before the fire, admiring the ring that now adorned my finger.

It was breathtaking—seeming to capture both lake and starlight in its faceted depths.

Kirill emerged from his shower wearing only a towel around his waist, steam still rising from his skin. The raised scar on his powerful chest served as a silent testament to everything he'd sacrificed for me.

He settled behind me, enveloping me completely in his arms. He lifted my hand with the ring, lowering his head to press warm kisses against the band, then my fingers, then the back of my hand.

"Do you like it?" His voice carried that post-shower huskiness that made my pulse quicken.

"I love it." I melted completely into his embrace. "Thank you, Kirill."

"I should be thanking you." He buried his face in the curve of my neck, his heated breath ghosting across my skin. "Thank you for saying yes."

I turned in his arms, framing his sculpted face with my hands and meeting his intense gaze. "I love you, Kirill."

"I love you too, Celia."

His kiss consumed me completely, so deep and thorough it seemed to reach my very soul, leaving me aching and ready for him.

His hands found the hem of my sweater, fingers tracing the smooth skin of my back. His calloused palms left trails of fire everywhere they touched.

"The bed," I whispered breathlessly when we broke apart.

Kirill swept me up effortlessly and carried me into the bedroom.

He laid me gently on the bed and moved to kiss me again. I pressed my finger softly against his lips.

"I want to taste you."

Something dark and hungry flashed in Kirill's eyes. He leaned back against the headboard, his gaze giving me silent permission.

I positioned myself between his legs.

My lips lingered on the jagged scar across Kirill's chest, the rough texture of the healed bullet wound a stark reminder of the night he'd thrown himself in front of me, taking the hit meant for my heart. My fingers traced the edges, trembling with a mix of reverence and sorrow. He'd bled for me, suffered for me, and the weight of that sacrifice pressed against my chest, heavy and aching. I kissed the scar again, slower this time, my tongue brushing over the raised skin, tasting the faint salt of him. My heart clenched, love and guilt warring within me as I pressed my lips harder against the mark, as if I could kiss away the pain he'd endured.

Kirill's breath hitched, a low, restrained sound rumbling from his chest. His hands, resting on the sheets, twitched, fingers curling into the fabric as if anchoring himself. His jaw tightened, the muscles in his neck straining as he watched me with those dark, molten eyes, their intensity burning through me. He was holding back, I could tell—his body taut, every muscle coiled with the effort to stay still, to let me worship him in this moment. The hunger in his gaze was almost too much, a storm of desire and restraint that made my skin prickle with heat.

I paused, my lips hovering over the scar, and looked up at him. "Does it still hurt?" I whispered, my voice barely audible, thick with emotion.

Kirill's eyes softened, though the fire in them didn't dim. "No, moya lyubov," he murmured, his voice rough and low. "It doesn't hurt anymore." He reached out, his fingers brushing my chin, tilting my face up to meet his gaze. His touch was firm but gentle, grounding me. "This was my choice. Don't carry guilt for it."

My throat tightened, and I shook my head, tears threatening to spill. "It's not guilt," I said, my voice trembling. "It's... I hate that you were hurt because of me. I know you love me, Kirill, but I can't stand the thought of you in pain." I leaned down, pressing one last, tender kiss to the scar, my lips lingering as if I could pour all my love into that single touch.

His hand slid into my hair, fingers threading gently through the strands as he exhaled, a sound that was half sigh, half groan. "You're mine," he said, his voice a low growl, laced with possessive adoration. "And I'd do it again, a thousand times, to keep you safe."

I smiled, my heart swelling, and let my lips begin their descent, trailing soft, open-mouthed kisses down the hard planes of his chest. His skin was warm, taut over muscle, and I savored the way his breath quickened as I moved lower, my tongue flicking out to taste the ridges of his abdomen. Each defined muscle tensed under my touch, and I could feel the heat radiating from him, the raw power of his body barely contained.

When I reached the edge of the bath towel draped around his hips, I paused, my eyes flicking up to meet his. The fabric was tented, his arousal unmistakable, straining against the soft cotton. My pulse raced, a delicious heat pooling low in my belly. I hooked my fingers under the towel's edge, tugging it free with a slow, deliberate pull. The towel fell away, revealing him—hard, thick, and pulsing with need. My breath caught at the sight, desire flooding through me.

I leaned forward, my lips brushing the sensitive skin just above his length, teasing him with featherlight kisses. Kirill groaned, a deep, primal sound that sent a shiver down my spine. His hand tightened in my hair, not guiding, just holding, his fingers trembling with the effort to stay in control. I took him into my mouth, slow at first, savoring the taste of him, the heat, the way he filled me. My tongue swirled around the tip, then slid down his shaft, drawing a ragged moan from his throat.

"Fuck, Celia," he growled, his voice raw, almost desperate. His hips twitched, but he held himself still, letting me set the pace. I moved faster, my lips and tongue working in tandem, drawing out every shudder, every low, guttural sound he tried to suppress. His fingers tightened in my hair, his grip firm but not forceful, guiding me just enough to let me know how much he wanted this. His breaths came in sharp, uneven gasps, and I could feel the tension building in him, his control fraying at the edges.

Just as I felt him throb against my tongue, his hand tugged gently, pulling me back. "Celia," he rasped, his voice strained. "I'm close." Before I could protest, he withdrew, his length glistening as he gripped himself. With a low, guttural groan, he came, hot and thick, spilling across my face. The warmth of it shocked me, but the sight of me—messy, marked by him—seemed to ignite something feral in his eyes. I looked up at him, my cheeks flushed, my lips parted, and the way he stared at me, like I was the most beautiful, depraved thing he'd ever seen, made my core ache with want.

Kirill reached for the towel, his hands surprisingly gentle as he wiped my face clean, his touch reverent despite the raw hunger still burning in his gaze. "You're so fucking perfect," he murmured, his voice dripping with filthy adoration. "My wife. My Zaitsev."

I shivered at his words, my body humming with need. He tugged at the hem of my sweater, pulling it over my head in one swift motion, his hands already working at the button of my jeans. "Look at you," he growled, his voice thick with lust as he stripped me bare, peeling away my bra, my panties, until I was completely exposed to him. "All mine. Every inch of you."

He pushed me back onto the bed, his body looming over mine, all hard lines and coiled strength. His lips found my throat, kissing and nipping as he worked his way down, his hands roaming my curves with possessive hunger. When his mouth closed over my breast, his tongue flicking against my nipple, I arched into him, a soft moan escaping my lips. He didn't linger, though—his kisses trailed lower, over my stomach, until he settled between my thighs.

His breath was hot against my core, and when his tongue finally touched me, a slow, deliberate lick, I gasped, my hands fisting the sheets. He devoured me, his tongue relentless, teasing and circling until I was trembling, my hips bucking against his mouth. He groaned against me, the vibration sending a jolt of pleasure through my body, pushing me closer to the edge. Just as I felt the wave about to crash, he pulled back, leaving me panting, desperate.

"Kirill," I whimpered, my voice pleading.

He rose above me, his eyes dark with triumph and desire. "You're mine, Celia," he said, his voice a low, possessive growl. "My wife. Say it."

"I'm yours," I gasped, my body aching for him. "I'm your wife. Zaitsev's."

He positioned himself at my entrance, his length hot and hard against me. With one slow, deliberate thrust, he filled me, stretching me until I moaned, my nails digging into his shoulders. He moved with purpose, each thrust deep and measured, his eyes locked on mine, claiming me in every way. "You're mine," he said again, his voice rough with emotion. "Forever."

I met his thrusts, my hips rocking against him, our bodies moving in perfect sync. The pleasure built, intense and overwhelming, until I was trembling, my breaths coming in sharp, desperate gasps. Kirill's rhythm faltered, his groans growing louder, more primal, as he neared his own release. "Celia," he growled, his voice breaking as he thrust one final time, spilling inside me, his body shuddering against mine.

We collapsed together, breathless and spent, his arms wrapping around me as he pulled me close. "My wife," he murmured against my skin, his voice soft now, reverent. "My everything."

I nestled against him, my heart full, my body still humming with the aftershocks of our love. "Yours," I whispered, and I meant it with every piece of my soul.

CHAPTER TWENTY-NINE

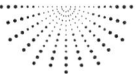

Kirill

Our wedding was held at a castle I owned.

The castle had stood for over five hundred years, its domed ceiling adorned with exquisite murals. Sunlight streamed through massive stained glass windows on either side, casting jewel-toned patches across the ancient stone floors.

Today, thousands of white roses flown in from Holland decorated every surface. They wound around the old stone pillars and covered the windowsills, transforming this heavy fortress into a secret garden that existed only in fairy tales.

I stood before the massive floor-to-ceiling windows in the study, wearing a perfectly tailored black tuxedo. The handmade suit fit flawlessly, its fabric expensive enough to buy several luxury cars. But right now, I felt like the damn thing was suffocating me.

Celia was still in another room getting her makeup done.

My heart hammered against my ribs. I was more nervous about this wedding than any gang shootout I'd ever been in.

"Fuck, I can't believe this."

Viktor sat on the couch nursing a whiskey, studying me like I was some rare specimen.

"Seriously, if your legs give out, I can have Dmitri carry you to the altar." He took another sip.

I ignored his bullshit and tugged at the goddamn bow tie. "Shut up, Viktor."

"Just stating facts." He shrugged innocently. "Look at you—wound tighter than when I first met your old man. I'm afraid when the priest asks if you take her, you'll panic and blow his brains out by reflex."

His crude words somehow loosened the wire-tight tension in my nerves, just a fraction.

I turned around, poured myself a whiskey, and knocked it back in one gulp.

"I can't believe this is real." My voice came out rougher than I'd expected.

Viktor's expression grew complicated. He knew better than anyone what I'd been through. He'd seen my pain when we buried my mother. He'd watched me seek thrills to numb myself.

"It's real, man." He stood up, walked over, and clapped my shoulder hard. "You're about to marry the woman you love most. Congratulations."

Yeah, it was real.

I wasn't alone anymore.

The ceremony was set in the garden behind the castle.

Ancient olive trees stood twisted and gnarled like silent guardians. White roses had been woven into an archway leading to happiness. The guests were already seated—their clothing and bearing spoke of extraordinary status.

Wall Street financial titans, reclusive European nobility, and of course, core members of our family.

I stood at one side of the altar with Viktor as my best man. The priest was an elderly man with white hair and beard. They said marriages blessed by him always ended in perfect happiness.

My eyes locked on the end of the red carpet. The elegant string quartet began to play, music flowing like water.

A small figure ran out from under the archway.

Lucas.

He wore a black tuxedo matching mine, his little face flushed red with nerves and excitement. He was our flower boy, carrying a small basket filled with white rose petals. He looked like a little prince from a fairy tale. Pride swelled in my chest.

I watched Lucas take a deep breath, then start down the red carpet on his short legs with solemn dignity. Every few steps, he grabbed a handful of petals from his basket and threw them high into the air.

The dew-kissed white petals fell like gentle snow, turning the red carpet into a flower path.

He scattered them with complete seriousness, his little brow slightly furrowed as if performing the most sacred duty. The guests' faces showed warm smiles.

When he reached me and threw the last handful of petals in my direction, I crouched down and pulled him into a tight hug.

"You did great, my little man."

"Of course, Dad." He puffed out his little chest proudly. "I made a flower path for Mom! Now you should welcome your bride!"

He ran to the front row of guests and sat obediently next to Dmitri.

The music's rhythm became more solemn.

Everyone's eyes turned with mine toward the end of that red carpet covered in white rose petals.

I saw Celia appear at the far end. Mia stood beside her saying something—I was too far away to hear their conversation, but I could see Mia dramatically pretending to wipe away tears before giving Celia a big hug.

"I bet that woman's saying some crap about how Celia will forget her bestie now that she has a husband," Viktor murmured beside me in his know-it-all tone.

I didn't respond. My entire vision was completely consumed by Celia's figure.

Her hair was swept up, the ethereal veil flowing behind her. The strapless wedding dress, encrusted with tiny diamonds, fit her body perfectly, outlining her slender neck, graceful shoulders, and tiny waist. Even the sunlight seemed generous, bathing her in a warm, sacred golden glow.

After Mia arranged Celia's train, she stepped aside.

Celia held a bouquet of white lily of the valley and walked slowly toward me along the flower path Lucas had created, the solemn background music accompanying her approach.

Jesus Christ, I thought I'd seen her every way possible.

I was wrong. Today, she was so beautiful that even breathing felt like sacrilege.

She walked through sunlight, through flower fragrance, through all the guests' blessed gazes, and through all the darkness and loneliness of my first half of life.

Finally she reached me and placed her hand—covered in a white lace glove—into my outstretched, slightly trembling one.

My heart finally settled like it had found home.

"Kirill Zaitsev, do you take this woman, Celia Cole, to be your wife? To love her, honor her, and protect her, in riches and in poverty, in sickness and in health, until death do you part?"

The priest's solemn voice reached my ears.

I looked into Celia's eyes and answered with the most resolute, clearest voice of my entire life.

"I do."

"Celia Cole, do you take this man, Kirill Zaitsev, to be your husband? To love him, honor him, and protect him, in riches and in poverty, in sickness and in health, until death do you part?"

"I do." Celia's eyes sparkled with joy as she answered firmly.

We exchanged rings. We gave each other our hearts.

"Now, groom, you may kiss your bride."

I gently lifted Celia's veil, revealing her breathtakingly beautiful face.

I leaned down and kissed her.

Cheers and applause from the guests washed over us.

When I pulled back, I pressed my forehead against hers, gazing into those green eyes that shimmered from our kiss, and whispered in her ear—words only we could hear.

"Mrs. Zaitsev, I think Lucas might get lonely by himself. Should we consider giving him a little brother or sister to play with tonight?"

Her cheeks flushed bright red the instant my words finished. She looked both shy and indignant as she lightly tapped my chest.

"Kirill!"

I couldn't help but chuckle softly at her adorable bashfulness.

She was my wife, the love who would be with me forever.

CHAPTER THIRTY

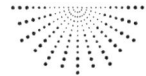

Celia

WEEKEND SUNLIGHT STREAMED through the massive floor-to-ceiling window of our bedroom, flooding the entire room with lazy, golden warmth.

I lay on my side, covered only by a thin silk sheet, quietly watching the sleeping man beside me. My husband. Even three months after our wedding, thinking that word still made my heart feel like it was soaked in warm water—soft and full.

Sunlight traced the peaceful lines of Kirill's sleeping face. Stripped of his usual coldness and authority, he looked like a handsome, harmless Greek sculpture. His breathing was steady and deep, one arm draped across my waist out of habit, as if even in the deepest sleep, he needed to keep me locked in his world.

My hand moved past Kirill's arm to rest on my flat stomach. There, new life was growing.

A gentle smile spread across my face unbidden. Three days ago, when our family doctor at the manor announced the news with pure joy in his voice, I saw the expression on Kirill's face—shock, wild happiness, and complete bewilderment all at once.

This man who controlled the massive dark empire, who could make the entire East Coast underworld tremble, stood frozen like a child receiving his first award when he heard he was going to be a father again. Then he pulled me into his arms. I heard him whispering thanks in my ear, over and over.

"Good morning."

Kirill's husky voice pulled me from my thoughts. I met his deep eyes, now filled with tenderness that wouldn't dissolve.

"Good morning, daddy of baby number two." I smiled. "Ready or not?"

His hand moved from my waist to my stomach. The warmth of his palm seeped through the thin silk sheet to my skin. He was feeling for that tiny life still taking shape.

"Hmm." He hummed low, then leaned down to kiss the corner of my lips. "Thank you, Mrs. Zaitsev."

"Not hard at all." I shook my head, savoring this tenderness. "Though we might have a new problem."

"What problem?" He raised an eyebrow, that scarred brow still giving him dangerous appeal.

"Lucas." I laughed helplessly. "Ever since he found out I'm pregnant, he's pulled out every single book about being a good big brother, and he spends all day agonizing over whether to buy blue dinosaurs for his brother or pink unicorns for his sister. I'm afraid he's too excited to sleep."

Kirill chuckled low, the sound deep and pleasant, vibrating through my chest. "Lucas will be an amazing big brother."

After lunch, feeling restless, I invited Mia over to the manor and had Kirill call Viktor too.

So there we were, four people around the patio couch, locked in what could only be called a catastrophic party game.

"No, no, no! You idiot!" If anger had flames, Mia's hair would be on fire. She pointed at her game partner—Viktor—and let out a roar. "You should've played the red seven! Not that damn yellow Plus Two!

Didn't you see Kirill only has one card left? You're helping him beat me!"

Viktor, the elite sniper who could hit targets two kilometers away on a battlefield, now stared blankly at the colorful UNO cards in his hands, brow furrowed like he was studying some incredibly complex battle plan.

"Rules don't say I can't play yellow," he shot back in that signature tone that could give people heart attacks. "And playing yellow is my strategy."

"This is UNO, not your combat manual!" Mia let out a desperate groan. "Can you see your strategy working?"

"Next round. We'll win next round," Viktor said flatly, then delivered the killing blow. "I'm still gathering intelligence."

"Well, right now we can't avoid getting turned into painted cats." Mia threw up her hands in defeat.

I leaned against Kirill, already laughing until my stomach hurt. Watching Viktor's seriously confused face, then Mia's face alive with exasperation—this was better than any comedy movie.

Kirill chuckled low too. He held me close, watching his mentally tortured best friend with pure entertainment.

Then he slowly drew a card from his hand and placed it on the table.

A yellow Plus Four wild card.

"UNO." He announced the end with calm finality, completely crushing Mia's last hope.

"Yeah! Mommy and Daddy won!"

Lucas, our game's only referee, immediately jumped up from his judge's chair, clutching a box of washable markers, running on his little legs toward Viktor and Mia.

"Viktor, Mia, you lost! Now I get to draw! Don't move!"

"Lucas, baby, since I'm always so good to you, make me look pretty," Mia's pleading voice echoed for the next few minutes.

Finally, under Lucas's artistic vision, Mia's face sported rainbow-colored cat whiskers and cute lettering that read "I love Mia." Viktor's left cheek got decorated with a giant pink butterfly.

Viktor stared at us with that butterfly on his face, completely stone-faced, his eyes full of "just you wait" threats. Meanwhile, Mia grabbed one of Lucas's markers and told Viktor, "Don't move, this side of your face is too empty. I'll add a bee for symmetry."

That scene was so ridiculous it made me laugh until tears streamed down my face.

Months later, Valentine's Day.

New York's winter night cut like ice. But our bedroom was warm as spring.

Lucas was already fast asleep in his own room. And I was in the bathroom, heart racing through my "pre-battle preparations."

I looked at myself in the mirror. My stomach already showed a gentle curve. I slipped off my robe and put on the "battle gear" I'd been secretly preparing for weeks.

Wine-red lingerie, lace and silk combined. Barely any fabric, just covering the most essential parts. Thin straps traced my collarbones, the deep V front pushed my pregnancy-enhanced breasts into a dramatic valley. Below, semi-transparent thong panties.

I took a deep breath and opened the bathroom door.

Kirill was half-lying in bed with a book, wearing only loose sleep pants. Hearing the sound, he looked up. The moment his eyes landed on me, I clearly saw flames ignite that could burn me alive.

Though what I was wearing was more revealing than being naked.

His book hit the carpet with a soft thud.

"Jesus, Celia..." His voice came out rough and breathless.

I felt nervous but more excited. I walked toward him step by step.

"Happy Valentine's Day, my husband." I knelt on the bed, whispering against his ear.

He didn't answer. I could see he was already straining hard against his pants.

This time, I was taking control. I pushed against his solid chest, making him lie flat. Then I straddled his waist.

His hardness pressed against me through the thin fabric.

I leaned down and started kissing him. From his lips to his sharp jawline, then to his Adam's apple bobbing with excitement.

Then I untied his pajama pants.

He sprang free instantly, already glistening at the tip.

My cheeks burned hot, but I didn't back down.

Pregnancy had made my body crave Kirill even more—I was ready almost the moment I saw him.

I guided him as I slipped off my thong with one hand, then lifted my hips and took him inside.

This position went so deep I cried out immediately.

I straddled Kirill, my thighs gripping his hips as I settled into the rhythm that set my nerves ablaze. His cock filled me, stretching me in ways that made my breath hitch, each slow rise and fall driving me wilder. Pregnancy had turned my body into a live wire, every sensation amplified, every touch a spark. I leaned forward slightly, my hands braced on his chiseled chest, feeling the heat of his skin under my palms. My hips rolled, deliberate and teasing, drawing out every inch of him before sinking back down, taking him deeper each time. The friction was exquisite, a delicious burn that made my toes curl.

"Fuck, Kirill," I gasped, my voice thick with need. "You feel so damn good."

His dark eyes locked onto mine, smoldering with hunger, but he stayed still beneath me, letting me take control. His hands rested on my thighs, fingers digging into my skin just enough to let me know he was fighting to keep himself in check. "You're killing me, baby," he growled, his voice low and rough. "Keep moving like that, and I'm not gonna last."

I smirked, loving the power I held over him. "Oh, you'll last," I teased, slowing my pace just to torment him, circling my hips in a way that made him groan. "I'm not done with you yet." My body was alive, every nerve singing as I rode him, my breasts heavy and sensitive, bouncing slightly with each movement. The heat between us was suffocating, the air thick with the scent of sweat and sex.

I quickened my pace, my thighs burning as I lifted and sank, the wet slide of him inside me sending jolts of pleasure through my core. Kirill's jaw clenched, his breath coming in short, ragged bursts. "Goddamn, woman," he rasped, his hands sliding up to grip my hips harder. "You're so fucking tight. I love you so much."

"I love you too," I whispered, my voice breaking as a wave of pleasure hit me. I leaned down, my lips brushing his ear. "You're mine, Kirill. Every inch of you." My words seemed to unravel him, his control fraying at the edges. I felt it—the subtle shift in his hips, a quiet thrust upward that caught me off guard. I gasped, my rhythm faltering as he pushed deeper, hitting a spot that made stars burst behind my eyes.

"Kirill," I moaned, trying to regain control, but he did it again, a slow, deliberate thrust that nearly unseated me. My hands slipped on his chest, my nails digging into his skin as I fought to stay steady. "You're supposed to let me lead," I panted, but the smirk on his face told me he was done playing by my rules.

"Can't help it," he growled, his voice dripping with need. "You're driving me fucking crazy." His hips bucked again, harder this time, and I cried out, my body trembling as he hit that perfect spot over and over. I tried to keep my rhythm, but his movements were relentless, each thrust making it harder to stay in control. My thighs shook, my core clenching around him as the pleasure built, sharp and overwhelming.

"Fuck, Kirill, you're gonna make me come," I gasped, my voice raw. I leaned back, my hands gripping his thighs for balance as I rode him harder, chasing the edge. His hands slid up to my waist, guiding me, urging me faster. "That's it, baby," he murmured, his voice thick with desire. "Come for me. Let me feel you."

I shattered, my orgasm crashing through me like a tidal wave. My body clenched around him, pulsing as I cried out his name, my hips grinding against him as the pleasure consumed me. Kirill groaned, his hands tightening on my waist as he thrust up one last time, deep and hard, before he sat up suddenly, his arms wrapping around me.

He pulled me close, his lips crashing into mine as he took over, his hips snapping up in a relentless rhythm. "I love you," he growled against my mouth, his voice rough with need. "You're so fucking perfect." His thrusts were deep, urgent, each one pushing me higher even as my body still trembled from my release. I clung to him, my nails raking down his back as he drove into me, his cock throbbing inside me.

"Kirill," I whimpered, my voice barely audible as he pushed me toward another edge. "I'm yours. Always." His thrusts grew erratic, his breath hot against my neck as he buried himself deep, his release flooding me with a warmth that made my toes curl. He groaned my name, his arms tightening around me as he came, his body shuddering against mine.

We stayed like that for a moment, panting, our bodies pressed together, slick with sweat. But Kirill wasn't done. His hands moved to the straps of my lacy lingerie, his fingers deft as he tugged it off, the fabric sliding over my sensitive skin. "You don't need this anymore," he murmured, his voice dark and teasing. He tossed it aside, his eyes raking over my naked body, lingering on my breasts. "Fuck, you're gorgeous."

I blushed under his gaze, but the heat in my core was already building again. He guided my hands to my breasts, his eyes locked on mine. "Hold them for me," he said, his voice low and commanding. I did as he asked, cupping my breasts, pressing them together as he positioned himself between them. His cock, still hard and slick, slid against my skin, the sensation sending a shiver through me.

He moved slowly at first, his eyes never leaving mine as he thrust between my breasts. Each stroke was deliberate, the tip of his cock brushing my lips every so often, teasing me. "You like this, don't you?" he murmured, his voice thick with arousal. "You love how I feel against you."

"Yes," I breathed, my lips parting as I leaned forward slightly, letting his cock graze my mouth. The taste of him was intoxicating, salty and warm, and I couldn't resist flicking my tongue against him. He groaned, his hands tangling in my hair as he thrust harder, the friction building between us.

"Fuck, baby," he growled, his voice raw. "You're gonna make me lose it." His movements grew faster, more desperate, and I felt the tension in his body as he neared his release. With one final thrust, he came, his release spilling over my lips, warm and wet. I gasped, my cheeks flushing as I licked my lips, tasting him.

He didn't hesitate, pulling me into a searing kiss, his tongue tangling with mine as he tasted himself on my lips. "I love you," he whispered against my mouth, his voice soft but intense. "You drive me fucking wild."

Before I could catch my breath, he slid down my body, his lips trailing over my skin, leaving a path of fire in their wake. He settled between my thighs, his hands spreading me open as he looked up at me with a wicked grin. "My turn," he murmured, his breath hot against my core.

His tongue flicked out, teasing my clit, and I cried out, my hips bucking against his mouth. He didn't hold back, licking and sucking with a hunger that made my head spin. "You taste so fucking good," he growled, his voice muffled against me as he bit down gently on my clit, sending a shock of pleasure through me.

"Kirill," I moaned, my hands fisting the sheets as he worked me with his tongue, his lips, his teeth. He pushed his tongue inside me, thrusting in and out, mimicking the rhythm we'd had earlier. My body was on fire, every nerve screaming as he drove me closer to the edge. "Don't stop," I begged, my voice desperate. "Please, don't stop."

He didn't, his tongue relentless as he pushed me higher, my thighs trembling around his head. "Come for me, baby," he murmured, his voice vibrating against my core. "I want to feel you come on my tongue." His words sent me over the edge, my orgasm crashing through me with a force that left me breathless, my body shaking as I screamed his name.

But Kirill wasn't done. He crawled back up my body, his lips glistening with my release as he kissed me, letting me taste myself on him. "You're not done yet," he growled, his cock already hard again as he positioned himself between my thighs. "I need you one more time."

I nodded, my body still humming with pleasure as he slid inside me, filling me completely. "I love you," I whispered, my voice raw as he began to move, slow at first, then faster, his thrusts deep and possessive. "You're everything to me."

"I love you too," he groaned, his hands gripping my hips as he drove into me, each thrust pushing me higher. "You're mine, always." His pace quickened, his breath ragged as he chased his release, and I met him thrust for thrust, my body aching for more.

When he released everything inside me, I screamed as I came, too.

We lay quietly embracing, still joined. I curled against his arm, catching my breath.

Outside the window, New York's night remained cold and endless. But in this room, in this man's arms, I had all the warmth and light in the world.

Our family photo and the picture of me with my mother sat together in a frame on the nightstand. I lazily gazed at it through half-closed eyes, completely at peace.

Now I had everything I'd always longed for about happiness.

CHAPTER THIRTY-ONE

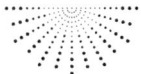

Celia

WEEKEND MORNING'S first rays of sunlight always kissed Sonia's hair first.

Our daughter. Our second child. A five-year-old girl with a tornado living inside her chest. She'd inherited everything from Kirill—that thick brown hair, those beautiful gray-blue eyes, and his strong build.

Right now, this little tornado was chasing a mini soccer ball through our massive dining room in her pajamas. Her footwork was... well, passionate and completely unpredictable.

"Sonia, careful!"

A worried voice called from the dining table—Lucas. Almost eleven now, attending some fancy prep school, becoming impossibly mature. He was elegantly cutting the steak on his plate with proper knife and fork technique. Then he set down his utensils, looked up at his bouncing sister, wearing the expression of a concerned professor.

Sonia ignored him completely. She giggled and kicked with everything she had.

The soccer ball went flying toward the man at the head of the table, who was focused on his tablet.

My heart jumped to my throat.

Kirill didn't even look up. He casually reached out with his left hand, caught that "cannonball" mid-air, then returned his attention to the screen, handling business as usual.

No matter how much chaos Sonia created, he remained unmovable as a mountain.

"Nice catch, Dad!" Sonia cheered, running over to steal the ball back.

Kirill set down his tablet, scooped his daughter into his arms, and rubbed his stubbled chin against her cheek until she shrieked and squirmed away.

"Little rascal," his deep voice was pure indulgence. "No soccer during breakfast."

"But I want to be a soccer player!" Sonia declared, hands on her hips.

"Good," Kirill nodded seriously. "When you can kick through Viktor's car door, I'll buy you a team."

I shook my head helplessly, lifting my coffee. This was our morning—Lucas's maturity, Sonia's energy, and Kirill's unique, mob boss approach to parenting.

I loved every bit of it.

The peace lasted until ten AM. The kids played in the garden while Kirill disappeared into his study.

I sat in the wicker chair on the terrace, watching Sonia charge across the lawn with her ball like a little cheetah, while Lucas sat under a tree with a book thick enough to use as a brick, occasionally looking up to make sure his sister stayed in sight.

He was the best big brother—so steady, so reliable. When Sonia was born, he'd been thrilled, always watching over her like a little adult.

Unlike other boys his age, obsessed with toy guns and cars, Lucas had an almost greedy hunger for knowledge. The family doctor said his IQ was far above average—he could remember almost everything he saw. I hadn't known this before, because around me, Lucas just seemed more well-behaved and thoughtful than his peers.

Suddenly my phone rang. Mia.

"Honey, turn on the TV. Financial news channel." Her voice sounded unusually serious.

My stomach dropped. I did as she said.

On screen, a blonde anchor was speaking in crisp, professional tones, "...the FBI and DEA conducted a joint operation today, raiding a Zaitsev Group cargo warehouse in Brooklyn. The action stemmed from an anonymous tip alleging the group was using its shipping routes for large-scale drug smuggling..."

Ice shot down my spine. Them again.

It had been months since they'd stormed the manor with the same accusations. I thought that mess had ended with Kirill's cleanup.

"...However, after five hours of intensive searching, law enforcement found no contraband. Zaitsev Group's attorneys claim this was malicious commercial defamation and reserve the right to pursue legal action. Group CEO Kirill Zaitsev has not yet commented on the matter."

The screen cut to a candid shot of Kirill leaving the corporate building. He wore a perfectly tailored suit, his face expressionless, eyes ice-cold. Even in a still photo, that overwhelming presence nearly broke through the screen.

I turned off the TV, my palms slick with sweat.

"Mom, what's wrong? You look pale."

Lucas had put down his book and appeared beside me, worried.

"I'm fine, baby." I forced a smile.

"Is it because of the news?" he asked quietly. "Are those people causing trouble for Dad again?"

I stared at him in shock. "Hey, sweetheart, how do you know about this?"

"I saw it," he explained calmly. "Last time they came to the house, I watched their cars from the window. And I know Dad's business is... complicated."

I looked at Lucas with complex emotions.

"Dad will handle it," he patted my hand with the composure of an adult. "Dad has his ways."

I pulled Lucas into a hug, kissing the top of his head. "Mommy knows. I just can't help worrying. Maybe I need to learn from you."

The study door finally opened before lunch. Kirill emerged. His face showed nothing, but the atmosphere around him was suffocatingly tense.

I asked him about the news.

He walked straight to me, cupping my face. "You saw it all?"

I nodded.

"Don't worry." His voice was soft but carried a force that made me believe. "The rats reporting us are just hiding in gutters. Since we married, I haven't touched the drug business. So nothing will happen to me."

He didn't explain more, but I knew another storm was coming.

That afternoon he didn't return to his study. Instead, he stayed with us—with his family. He changed into casual clothes and played soccer with Sonia on the lawn.

He jogged on defense while Sonia used a beautiful fake-out to get past him, kicking the ball into the goal.

"Yeah! I beat Dad!" She jumped with excitement.

Kirill broke into a genuine smile. He walked over, hoisted his sweaty daughter onto his shoulders, letting her survey her domain like a victorious queen.

Lucas sat nearby, closing his book with a faint smile.

Watching this scene, the fear and anxiety in my heart slowly dissolved.

This was him.

He could issue orders in Russian that would destroy entire families, then in the next second, pretend to lose to his daughter just to make her happy. He was a ruthless boss and a gentle father.

He was the man I loved most.

That night, after the children were asleep, I lay in Kirill's arms, listening to his steady, strong heartbeat.

"The person who reported you—did you find them?" I couldn't help asking.

"Yeah." He nodded. "A distant relative of the Moretti family. Theodore's death still eats at some of them. They thought feeding information to the FBI would let them get revenge."

"And he..."

"He won't get another chance." Kirill's tone was as calm as discussing the weather. "People disappear in this city every day for all kinds of accidents. He's just one more."

I didn't ask further. I didn't need the bloody details. I just needed to know Kirill was safe. We were safe.

"Sleep, my angel." He kissed the top of my head. "When you wake up tomorrow, everything will be just like today."

I knew he was telling the truth.

The sun would rise as always. Sonia would continue her dream of soccer stardom. Lucas would keep exploring the mysteries of his books. And he—Kirill Zaitsev—would stand at the center, using his body to shield us under an eternal, peaceful sky.

Printed in Dunstable, United Kingdom

72270565R00147